INTRODUCTION

In Regencyland, Patrick Daley and Elizabeth Shea fell in love, but when their memories are rebooted, they'll have to find their connection again in this classic retelling of The Count of Monte Cristo.

When 18-year-old Patrick Daley arrives home in Sacramento with his traveling circus, he's desperate to look into his mother's missing person case. After a reckless attempt to shine a big, obnoxious light on her disappearance, Patrick finally gets the help he's wanted. It's not until he's kidnapped, and thrown into a Siberian work camp, that he discovers how close he was to solving his mom's case.

Ten years later with revenge in his heart and a fortune hidden in a secret account gifted to him by a spiritual, old coot, Patrick escapes and finds his way home. He's all set to face the men who betrayed him until he meets the girl he left behind all those years ago. As a girl Elizabeth Shea had a high moral code, as a woman, she wears a badge. Proceeding as planned will not only cost him his freedom, but the one person whose memory gave him the strength to survive the unthinkable.

ACCOUNT 13,14...

THE CONTEMPORARY REBOOT SERIES BOOK 2

ELLIE THORNTON

DEDICATION

For my Grandma Betty and Grandpa Bill Thornton. After 74 years of marriage and 75 years together, you've shown me what true love really means. I miss you and love you, grandma.

And for Sebastien-Remi Le Morillon. I will forever love you as a little brother. I valued your friendship and kindheartedness. Until we meet again, my dear friend.

"A life well lived is the most exquisite work of art."
- Erwin Raphael McManus

PROLOGUE

PRESENT DAY

Crossing the street from Mahoney's Pub and Grill, Elizabeth Shea reached into her pocket and removed her keys. She glanced over her shoulder at Patrick Daley as he trailed behind her. The sun streamed through his wavy, golden locks. He was staring at her and smiling. It sent a pleasant tingle up her spine.

It'd been five months since she'd first met him at Bristle Park and a month since they'd started dating and she still wasn't used to it—being in a relationship. She stopped at her car and quirked a brow.

He rubbed the pad of his thumb over the side of his index finger.

"What?" She sighed.

"Remind me again why you can't play hooky?"

"Some of us have to work for a living." Sergeant Brown would be ticked, and besides, she'd never played hooky before. It felt too much like cheating. Though, if Daley had been around when she was a teenager, and he'd asked her to play hooky then, she might have. She'd been pretty stressed after her mom had died. A day of hooky with him might have done her good.

He took her hand, interlacing their fingers. "You said that yesterday. And the day before that."

"Funny how jobs work like that, isn't it?" Not for him, of course. He only worked for the fun of it, doing his Private Investigating only when it interested him. He'd invested well from a young age and lived modestly now to accommodate a work schedule he wanted. "I should be home by six unless we get a case. Want to have dinner?"

He hummed low in his throat as though he were thinking it over. "Will there be hot chocolate?"

She rolled her eyes. "Yes."

"You drive a hard bargain." He leaned in and gave her a quick kiss, then turned and headed to his car, parked three down from hers. "Call me."

Smiling, she reached into her coat pocket for her phone. It wasn't there, or in her other coat pocket or her pant pockets. *Right. Der.* Her partner, Detective Lee, had called her halfway through lunch. She must have left it on the table. Turning, she ran back into the restaurant, waving at Daley as he pulled away.

Reaching the table where they'd had lunch, she found her phone sitting next to her napkin. She grabbed it and weaved back through the tables. As she went out the door, a man about the same height as Daley bumped into her, sending her off-balance.

"Hey!" She reached out to the door-jamb to keep from tipping over.

"Pardon me." He didn't stop.

A pulse shot through her skull, the pain so intense her vision blurred. Quick images of different memories flashed in and out of her mind, the last clearer than all the others: a man with curly, blond hair and an infectious smile. Another intense pulse of pain hit her, and the man was gone.

The pain stopped, and she sucked in a gasp.

A young woman in a waitress uniform stood in front of her. "Miss, are you all right?"

"Daley."

"Daley?" the girl repeated.

Shea glanced around at the dark bar with cherry-wood tables and green booths. She blinked as she tried to remember what was happening. "Where am I?"

"Mahoney's Bar and Grill?" The girl spoke slowly.

Shea pulled her chin back. Why on earth was she here?

"Are you all right?" the server asked.

Shea shook her head. "Yes. Thank you."

Spotting her car through the stained-glass windows on the front doors, she pushed them open. *Daley.* Is that what the waitress said? She turned to her. "Did you just say 'Daley'?"

The girl furrowed her brow. "You said it."

"I said it?" Shea reached for her crucifix.

"Yes." The girl took a step back. "I have to get back to work."

Shea headed for her car. She hadn't heard the name Daley, let alone said it out loud, in years. Opening her car door, she sank into her worn leather seats and took several calming breaths.

"Patrick Daley." She tested it out, remembering why she hadn't said it for so long or even thought it as a tide of sorrow and regret washed over her. He was her friend from the circus, who'd disappeared almost a decade ago.

Her gaze went back to Mahoney's. Was that why she was here? Maybe she'd found something out about him that brought her here? But why would she have been looking into him in the first place? As far as she could remember she hadn't thought about him in years. She'd blocked him in self-perserverance.

His disappearance had been a terrifying experience for her. Just gone, without a trace, as if he'd vanished into thin air. And now his memory was back to haunt her.

She turned on her car and merged into traffic. When she got back to the precinct, she was pulling Patrick Daley's file.

REBOOT: THE COUNT OF MONTE CRISTO

CHAPTER ONE

Patrick Daley glanced around the park and camp grounds that the circus he worked with called home for five or so months of every year. Jay, the circus's strongman, and bullman, or elephant handler, lowered the ramp on the trailer they used to transport their elephant, Maggie. They hadn't been back for half an hour yet, and already the workers and performers—or kinkers as they called them in the circus—were setting up the food carts, striped orange and yellow tents, and the rides.

The circus wouldn't be open until tomorrow night, but it'd be ready for the grand opening before anyone went to bed. It always reminded Patrick of an ant farm, the way they got to work putting up and pulling down everything—and always without complaint.

Once the ramp was down, Jay, who stood at six feet six inches, reached up and patted Maggie beneath her shoulder. Maggie stood at only eight and a half feet tall.

Patrick removed an apple from a basket in the cab and sauntered over.

From a distance, Jay was pretty intimidating, up close he was a big teddy bear and nearly as hairy. The hair on his head was always a messy mop of brown, as was his full, scruffy beard; he had hair coming out the top of his button-up shirt, and his arms and legs were covered, too. Not that that stopped him from wearing shorts and short-sleeve shirts all year round. And his pasty white skin sure was in contrast to his dark hair.

"Now don't you go feedin' her the entire bushel o' apples." Jay pointed one of his bratwurst-sized fingers at Patrick. "She don't need it; it spoils her app'tite."

"Yes, sir." Patrick grinned as Jay wandered off to get work done elsewhere.

Jay was the bullman, but for the last two years, Patrick was the only one who could get Maggie down. Before that, only Patrick's mother could.

"Come on, Maggie." Patrick coaxed her with the shiny red apple. "If you come down, I'll give you a whole bushel of these."

"I 'eard that!" Jay's voice boomed across the backyard of the circus.

"You were meant to!" Patrick returned.

Moving her weight from one foot to the other, Maggie stared from the ramp to the apple, making soft rumbling sounds.

Patrick rubbed the apple against his vest, then sniffed it. "Mmm. Maybe I'll eat it." He opened his mouth as if to take a bite, and Maggie let out a warning blast.

Patrick chuckled.

Tilde, the resident jack-of-all-trades, and Jay's wife, came up beside Patrick and slapped him on the back of the head. "Stop teasin' her and help her down."

Tilde's dark brows rose over her bronzed-brown skin, her chocolate-colored eyes focusing in on him like laser beams. She was almost a foot and a half shorter than her husband, but about ten times more threatening.

Ten years ago, when Patrick was eight, the ramp hadn't been

connected properly, and Maggie had fallen, spraining her foot. It'd taken five months for her to walk normally after that, and another six months before she could perform again.

Patrick winked at Tilde. "What do you think I'm doing?" He climbed the ramp.

"Being your own obnoxious self." Tilde fluffed her tight, black curls with one hand.

Reaching Maggie, Patrick placed a hand on her jaw and rubbed over the rough skin up to the soft, paper-thin section behind her ear. She sought out the apple with her trunk, her nostrils whipping up and sniffing loudly. Patrick gave her the apple. Her gray snout wrapped around it and she plopped it in her mouth.

"Your favorite, Red Delicious." He gave her encouraging pats. "This is the last time you'll have to do this for a while."

Her trunk found his hand again, searching for another apple, then wrapped around his arm.

"Gotta get out first." Placing a little pressure behind her ear, he guided her down the ramp. "Good girl."

Halfway down, the ramp creaked. Maggie stopped, a front foot hanging in the air, too nervous to set it down.

"It's all right, girl. You're almost there," he urged.

After easing her foot down, Maggie rushed the rest of the way off the ramp.

"Thatta girl." Tilde approached her and rubbed her side.

Maggie leaned forward on her large front feet in a stretch, and Patrick and Tilde stepped back. Maggie straightened up, turned, and ran a circle around the trailer. Her tail went up; she wagged her head, ears, and trunk from side to side and made nasal play-trumpets as she went.

Everyone stopped to watch Maggie's routine show of freedom that she only performed here, on the outskirts of Sacramento. The circus paid rent on it all year, so it would always be available when they got back.

"Old girl knows we're home." Tilde smiled then faced Patrick. "Where's your pa? Jay and he need to get going on Maggie's tent, and if you two want to do your show on opening night, you'll need to get your tent up as well."

Patrick retrieved the bucket of apples from the cab of the trailer so he wouldn't have to look Tilde in the eye. "He left, said we'd hold off on our act for a night." Their act was psychic readings—not that either of them was psychic, but Patrick doubted there was anyone in the world who wouldn't buy their performance. Everyone always bought it, at a less than reasonable price, too. Patrick didn't much care for the routine, but he could admit that he liked being able to read people.

"He left already?" She threw her hands up. "We just got here."

Patrick came to her side again. "The poker tables were calling."

She shook her head. "We're not going to see him for a couple days at least, are we?"

"No." Patrick took one of the apples from the bucket and tossed it in the air. "Maggie!"

Maggie charged him, and Tilde moved to the side. Just before crashing into him, Maggie slid to a stop and grabbed the apple from his hand. Patrick set the bucket in front of her and patted her leg.

"I'll help Jay get the tent up before I leave." Patrick faced Tilde.

"And twenty-five minutes after the father abandons his duties, the son follows suit."

"I'm going to the police station."

She schooled her expression. "Patrick—"

"Spare me the lecture, Tilde. I'm going."

"Ain't no lecture comin' from here. But it's been two years."

He nodded. "Exactly. Someone needs to remind them that there are still people who care. I'll stay up all night to get my work done if I have to."

She pointed at him. "You're gonna have to do your pa's work too, you know."

Patrick tightened his fist as he thought of his dad sitting in the back of some bar with his feet up, cards in his hand, and a wad of cash that consisted of all their earnings over the last few months. He wondered how much they'd be down tomorrow or the next day, or whenever it was his dad decided to come home. "How could I forget?"

She patted his cheek. "You're a good boy, Patrick Daley. Your mama would be proud."

He swallowed the lump in his throat. Tilde was only twenty-five and Jay twenty-eight, but the two of them seemed to think it their responsibility to look after him. He was grateful they cared, but they had their own responsibilities, too, and he never wanted them to feel they had to choose. "Thanks"

"She'd want you to be happy, you know," Tilde said.

"I am."

"Mmm-hmm." She rested her hands on her hips. "Are you going to see that pretty towner girl, Elizabeth?"

Last time they'd gotten home, it'd taken Tilde two hours to mention Elizabeth, now they were down to forty minutes. Patrick snorted.

Then Maggie snorted. Patrick's and Tilde's gazes went to the elephant. Her head was up, her gaze fixed behind them. She let out a low growl, then a warning blast.

Tilde moved toward her. "What is it, girl?"

The fast plunks of heavy footfalls flew toward Patrick. He turned, and someone slammed into him, knocking him to the dirt. The culprit landed on top of him. *Sean.*

Maggie let out another warning blast.

"Sean! Get off me." Patrick shoved Sean and jumped to his feet.

Sean had grown a lot since the last time Patrick had seen him. Like Patrick, he now stood just over six feet. Unlike Patrick, Sean had bulked up since last fall. Patrick was lean, had always been, especially compared to his best friend.

Tilde always called them night and day, not only because Sean had dark hair and dark blue eyes and Patrick had blond hair with light blue-green eyes, but because of their personalities. She said Patrick had a free and sunny disposition and Sean was dark and mysterious as the night. She said they balanced one another.

Patrick had to agree.

Maggie stomped her foot.

"It's all right." Tilde patted the elephant's side. "It's just the other ruffian."

The two boys circled, grinning as they sized one another up. Knowing Sean the way he did, Patrick had had a pretty good idea that he'd show up today. He was glad. Sean was one of the few constants Patrick had in his life, and he wanted his support today.

"Hey, Tilde." Sean waved, waggling his fingers in the process.

She folded her arms. "You better not be breakin' any of his bones, Sean Jones. Patrick has work to do 'round here."

Patrick shot her a dirty look. "Thanks for the vote of confidence, Tilde." So he wasn't a strongman, but Patrick wasn't exactly a light-weight either.

"Don't worry," Sean said. "I'll go easy on him."

He wouldn't. Sean got some perverse pleasure out of stomping him, but Patrick could hardly blame him. Patrick always got even.

With a shake of her head, Tilde led Maggie away.

"Been working out?" Patrick dashed out of Sean's reach. "You might consider working on your personality first."

"I see you're still curling your hair, Goldie Locks," Sean returned.

Patrick lunged, managing a smack on Sean's shoulder before Sean lurched away. Patrick's curls were natural! A genetic gift from his mother, as was the blond that he'd inherited from his father. Curl it? Please. Dye it? Never.

Looking up, Patrick feigned interest in something in the sky until Sean looked too; then Patrick rushed him. Sean was an easy target like that. Patrick knocked him to the ground, but in a matter of seconds, Sean had Patrick face down in the dirt, with an arm up behind his back.

Patrick tried to spit out a chunk of straw and mud from the corner of his mouth. "Still wrestling at school, huh?"

"And boxing in the evenings." Sean bounced once, winding him.

"Oof!" Patrick wriggled under Sean's powerful grip. "Show off."

With his free hand, Patrick patted the compacted dirt, the wrestler's way of conceding.

Sean released him and pulled him to his feet. "How are you?"

Patrick shrugged as he rubbed his arm. "Sore."

The boys embraced, patting each other on the back, then stepped back to face one another.

"Good," Sean said. "I can't believe it's been seven months already."

"Time flies."

"Speaking of which, wait until you see the Sheas. They've grown a lot since last year. I promised the kids I'd bring them tomorrow night. They can't wait to see you."

Patrick smiled. The Sheas were his only other friends outside of the circus, the only normal family he knew.

"The boys are getting so big, and Elizabeth—" Sean let out a low whistle. "She's really grown into herself."

Patrick shook his head. "How are they?"

Sean ran a hand through his dark brown hair. "You mean considering their mom just died? Good, surprisingly. Elizabeth's strong and is keeping them from falling apart. It was rough there for a while, but you know all about that."

Patrick rolled back on his heels. "That's why you're here, isn't it? You've come to take me to the police station?"

"Sometimes I think you really are psychic."

Patrick stared at his feet. "You're the one who knew to come."

"Well, considering the last two years you've come back your dad's taken off to gamble, I figured you'd need a ride, and Tilde and Jay are always too busy." Sean raised his hands. "So, here I am."

Patrick stared across the camp where Maggie stood with Tilde and Jay. Jay was hard to miss even from across the park. The two were giving Maggie a good rub-down. "It's not that they don't want to. This place is their livelihood—"

"And with the cops refusing to dig deeper into your mom's missing person case, they figure there's not much they can do?"

"Not after two years." They'd never had much to go on from the beginning. Six at night she'd left to go grocery shopping, a teller recalled checking her out, and then nothing. She was just gone. No witnesses, no leads, no nothing.

"So, what are you going to do? Talking to the officers in charge... what are their names?"

"Brown and Benson." Patrick didn't like Brown, but he did like Benson. That said, he didn't trust either of them. How could he? The one thing he'd trusted them to do, they'd failed at.

"They haven't been exactly helpful, have they?"

"I have a plan." I needed in the records room, so that's where I was going. "You sure you want to do this?"

Sean scoffed. "Please. Like I'd let you have all the fun without me."

Patrick snickered. "Before we go, we have to help Jay and the others put up Maggie's tent."

"Sure thing," Sean said. His willingness to help with anything was one of the reasons Patrick liked Sean so much. He was reliable.

"I won the fight, by the way. Hand it over." Sean held out his hand.

Patrick reached into his vest pocket and searched until his fingers ran over the cool metal. He pulled out a silver dollar and ran his thumb over it. The two of them had been passing the coin back and forth for years. Sort of a man-of-the-hour thing with boasting rights. Patrick had had it for the last five months and had lost it within an hour of coming home.

Let the game begin. He grinned.

Sean crooked his fingers of his extended hand. "Toss it over. It's mine fair and square."

Patrick flipped the coin in his direction. Sean caught it and planted a kiss on it.

"Don't get too comfortable," Patrick said. "It'll be mine again by the end of the night."

CHAPTER TWO

Riding her bike down her street, Elizabeth Shea kept a tight grip on the handle bars. From each handle hung several grocery bags, swaying back and forth, threatening to tip her. She hit a small rock, making the bike swerve. Her muscles stiffened as she fought to get it back under control. She was asking for it, way overloaded, but she didn't have much choice. They needed the food. Next week she had midterms and wouldn't have time to do the shopping.

Two more houses to go. She pedaled at a steady rhythm, ignoring the awkward pull of the weighted, swinging sacks until she reached her house. She planted both her feet and duck-walked the bike up the driveway. *If Donald could see me now.* She chuckled.

"Boys!" She dropped the kickstand in front of the garage and with finesse lowered the bags one at a time to the ground. "Boys."

Luke and Jake, the two youngest boys, were out the door immediately. She knelt next to the groceries as they rushed up to her. Her thirteen-year-old brother was nowhere to be seen.

"Where's Kyle?" she asked.

Jake, the ten-year-old, held out his arms for her to load. His head came to her chin, and he had the same dark raven hair they all had, but his eyes were emerald like Kyle's.

"Watching TV," Jake said.

She loaded his arms. All the boys were tall for their age and skinny, but man, were they buff. They had six-packs—even the six-year-old. Sure they ran around like a pack of wild hyenas, but she was athletic too, even ran on her track team, but with no six-pack in sight. How was that fair?

Luke, the six-year-old, grabbed the gallon of milk and started waddling toward the house, his arms wrapped precariously around the jug.

She cringed as she pictured a milky version of Lake Erie across the kitchen floor. They'd lost many a gallon to his uneasy grasp. "Wait," she called after him, then looked at Jake. "Go help him, then tell Kyle if he doesn't get out here, he's getting onions for dinner."

Jake ran off after Luke and slammed the door behind him.

She slid the rest of the bags up her arms and inched toward the house. Stepping up onto the patio by the front door, she stopped and stared at the doorknob. She hadn't thought this through very well. The front door swung open, and she stepped back, the wood frame of the screen barely missing her nose. Her foot hit the edge of the step, and she almost careened backwards before Kyle caught her around the waist.

When she was thirteen, she'd been nowhere near as tall as he was. He already had an inch on her. His emerald eyes widened in surprise. "Whoa, El, what are you doing?" He pulled her upright.

From the living room TV, the Oompa Loompas sang of perfect puzzles.

"Trying not to fall."

"Oh, well, you're welcome." Kyle grabbed several bags from her, turned, and marched back into the house.

In the kitchen, Luke had the fridge open and was on his tiptoes, pushing the milk onto the top shelf. She rushed over just as the carton was about to tip out of his grasp and pushed it into place.

"I can do it," Luke protested, before catching sight of Willy Wonka on the TV. He ran into the living room and plopped down on the couch. "Play this song again."

Kyle and Jake dropped the bags on the counter and followed. From where she stood, she had a good view of her dad sleeping in the recliner, his hair was messy and his face flushed.

"Kyle," she called.

He turned. "Yeah?"

"How long has Dad been home?" she asked.

"He was home before I got out of school," Kyle said.

Kyle got home at 3:30, which meant her dad had left work early again. She took a deep breath. She hoped he was okay.

After unloading the groceries, she went back into the hall and picked up her dad's wallet off the hall table. Opening the buttery leather, she counted what was left of his last pay check and frowned. Just enough to get them to his next paycheck, if her dad didn't have one of his "weak" moments again. It'd been two weeks since he'd last gone out drinking all night, and he promised he wouldn't do it again. Opening her purse, she removed the change she'd gotten from the groceries and shoved it back in her dad's wallet with the rest of his money.

Luke came skidding around the corner. His honey-hued eyes, the exact shade as her own, stared at her wide and excited. At the top of his lungs, he sang the Oompa Loompa song fixating on the part about how much elephants eat.

Elizabeth grinned.

Luke hopped up and down in a circle. "We still going to the circus tomorrow?"

She breathed out. Not with their dad's money, they weren't. Not if they wanted to eat next week.

"I want to see Maggie and Patrick!"

It was a good thing Elizabeth had saved her allowance and babysitting money religiously for years. It was intended for college, and while she'd promised her mom she wouldn't touch it, they'd had a rough month. Plus, she wanted to see Patrick. He always made them laugh.

She was a little nervous about seeing him, too, not just because her mom had passed, but because she'd turned sixteen. Her face flushed with heat as she remembered a conversation she'd had with Patrick two years ago, when *he'd* turned sixteen.

Naively, she'd asked him if he would be going on his first date now that he was old enough, not realizing that the sweet-sixteen-dating rule only applied in her house. Of course, she had friends that'd dated before they were sixteen, but for some reason she hadn't put it together. It'd been humiliating.

Patrick and Sean had nearly burst from laughing. And then Patrick had claimed *her* very first date. At the time she'd been equal parts perturbed and excited.

Now she was equal parts hopeful that he'd remember and wishing he wouldn't. She thought of her dad slumped in his chair. Love hadn't done her family any good.

Luke grabbed the hem of her shirt. "Are we going?"

She could spare a hundred bucks it'd take to get them in. She swallowed the thick lump in her throat and smiled.

"Are you kidding?" She dropped to a knee. "We wouldn't miss it for the world."

~

"YOU KNOW you just ran that light, right?" Patrick pulled on his seat belt, making sure it was secure. Sean's Jaguar was always a joy to be in... when Sean wasn't driving.

"Don't be such a crybaby." Sean sped through several neighborhoods and toward the 35th precinct. His car kicked up colorful leaves that lay like a red and orange blanket over the streets. "Every cop within a hundred-mile radius knows who I am. You don't really think anyone would give me a ticket, do you?"

"Yes, I do." Just because Sean's dad was a judge—okay *the* judge that everyone feared—that would mean nothing to a self-respecting cop.

"Three years with a license and my record is clean. You just need to know how to negotiate." Sean rested a hand on his gear-shift.

Patrick shook his head. And Sean thought Patrick was the master manipulator? *Right*. Something poked him from the back of the seat, and he shifted. The object scraped across his back. He reached down and pulled the offending item from between the bend in his seat. It was purple and lacy and...

A bra. Patrick chucked it into the back seat.

Sean chuckled.

"You started wearing bras?" Patrick wiped his hands on his pants, picturing its real owner.

"Just the lacy ones," Sean deadpanned. "They're pretty."

"I can't believe you left that in your car." That was something Sean would never have done a year ago. "What if your dad found it?"

Since when had Sean gotten so careless? Sean's number one rule had always been to present as the perfect son. He kept all his shenanigans so secret, not even Sherlock Holmes could've figured it out. Leaving a bra in his car like that was just asking for it.

Sean pursed his lips.

Oh. He *was* asking for it. "You want your dad to find it, don't you?"

"What? No. I don't care anymore. He doesn't care, why should I?" Sean took a right at Patrick's favorite outdoor café, almost hitting a couple about to cross the street.

"Hey, watch it." Patrick dropped his hands to the dashboard.

"I forgot about it. The girl it belonged to was crazy. Attacked me and everything." Sean shifted up a gear, zooming down the residential street with quaint little bungalows.

Something had happened between Sean and his dad, but Patrick wasn't going to pry. Sean would tell him when he was ready. He always had. They came to each other about everything. "Just be careful, man, and maybe you should stay away from the crazy girls for a while, huh?"

Sean chuckled. "Two things: I had nothing to do with that bra coming off, and I haven't gone out with a crazy girl in months—or any girl."

"I find that hard to believe."

Sean shrugged. "Have you ever considered that my tastes might be refining?"

"No, why would I?" Patrick's phone rang, and he pulled it from his pocket. The caller ID read Rafferty. He shoved the phone back.

"Who was that?" Sean glanced over.

"No one. Keep your eyes on the road."

"It was him, wasn't it? Sergeant Rafferty?" Sean slowed the Jaguar infinitesimally. "Why didn't you answer?"

Patrick fought back a grin. "I want my visit to be a surprise."

"Oh, come on. If *I* knew you were back, then *he* definitely knows. I swear he keeps tabs on the circus." Sean's grip on the steering wheel tightened.

That probably wasn't far from the truth after Patrick's last visit to the station. He doubted he'd be getting a welcoming cheer, but his intention had been to shine a big, bright, obnoxious light on his mom's case and that's what he'd done. Of course, it hadn't helped find her, but it kept them from forgetting her. The fact that Rafferty was calling was proof of that. Two of Rafferty's detective's, Brown and Benson, were over his mom's case and he'd been present for all of Patrick's visits.

Patrick's phone beeped, alerting him to an incoming text. He pulled the phone from his pocket and read: *Don't come to the station today. Have crisis. Won't have time to talk. Will be in touch.*

Patrick grinned. If they were in crisis, then this was the *perfect* time to come in.

"Now what? Why are you smiling?" Sean ran a stop sign, but started to slow now that they were only a block from the station. "That was him again, right?"

"Yep. Apparently they're in a crisis and don't want me to come in."

"And that's a good thing... because?"

"It'll make sneaking into the records room a lot easier."

Sean sped into the station's parking lot and slammed on his brakes, making his car swerve into a parking spot.

Patrick took a deep breath and released his death grip on his seat.

Sean asked, "You want to break into the records room?" His tone asked, *Are you crazy?*

"Detectives B and B won't tell me what's happening with her case. This is the only way to find out. Besides, if we get caught, you can use those negotiation skills you've been bragging about." Patrick clapped Sean on the shoulder. "I can't wait to see you in action."

"You wish. If we get caught—" Sean pointed at Patrick. "I'm rolling over on you."

"'Courage is the price that life exacts for granting peace.'"

Sean glowered. "That's annoying."

Patrick shrugged.

"Who said that?" Sean asked.

"Amelia Earhart. Smart woman. Brave woman."

"Yeah, and look where that got her." Sean opened his door. "Let's get this over with."

CHAPTER THREE

Inside the station lobby, Patrick leaned against the tall, gray, front desk. He held his hand suspended over a little bell as he made eye contact with the officer sitting there. She kept her poker face as she held a phone between her shoulder and ear. Her posture was perfect, her blue uniform starched and ironed stiffer than her posture, and her hair was pulled back into a tight bun.

Patrick had never seen her before, but he liked her. She managed to keep calm on the phone despite his pestering, and she seemed competent. It almost made him feel bad for the shenanigans he was about to unleash.

Patrick had visited the station enough to know that the hall that ran vertically behind her led toward the bullpen and break room and that the hall running horizontal of the front desk and behind it led to the records room. Patrick wiggled his fingers over the bell as she wrote on a small pad of paper.

When she finished, she attached her note to a file with a green paper clip she'd pulled from a cup of them. "Yes, sir," she spoke to the person on the other end of the line. "I'll let Rafferty know you're on your way. Yes, the war room is set up. Okay."

Patrick grinned, bringing his hand down toward the bell—she snatched it before he could ding it. He'd already hit it twice while she'd been talking. While she moved the bell out of the way, he snuck a quick glance at the picture hanging from her side of the counter. In the photo, she stood with a group of five men in the middle of a desert, in heat enough to make everyone sweat though their ARMY desert camo.

The fluorescent lights flickered overhead. He leaned back just as she glanced up at him.

Sean stood next to Patrick with his arms folded over his chest. "Does it bring you joy to harass people?"

Patrick rolled back on his heels and smiled. "Usually."

Hanging up, the officer stood and leaned the bulk of her weight on her right leg, still making sure to keep her hips as straight as possible. "Mr. Daley."

She had a wound—probably from war. That would work.

Patrick shoved his hands into his pant pockets. "You know me?"

"Yes, sir," she said.

Patrick thrummed his fingers on the counter and glanced sideways at Sean. "Hmm, 'sir.'" He liked that.

Sean grinned.

She lifted a picture of him that sat on her desk next to her notepad. "Sergeant Rafferty brought this to me earlier today—told me that under no circumstances was I to let you through."

He lifted it. "That's not a bad picture." Okay, so the low light in the station did him no favors, and at the time the picture was taken he hadn't slept in a week, but considering all that, he didn't look so bad. Just a little ruffled with his normal button-up partially untucked and wrinkly, and vest-less.

"It looks like a mug shot," Sean said.

Okay, it did. Patrick pivoted toward Sean. "That's weird, isn't it?"

"That they took a mug shot of you?" Sean shook his head. "No, not really."

Patrick furrowed his brow, and they were off into their

distraction. They'd gotten so good at their routine that they didn't need to signal each other anymore. "It's not a mug shot."

The officer stared at them with the same blank expression she'd worn while on the phone.

Patrick held the photo up. "Do you see any lines in the back to indicate height? They just stood me up against a wall in the bullpen. It's weird that Rafferty doesn't want to see me."

"No, it's not," Sean said, and faced her again. "You'll have to excuse my friend, Officer—" Sean lifted his hand to her, questioning.

"Officer Mitely." Her fingers ran over a spot on her thigh on the leg that wasn't supporting her weight.

"Officer Mitely," Sean said. "He likes to harangue people."

"Whoa, whoa." Patrick raised his hands. "Harangue?"

"Yeah," Sean said. "Last time we were here, you stole Detective Brown's badge, remember?"

Officer Mitely's eyes went round as bulbs, and her gaze whipped between the two.

"Oh, yeah." Patrick laughed. "Wait, no. I borrowed it. Gave it right back the next day."

"I bet Brown doesn't feel that way." Sean rubbed the back of his neck.

"You're only saying that because he chased me around the station." Had almost caught him, too. Patrick shuddered a little just thinking about it. Brown was a large man and burly. Patrick was pretty sure the only reason he'd come out unscathed was because of Benson.

Benson was nowhere near as big as Brown, but when he'd jumped in between them, Brown had backed off. Patrick liked to think it was because of the fact that Benson was a prize fighter, but he knew the reality was that Benson and Brown were like brothers.

Sean pointed a finger at Patrick. "If Sergeant Rafferty hadn't been here, Brown would've done more than that."

Patrick turned to Sean. "What is it with you and Tilde? I can take care of myself." He wasn't that weak; he just didn't have the same training as Sean.

"Gentlemen," Officer Mitely tried to cut in.

They couldn't let her, yet. They had to make her work for it.

Sean pivoted toward Patrick. "Oh yeah? You want to go another round?"

"Anytime."

"Hey!" Mitely's hand ran over the same spot on her thigh it had a moment ago. She was properly flustered. Time to move this gag along.

Patrick reached down to his leg, clasping it in the same spot where Mitely had been touching her own leg, and doubled over, moaning.

"Patrick," Sean's worried voice called out. He was getting better at faking worried.

"What's he doing? What's wrong with him?" Mitely's voice was strained.

It was almost too easy. "There's light. Bright light everywhere. Pain. My leg." He stood tall and stared at a fixed point behind her.

Her gaze trailed to the photo she had taped to the counter.

"You were in an explosion," Patrick murmured.

She took a step back, a small limp appearing in her movement. "How did you know that?"

He leaned on the counter. One guess spot on!

"Patrick." Sean rested a hand on his back. "Are you—?"

"I can see them," he said. "Ghosts."

Her eyes narrowed in confusion.

Okay, not ghosts, just one ghost. Not all of her platoon had been involved. His guesses weren't always right, but this wasn't something he couldn't fix. He shook his head. "A man."

"Not again." Sean grabbed Patrick's arm, supporting his weight. "He's having a psychic vision."

She gasped.

Patrick pointed at Mitely. "He's here."

Mitely stepped forward. "Who? Who's here?"

He sucked in a ragged breath, then lifted a hand to indicate height. "Tall, thin, brown hair and—"

"Blue eyes?" Mitely grasped the counter.

He huffed and nodded his head. "He says it's okay. He wants you to be happy."

"David?" She glanced around the lobby behind them, looking from one empty plastic chair to the other. "Where?"

Patrick went slack, and Sean caught him. "I can't. He's not... he's gone. I'm sorry." He wiped his brow.

Sean stuck one of Patrick's arms around his neck and led him to a plastic chair behind them. The chair was cold and chilled him to his bones, to the core of him. Sometimes doing this was fun but this wasn't one of those times.

Sean took the seat next to him, his arm still around his back.

"Water," Patrick wheezed out.

Sean turned to Mitely, and with all the urgency he could muster, he said, "He needs water."

"Okay. I'll get it." She rushed down the blue, mat-carpeted hall behind her leading to the bullpen.

Sean watched as she went. "She's gone."

Patrick jumped to his feet and rushed to the counter, Sean following close behind.

"That was fun." Sean chuckled.

Patrick grabbed two paper clips from the paper clip cup as they passed and shoved them into his coat pocket. He turned down the hall to the records room.

"She believed you. I could see it in her eyes. You had her hook, line, and sinker," Sean said. "How did you know all that about her?"

"I didn't. It was targeted guessing."

At the records room, Patrick opened the door. Not locked. He entered, then held the door for Sean to go in before he eased it closed behind them. He flipped the light on, filling the room with a dull yellow glow.

"There's no way a person could guess all that," Sean protested.

"She had military posture and presence, she held all her weight on her uninjured leg, and she kept touching her injured leg in the same spot while we were arguing." He made his way through dusty filing cabinets, each adorned with sets of numbers. 178-34 through 184-27, 184-30 through 190-02, and on and on.

"What about the explosion?" Sean whispered even though they were alone in the musty room. "I didn't see her limp until she left to get your water. And she could have been shot."

"When I mentioned the pain in my leg, she looked at the photo of her platoon on her desk. Like more than just she had been involved." He found the cabinet he was looking for. "I took a shot."

Patrick opened the drawer marked 231-73 through 239-65 and flipped through the files, the rough edges of the manila folders scratching the tips of his fingers as he went.

"I can't believe that worked." Sean leaned against the chest-high cabinet next to him, his elbow resting atop it.

"Me neither," Patrick said. "That argument was quick thinking on your part."

"I can't read people the way you can, but I know that you like your targets off-balance. The talking-to-ghosts thing caught me off guard. Learned that while you were gone, did you?"

Patrick paused when he reached his mother's file. "237-34, Samantha Daley."

He pulled it out of the drawer and set it on top of the filing cabinet. Sean leaned closer as Patrick opened the file.

On the very top page, which held a picture of his mother with some other information about her disappearance, stamped in big red letters, were the words "Case Closed."

CHAPTER FOUR

Patrick and Sean sat handcuffed in front of Rafferty's desk, staring at the man. Rafferty was in his early forties with light ash-brown hair that he kept short. He was a little shorter than Patrick in height, but loads taller than him in presence, and just about anyone Patrick had ever met. He was tough and a no-nonsense type of guy, but there was also an infinite kindness behind his baby blue eyes that had made Patrick trust him from the moment they'd first met.

Patrick sat with his legs crossed and wore a cool expression on his face, though his insides were a rolling tide of emotions. How could Rafferty not have told him? How could his mother's case be closed? They hadn't found her.

"He broke into the filing room." Detective Brown's face was redder than a beet. "What was I supposed to do?"

Since last time Patrick had seen him, Brown had gotten a military buzz cut. Patrick hoped it was because he'd insulted his receding hairline last year while Brown had been chasing him around the bullpen.

Rafferty pointed at Patrick. "You're not supposed to hit him!"

Being as dramatic as he could muster, Patrick dabbed at his

swollen lip. It'd been a while since he'd been punched. He'd forgotten how painful it was.

"He's a lunatic." Brown threw his hands in the air.

"And the teenage son of a missing woman," Rafferty said.

"So we should just put up with him? Deal with his—"

Rafferty held up a hand. "Holding him accountable for his illegal behavior and punching him are two completely different things."

Sean lifted his cuffed hands as if to ask a question. "In Brown's defense, Patrick did egg him on."

Brown signaled to Sean. "There. I was provoked."

"Thanks, pal." Patrick smiled at Sean.

Sean returned it. "I told you I'd roll over on you."

"Understood," Patrick said.

Rafferty came around his desk to Brown. "You're an officer of the law, and you will behave like one. Now, get out of my office."

Brown faced Patrick before exiting. "I'm sorry your mom's gone. I am. But you need to get on with your life. You're not a cop. You're a victim. All your interference is doing is impeding our investigation."

"Brown," Rafferty warned.

"I'm done." Brown left.

Patrick kept a smile planted on his face, but had to swallow the thick lump in his throat. His mom was the victim.

Rafferty narrowed his eyes at him. "What part of 'don't come in today' don't you understand?"

"Have you found my mother?" Patrick asked.

"You know the answer to that." Rafferty went back around his desk. He ran a hand through his brown hair, which was starting to gray in patches at either side of his head. "I was going to tell you. Going to have a rational conversation with you about what happened—"

"Case closed?" Patrick inserted.

Rafferty's blue eyes shot daggers at him. "But no, you had to go against my request, come in here anyway, and commit a felony. What were you thinking? And now here I am, in the middle of a kidnapping case, having to worry about you."

Patrick leaned forward, his cuffed hands out in front of him. "You wouldn't have to worry about me if Brown and Benson could be bothered to do their jobs." That wasn't entirely fair. Detective Benson had always been kind to him.

Rafferty cussed. "You think we haven't looked? That no one tried?"

"You could have done better. Why is her case closed?"

"It's cold!" Rafferty took a deep breath. "It has been for two years now."

"Right," Patrick barked back. "Cold. Not closed. Her file read 'case closed,' with approval of the captain."

Rafferty glanced up and furrowed his brow. "It said what?"

Sean leaned forward. "I saw it too—'case closed.'" He always had Patrick's back.

Detective Benson poked his head in the door. "The kidnapper is on the line." He gave a quick nod to Patrick.

"I'll be a minute," Rafferty said. When Benson left, Rafferty continued. "I can't imagine what it would be like to lose your mother at such a young age, and in this way—a tragedy. But you're not the only victim in the world, not the only one who needs help. And right now I have the parents of a thirteen-year-old girl praying that we'll find their daughter alive. You know what that's like, son. The clock's counting down."

Patrick felt sick but didn't let it show. Being called a victim twice in one night sucked, but worse than that was Rafferty's comment about the clock counting down on the little girl. He remembered that the first hour, first twenty-four hours, first forty-eight hours, and first seventy-two hours were the most critical. Then he remembered the despair once that time had passed.

Rafferty pointed at him. "Stay put."

Patrick lifted his hands. "It's not like I can go anywhere."

Rafferty marched out of his office, pulling the door closed behind him.

"That could have gone better. At least he didn't say anything about arresting us." Sean looked at his hands. "Then again, we are in handcuffs."

Patrick went to the door. He peered out the window and into the bullpen. Officers were gathered around a couple. The woman's eyes were red and her face was blotchy. The man had dark circles under his eyes. He spoke into a cell phone and looked like he was pleading with whoever was on the other end.

Patrick hoped they got their daughter back. Life after losing a loved one sucked.

"Patrick?" Sean said. "Are you okay?"

Patrick glanced around the bullpen, noting several white-boards that had notes on them, photos, and other forms of some kind. Curiosity struck. He hadn't been at the station for this part of his mother's case, probably because there had been no ransom demand—who would demand money of circus folk? He had an overwhelming urge to know how the process worked. What went into finding a missing person?

He reached into his vest pocket, pulled out one of the paper clips he'd pilfered earlier and inserted them into the lock of his cuffs.

"Whoa, what are you doing?" Sean peered into the bullpen.

"Picking the lock." The cuffs popped and Patrick rubbed his wrists; they were red and sore. Brown had tightened the cuffs until they were digging into his skin. Patrick had played apathetic to it, which had only made Brown angrier.

Sean stared at the paper clip. "That's the paper clip from the front desk. You knew we were going to get caught, didn't you?"

Patrick grabbed Sean's cuffs and picked them. "We're in a police station, Sean."

Sean shook his head. "You're a glutton for punishment, aren't you?"

Patrick freed him. "If I am, then what does that make you?"

"An accessory to gluttony?"

Coming out of the office, Patrick kept his shoulders back and meandered toward the suspect boards. He passed Brown's desk at the edge of the bullpen, and Patrick's gaze landed on a red ball on the desk just slightly smaller than his fist. Benson sat at his desk with his back to them. His broad shoulders, super tan skin, and nicely styled dirty blond hair made him stand out just about anywhere. He was just cool and not someone they wanted on their bad side. Patrick was glad he had his back to them.

Patrick made his way toward two-white boards covered in information. Sean followed him, bumping into Patrick more than once.

"Relax," Patrick said.

"Easy for you to say. You're used to conning people."

"Like you're not? I believe I recall a story about how you've never gotten a speeding ticket. No one's paying attention to us."

Most of the officers stood around the parents. Others were off working on different cases, all busy doing something else. The missing girl's dad had hung up with the kidnappers.

"Do you have eight-hundred thousand dollars?" Rafferty asked.

The mom gave a little hiccupping cry.

"Yes," the dad said. "But it's mostly in stocks and bonds."

Rafferty looked at his watch. "Can you pull it together in five hours?"

Patrick stopped at the first white-board, his gaze traveling over the notes to a picture of a little girl. His stomach dropped. She looked like she could be a Daley, but it was her eyes that drew him in. So, so similar to his mom's and his own.

"You okay?" Sean asked.

Patrick nodded and pulled his gaze from the girl. Having sympathy for her wouldn't help her, and it wouldn't help him. Several photos showed neighborhoods in places where they believed she might have been abducted and her walking route to and from school every day. There was a photo of a van taken from a surveillance camera, but the picture wasn't clear enough to help, and the vehicle had no distinguishing marks on it.

His gaze trailed from a piece of the girl's homework that had been wadded up, the name Sophie scribbled at the top, to a photo of a man's corpse. *Why would a picture of a corpse be in a missing person case?* In the photo, the man lay on his stomach in a ditch filled with tall grass, one arm above his head, the other at his side. His long brown hair was splayed over his face, and he had five bullet holes in his back.

In Patrick's peripheral vision, cops were moving around the bullpen and still hadn't noticed them. His heart rate rose, and he took a deep breath.

Patrick stared at the man's left hand, the one at his side. It was twisted a little, his palm almost facing up. He leaned in. There was something written there. Something that he couldn't make out with his hand twisted the way it was.

"What are you looking for?" Sean asked.

"Nothing in particular." There were other photos. One showed a wadded-up piece of paper, the same on the board, lying feet from the body.

"You'd better find your 'nothing particular' quick because Rafferty saw us, and I'm guessing from his expression that he's not happy."

"You sure?" Patrick lifted the photo, flipping through the ones under it.

Sean shrugged. "I'm no expert, but his face is red, and he has steam coming out his ears."

Patrick lifted the second to last photo and smiled. It was a picture of the man's hand. There was a sequence of numbers tattooed there. He pulled it down. Nope, not tattooed but written with a permanent marker, looked like. They read:

D 10 5 9 13 / 17 7 16 5 22 9 18 /
23 5 7 / 14 9 24

Patrick should turn and see what Rafferty was doing, but he was fascinated with what he saw. The way the numbers were separated suggested... words. His heart jumped in his chest.

It's a cipher! It had to be. It had all the common elements of one. He'd known reading those books on code breaking would come in handy one day.

"Rafferty's headed this way," Sean said.

Working at a mile a minute, Patrick started going through all the possible ciphers it could be, starting with the easiest ones. First, he tried an A1Z26, but when he changed the numbers into their corresponding letter of the alphabet, they made no sense.

Base 10? No.

ROT1? No.

How about a shift?

"I thought I left you boys handcuffed in my office," Rafferty said from behind him.

That was why the D was there! It was a shift. Patrick spun around, coming face-to-face with a frowning Sergeant Rafferty. "It's a shift code!"

Rafferty shook his head. "We already explored that possibility."

Patrick's excitement deflated faster than a balloon pricked by a pin.

"But without any real code key, it will take us longer to break this than we have time for." Rafferty turned to Sean. "I get why Patrick left my office, but I thought you had more sense than that. I thought you had a mind of your own. Looks like you proved me wrong."

Sean's face fell, and he stared at the floor. Sean's disappointment hit Patrick harder than Sean had actually hit him at the circus earlier.

Rafferty turned back to Patrick. "Maybe you think this is all fun and games but it's not. And every minute I stand around here explaining things to you that are none of your concern, it's wasting what precious little time this girl has." He waved over Detective Benson.

Precious little time. Dark tendrils crept through Patrick's mind, wrapping themselves around his thoughts, suffocating them. The shadow man from his dreams, the one he imagined took his mom, crept forward.

Benson weaved his way through the busy bullpen, and Patrick pictured a clock counting backwards.

"You think they're going to kill her?" Patrick made eye contact with Rafferty.

"I can't discuss an ongoing investigation with you," Rafferty said.

"It wasn't a question." Patrick pointed to the picture of their John Doe. "This man kidnapped the girl, which was why he was found with her homework, but she's still being held for ransom. That tells me that John Doe messed up and that whoever he was working with killed him when they took the girl."

Rafferty lifted a hand in a staying motion. "This isn't our first day on the job."

So Patrick *was* right. Statistics showed that only one in ten-thousand kidnapped children ended with a death. Most kidnappers asking for ransom just wanted their money, and they didn't want to kill anyone, but if they'd already killed one of their own, then what was to stop them from killing the little girl? *Sophie.*

Nothing.

Benson stopped at Rafferty's side—his brown eyes shifting from Patrick and Sean to Rafferty.

Patrick glanced at the photo in his hand. He had to do something, but Rafferty was going to take the photo from him and lock him up. Finding the smallest grouping of numbers, the third grouping, he put the numbers to memory. 2357.

Rafferty signaled to Patrick. "Take him down to holding. If he does anything crazy, you have my permission to Tase him." He took the photo.

Benson grabbed Patrick's arm and led him away.

Sean stepped forward, hands up. "Whoa, don't you think that's a little overboard? He was just looking."

Rafferty turned his angry gaze on Sean. "Brown."

Brown came over with a grin pulling at his lips as Benson escorted Patrick away.

"Take this one downstairs, too," Rafferty said. "If he thinks breaking the law is so much fun, then he can partake in the consequences."

"Hey," Sean called. "That's not fair."

"Life isn't," Rafferty said.

Everything slowed in the room. Patrick's heartbeat sped up, and his mind raced through the information he had. He started shuffling through all the possibilities. One after another, after another. His gaze fell on the little girl's parents, on their questioning, almost hopeful gazes, and it hit him.

He planted his feet as time came back like a whip. "Wait," he said.

"Don't make me drag you out of here," Benson whispered to him, his tone not unkind, but not joking around either. "You know I can."

Bargaining with him wasn't going to cut it. So, Patrick did the only thing he could think of.

"It's an address!" he yelled across the bullpen and grabbed onto a desk, Brown's desk, jerking it forward. The red ball rolled toward him.

Brown released Sean and made his way to where Patrick held on.

Benson grabbed one of his arms and yanked it free, pulling it up behind his back. He then slammed his face into the desk. "I don't want to hurt you, Patrick."

Patrick tried to angle himself toward the parents. "The little girl might still be there."

Benson yanked Patrick away from the desk. Patrick grabbed the ball as he went, shoving it in his pocket. *Might want that later.* He then hooked his foot around the leg of the next desk over, pulling it, screeching across the green tile as Benson towed him away.

At that moment, Patrick had a weird out-of-body experience where he could see himself as though from above. He looked like a freak, which was disconcerting.

He shook it off. "They're not holding her for ransom. You have to listen to me."

"Shut up," Sean snapped.

"Get them out of here," Rafferty yelled.

Brown reached them and shoved the desk away from Patrick's foot—it hurt like crazy. Brown pulled out his Taser.

Patrick's eyes went wide. He'd thought Rafferty was joking when he'd said that Benson could Tase him, but he was pretty sure Brown had been looking for an excuse to do it since last year. The man's eyes were giddy with excitement.

The girl's father moved forward. "Wait, please."

Patrick took his chance, making eye contact with the man. "It's an address, I swear. They're not going to give her back. They're going to fly her out of the country."

The Taser sparked, and the little girl's father ran around the table, placing himself between Brown and Patrick, his hands up, palms out. "Rafferty, please! Let's hear what he has to say."

Patrick glanced at Sean.

Sean shook his head and mouthed, "Stop talking."

Rafferty moved in, the muscles in his jaw pulsing. He glanced from the father to Patrick, then looked down and shook his head. "Let him go, Benson."

Benson let go.

Brown turned the Taser off and faced Rafferty. "Boss."

Rafferty shook his head, but otherwise ignored Brown as he moved closer. "This had better not be a game."

Patrick shook his head. "It's not. It was a skip inside an A1Z26 inside a shift. Three easy codes that when paired make something opaque, each simple until layered."

"What makes you think they're going to fly her out of the country?" Rafferty asked.

"2357 decoded is SAC. If the next sequence is JET like I think it is, then they might be." SAC JET was one of the smaller airports in Sacramento.

Rafferty dropped his hands to his hips. He glanced at the father and then the mother, then turned back to Patrick. He breathed out and stepped aside.

"You can't be taking him seriously!" Brown stepped forward.

Patrick went to the board, grabbed a marker from it, and decoded the rest.

Rafferty came up to him as he wrote out the address. "You better pray you know what you're doing."

Patrick shushed him, then wrote down the last word.

6159 McLaren

Sac Jet

"There. That's it." Patrick put the lid back on the marker and stuck it on the board.

Rafferty cursed under his breath.

"There's something familiar to you about this, isn't there?" Patrick faced him. A chill shot through him when Rafferty turned his stare on him. This wasn't just familiar; he knew what this was. "You've had these kidnappers before, haven't you?"

Rafferty narrowed his eyes. "Brown, Benson. Take these two to holding. We have to move. Fast."

CHAPTER FIVE

"It's too bad Brown didn't have more than one of these." Patrick squeezed the red ball he'd pilfered from Brown's desk. He sat with his back to the bars and across from Sean. They tossed the ball back and forth. "If he'd had three, I could practice my juggling."

Sean said nothing. He had two predictable reactions when he got mad. One, he punched it out, and two, he gave the silent treatment. Patrick had never been much of a fighter, and once Sean figured that out, more often than not, he'd gone with the silent treatment. Patrick guessed Sean was playing catch with him to stave off boredom.

Patrick remembered once, two years ago, when he'd inadvertently flirted with a girl that Sean had called "dibs" on. The memory made Patrick's chin ache; he reached up to rub it. That time, Sean had opted to do both. He'd punched him in the jaw when he caught Patrick kissing the girl *and* had given him the silent treatment.

Though, that time it wasn't all Patrick's fault. Sure, he'd flirted with the girl, but she'd flirted with him first. And he hadn't kissed *her*; she'd ambushed *him*. If Sean hadn't caught them, Patrick would have pushed her off anyway. Not that it'd mattered—an hour later she was gone, and they were back to normal.

Despite the silent treatment, Sean was eerily calm. Had been since coming down here. That wasn't like Sean at all. Sean squeezed the ball and tossed it back.

Patrick caught it one-handed, switched hands, and tossed it back. "Juggling has never been my strong suit." He continued filling the silence. "I can do magic tricks, of course, but juggling isn't the same thing, is it?"

Sean let out a breath.

Patrick held back a grin. "I could take my shoes off and practice with them. Who knows how long we'll be in here. Hours? Days? Weeks? I've never seen Rafferty that angry. Which makes no sense, considering I blew the case wide open."

"Shut up," Sean said. "Just shut up."

"He speaks." Patrick grinned.

Sean tossed the ball. "Self-preservation. I can't take your verbal diarrhea anymore."

Patrick caught it and chucked it again. "What's on your mind?"

Sean sat the ball on the bench next to him. "Nothing."

"Then why have you kept your responses to yes or no for the last fourteen hours?" Sean opened his mouth to speak, but Patrick lifted his hand palm forward in a staying motion. "And don't say it's because I got you thrown in jail because that's not true."

Sean knew what the stakes were and had insisted on coming. He was in jail because he wouldn't be left out.

The muscle in Sean's jaw twitched. He leaned forward and placed his elbows on his knees, clasping his hands. Sean ran a hand through his dark brown locks. "Why'd you do that?"

Patrick furrowed his brow as he tried to recall the "that" he'd done. "Do what?"

"You should have negotiated."

Uh... yeah. That didn't help either. "You've lost me. What are you talking about?"

"You want to know what's going on with your mom's case, but no one will tell you. You finally get some leverage—"

"Leverage?" He'd had leverage?

"—and what do you do? You tell them what the cipher means." Sean stood.

Patrick's mind reeled. That *had* been leverage, and it hadn't occurred to him for even a split second. "The cipher..."

Sean extended both hands in front of him, palms up and shrugged. His expression said it all: *Yes, you idiot.*

The fact that Sean always had his back, no matter what, was the biggest reason why Patrick trusted him. Even though trust wasn't something that came easily to him.

Taking a deep breath, Patrick pulled himself off the cement floor. His muscles ached from hours sitting and sleeping there. That was why Sean kept telling him to shut up. He was an idiot. But then again, he'd helped that little girl. At least, he hoped he had. At this point, she could just as easily be dead as rescued, for all he knew.

He rolled back on his heels and shook his head. What was he thinking? He was no hero.

When he'd picked the lock on his handcuffs and had come out of the office, helping that little girl had been the last thing on his mind. If he hadn't seen her picture, hadn't looked into the eyes of her parents, it would never have occurred to him that he should help. That was the simple truth of it. He'd seen the cipher, he'd known he could help, and he had.

"They were desperate," Sean said. "They would have traded."

That wasn't true. Patrick shook his head. Hadn't Sean been there? Hadn't he seen them dragging him away? If Patrick had tried to leverage his help for information, Rafferty probably would've done the honors of Tasing him. "No."

Sean breathed out. "All I'm saying is that you should've thought it through."

Patrick slumped his shoulders. Had he lost his only bargaining chip? And if that were true, why wasn't he angrier with himself?

A creak of a door opening at the end of the hall echoed through the cement room.

Sean sat back down and grabbed the ball.

Footsteps plodded down the hall, and then Judge Dread, Sean's dad, came into view with an officer right behind him. Mr. Jones and Sean looked very much alike, both tall and lean with dark brown hair and deep blue eyes, but Mr. Jones' hair was starting to gray, and his skin had a pale gray sheen to it. Sean jumped to his feet, and Patrick took a quick step back from the bars and Judge Dread on instinct.

"Dad, what are you doing here?" Sean swallowed.

"You didn't think I would hear about this?" His tone was cold and calculating.

Patrick swallowed and stepped forward. "It was my fault, Mr. Jones. He didn't—"

"Shut up!" Sean snapped at Patrick. "I can handle my father on my own."

Patrick stared at Sean in shock. Sean had never really been mad at him, not really, but the hatred and bitterness in Sean's tone startled him. What had happened while he'd been gone?

The tension between the two was thick enough to swim through. The fact that Patrick hadn't noticed right away was a testament to how freaky Sean's dad was.

Mr. Jones signaled to the guard, who stepped forward and opened the cell.

"Let's go," Mr. Jones said.

Sean planted his feet. "I'm not going anywhere with you."

Mr. Jones stared Sean down, but Sean didn't move. "Now."

"I'm nineteen. I don't have to go with you," Sean said.

Mr. Jones took a quick step into the cell and toward Sean. Sean flinched, but held his ground. Patrick took a step back.

Mr. Jones' glare moved from Sean to Patrick for the first time, and he sneered before looking at Sean again. "You're a disgrace." He stormed out of holding.

The officer locked the cell again.

Patrick swallowed. He'd met Sean's dad before, and while he'd never considered the man pleasant, he'd never been cruel. "You okay?"

"Never better." Sean clenched his fists.

Yikes.

Another set of footsteps entered, and soon Rafferty came into view, stopping in front of the bars. "How'd you boys sleep?"

Aside from dark circles under his eyes, Rafferty's posture was tight, and his countenance was confident.

"Best sleep I've had in months," Sean said. And at very least, to Patrick's ears, the sarcasm there was palpable.

Yeah, right.

Rafferty wore a poker face, which for a minute confused Patrick, if Rafferty were mad he wouldn't be blank-facing it. He'd be frowning or scowling.

"Brown's been looking for that ball." Rafferty pointed to the bench where Sean placed the ball.

All the uncomfortable tension fled the moment Patrick realized what was happening. He smiled. "You got her."

Rafferty raised a brow.

"You got the girl."

Rafferty nodded. "We got the girl." He opened the gate again and motioned for them to follow. "I want you boys to see something."

Walking at a swift pace, Patrick followed after Rafferty with Sean close behind him. Rafferty led them to the bullpen. They stopped outside Rafferty's office, and he pointed across the room to where the parents of the little girl knelt on the floor with their daughter embraced between them.

Sean leaned against the door-jamb of Rafferty's office as Patrick's gaze fixed on the family. He'd done that. Or he'd helped. A warmth swirled inside him, a feeling he'd never felt before. This was the first time in his life that he could remember ever *really* helping someone.

Rafferty rested a hand on Patrick's shoulder. "You saved her, son. You saved her life."

He swallowed the sudden lump in his throat.

"How'd he do that?" Sean's voice was barely there. "I mean, what happened exactly?"

"We found her at the address he gave us. We also found plane tickets, a passport for her under a different name, and sedation drugs. These men weren't kidnappers."

Brown and Benson came out of an interrogation room escorting a man to holding. The man was in his mid-forties with a pockmarked face and a long, greasy-blond ponytail.

Rafferty pointed at the man. "Human traffickers; thought they'd make a little extra by ransoming the girl."

Patrick faced Rafferty. While in holding, he'd had a lot of time to go over the different possible scenarios of why these men would kill one of their own, would use ciphers, and would be keeping the victim near the airport. His mind had supplied "human trafficking," but he'd pushed it out. The idea had been too terrifying.

Getting a fake passport and airline tickets for a minor wouldn't be easy, unless they already had a system set up to do it. "They've done this before," Patrick said under his breath.

Rafferty gave him a look he'd seen hundreds of times on countless faces, a look that asked how he'd known that. Rafferty didn't ask, for which Patrick was grateful. He hated going through his deduction process. A process he could go through in seconds in his mind could take forever to explain to comprehension.

Rafferty nodded. "He'll never do it again. He's going away for a long, long time."

"Sergeant Rafferty." They all turned to look at a distinguished older man as he made his way down the hall. He wore a dark suit with a blue tie, his brown hair was combed neatly back like a businessman's, and he had a confident gate. He grabbed a candy bar from a vending machine that was being stocked as he passed, and then winked at Patrick.

Patrick glanced at Rafferty out of the corner of his eye.

"Is this the young man who solved the cipher?" He opened his candy bar.

"Yes, Captain Wright," Rafferty said. "Patrick Daley."

Captain Wright extended his hand to Patrick. "Well done, young man."

Patrick took the proffered hand and glanced at Sean. Sean quirked a brow.

Rafferty signaled to Sean. "And Sean Jones."

Wright took Sean's hand. "You boys should be proud." Captain Wright's friendly brown eyes strayed back to Patrick. "Now, tell me, how did you manage to solve that cipher?"

Rafferty lifted a hand to Patrick, palm up.

"It was, uh, simple." Patrick shoved his hands in his pockets. "It was a skip inside an A1Z26 inside a shift. The use of several simple codes together is what made it so difficult. I'm sure I only figured it out so quickly because I didn't start with the first set of numbers—I started with the third set."

"Go on." Wright took a bite of his candy.

A soft snigger came from Sean's direction.

Patrick stopped himself from smiling. "The code started with a D. I simply converted the D to a four using the A1Z26. Then I shifted all the numbers by four. That's where starting with the third set came in handy. After I figured out that that set changed to 1913, I used the A1Z26 cipher and got SAC. With that as my base, it wasn't hard to figure out the fourth set of numbers converted to JET, and once I had SAC JET, it wasn't hard to change the second set to McLaren.

"I'll admit that I did get momentarily stuck on the first set, until I realized that if you shift 105913 by four, you get four numbers. 6159. That's where the skip cipher came in. The D or 4 at the beginning told us not only how many numbers to shift, but also how many to skip. So, I skipped the first four numbers and got 6159 McLaren, SAC JET."

"You're right." Wright smiled. "That wasn't so hard after all."

Patrick frowned. Yes, actually, it was hard. He'd had less than a minute to figure out SAC, and even after that, he'd still had to figure out what numbers he was supposed to be shifting for each word, not to mention the skip.

Wright laughed. "I'm kidding."

Patrick faked a laugh.

"You did well. I wouldn't be surprised if you boys got medals after this." Wright faced Rafferty. "As soon as you're done here, come up to my office."

Rafferty nodded as Wright walked away.

Rafferty removed a dollar from his wallet and gave it to the man at the vending machine, then came back. "Sean, why don't you take that ball Patrick stole and put it back on Brown's desk?" He turned to Patrick. "I need to have a word with you alone in my office."

Patrick and Sean locked gazes as Patrick handed over the ball.

Sean frowned. "Sure."

Patrick shrugged as Sean passed him heading to the bullpen and to Brown's desk. Benson approached Sean as he went.

Rafferty led Patrick into his office and closed the door behind them. He sat at his desk.

Patrick sat on the edge of his chair. "What's up?"

Rafferty laced his hands on his desk. "You saved a little girl's life today."

Patrick stared at his hands on his knees. *Okay, okay already.* Sure, he was glad that he'd helped—more than glad—but this was getting uncomfortable. "It was nothing."

"Not to that little girl. Not to her parents."

He breathed in. "Okay."

"You could've bargained her life for information on your mom's case, but you didn't," Rafferty continued.

Patrick shook his head. He wasn't entirely sure that was true. If he'd thought of it, he might have... maybe.

"Stop. I'm not a good person." He signaled to the door with his thumb. "That was a fluke. I mean, I scammed Mitely, riled Brown, broke into the records room with the intention of stealing my mom's file, picked the lock on my handcuffs, and made a risky move forcing my way into this case. What if I'd been wrong? She could be dead because of me. And the truth is I'd do a whole lot worse if it meant getting my mom back or figuring out what happened to her."

A small grin spread across Rafferty's lips. "All true. Except the little girl's not dead. And you didn't do a lot worse. Whether you want to acknowledge it or not, you made a good choice. A choice that, as far as you could tell, had no way of benefiting you."

Patrick shook his head and tightened his jaw. Wasn't Rafferty listening to him at all? Hadn't he heard what he'd just said?

"I'm going to look into your mother's case again."

Patrick's gaze flew up. "What?"

Rafferty stood, went to the door, and pulled it open. "Go home. I'll be in touch once I've had a chance to go through her file."

Patrick scrambled to his feet. "Oh, okay." He started for the door, then on an impulse stopped by Rafferty and threw his arms around him. "Thank you."

Rafferty patted his back. "You're welcome, son."

CHAPTER SIX

"You're still coming tonight, right?" Patrick stared out the front window of Sean's car at the circus beyond. As expected, all the tents, rides and stands were up and ready for opening. The Ferris wheel was going with several of the performers taking a ride. Even from inside the car he could smell the popcorn stand behind the entrance.

"I promised Elizabeth and the boys I'd give them a ride." Sean put his Jaguar in neutral and left his hand resting on the gearshift.

"Great." Patrick reached for the handle.

"Did you know that Rafferty was up for captain before Wright?"

Patrick turned back to Sean. "What?"

"Benson told me. Everyone was pretty angry when Wright got the job," Sean said.

"Did Benson tell you why Wright got it instead of Rafferty?"

Sean shook his head. "Nope, but he's got to be better at it, right? Why else would he be promoted over Rafferty?"

To Patrick, it almost sounded like Sean was rubbing it in. "Why are you telling me this?"

Sean shrugged. "Maybe we could talk to Wright about your mom?"

Patrick's grip tightened on the car door. "Yeah, maybe." He started to get out and stopped. "Listen, about what happened with your dad earlier—"

"It's not a big deal." Sean's hand tightened on the gearshift until his knuckles turned white.

"Sean—"

"Just drop it!" Sean barked.

Patrick nodded and got out of the car.

"You have no idea how lucky you are," Sean whispered.

Patrick faced him and rested a hand on the roof of the car. "What?"

"You're free. You can do whatever you want, whenever you want, and you'll always be able to."

That's what Sean thought of Patrick's life? Patrick signaled to the fair. "This isn't as freeing as you might think. It's a lot of hard work; it's every man for himself. Even Tilde and Jay can only do so much for me. At least your parents are around, and you get to go to school. Even when my mom was here, the only structure I had was in setting up and tearing down the circus and our nightly shows."

Sean kept his gaze straight ahead but nodded. "I'll see you later tonight." He pulled the silver coin from his pocket. "Hey, this goes to you. It was your night, after all." He tossed it to Patrick, who caught it in his left hand. "I'm glad Rafferty is going to look into your mom's case."

As Sean drove away, Patrick flipped the coin in the air, watching it glisten in the fading, yellows, reds, and oranges of the sunset. He shoved it in his vest pocket. Something wasn't right with Sean. Aside from being more careless than Patrick had ever seen him, there was an intensity about him that wasn't normal. Like he was a powder keg about to explode.

∾

THE FRESH SMELL of caramel apples and cotton candy surrounded Patrick as he sauntered from the back-yard and into the circus grounds. The crowd was enormous as always. Parents and kids ran in every direction, playing games, eating, going on rides and to the shows.

Patrick rolled up his shirt-sleeves and fiddled with the buttons on his vest. For years he'd envied the kids that got to go to proper schools, but now that he was older, he realized how lucky he'd been to grow up in this magical place. He stopped back by one of the game tents and kept an eye on the front entrance until Sean and the Shea's arrived.

His stomach clenched at the sight of them. He saw the boys first; their tall, lanky frames and their straight-as-a-pin raven hair made them stand out. He'd missed them a lot. Luke had been two-years-old when they'd first met, and Patrick had loved carting him around the circus in his arms, listening to his baby squeals whenever he saw something new and exciting.

Now Patrick was most excited to see Elizabeth.

Sean passed the box office and went straight through the gates. The boys raced after him, then came to an abrupt halt and turned back. They'd gotten so much bigger.

Elizabeth sprinted up to them and took Luke's hand. She signaled for the two older boys, Kyle and Jake, to follow her back to the box office. Even Sean was waving for her to come in. She shook her head at them, making her ponytail shimmer in the Edison lights that hung all over the grounds.

Patrick grinned. How many times did she have to be told that the Sheas had free admittance before it sank in?

A moment later, they rounded the box office as Elizabeth put her change in her purse. He'd make sure she had her money back before she left.

Patrick headed toward them, his hands in his pockets, and tried to look as uninterested as possible. Tried and failed.

Jake saw him first. "Patrick!" He'd grown at least an inch since the last time Patrick had seen him and ran twice as fast.

Luke saw him next. "It's him! It's him!" He jumped up and down, then chased after his big brother. Luke didn't look all that different than the last time Patrick had seen him. Still cute and round-faced, but if he was anything like Jake, that wouldn't last much longer.

Patrick picked up his pace, going into a jog until he reached Jake, who careened into him. Jake threw his arms around Patrick's middle and Patrick hugged him back.

"You're a week late." Jake stepped back.

Patrick forgot that the boys kept track of their arrival dates. "We had some car trouble."

Luke reached him next, and Patrick swooped him into a big hug.

"Where's Maggie?" Luke used his new, higher vantage point to stare over heads.

"Hey." Patrick sat him down. "I thought you were here to see me."

Luke nodded and shrugged. "But mostly Maggie."

Kyle, the oldest of the boys, was the next to arrive. He'd grown at least two inches. It wouldn't be long before he was as tall as Patrick.

"Hey, man," Kyle said. "How are you?"

"Good. And you?"

Kyle leaned in and lowered his voice. "We're okay." He nodded over his shoulder to Sean and Elizabeth as they approached. "Mostly."

Patrick's gaze fell on Elizabeth, and for the life of him, he couldn't look away. Her petite stature and perfect posture, her hair and golden eyes, and her tomboy walk were the same as always, but in other ways, she was irrevocably changed.

She'd turned sixteen since the last time he'd seen her, but the way she held herself was not like a typical teenager. It was of someone responsible for others, someone whose world didn't revolve around herself, or boys, or school, or any of the normal things most teens' lives revolved around.

She caught his eye and smiled; the moment short lived because Luke darted away. "Luke," she yelled after him. "Get back here."

Luke stopped and threw his head back. "Aw, but El, I want to see the petting zoo."

She quirked her finger at him. "We'll go in a minute."

He stomped back.

She came up to Patrick and smiled wide. "Hello, Peter Pan."

The first time he'd met the Sheas the trapeze artists were doing a version of Peter Pan, and he'd been roped into playing Peter. They'd only done it the one year, and because Patrick had never loved the aerial stunts after falling to the net several times, he'd given up flying. Elizabeth liked the nickname, however, so it stuck.

Patrick crowed, throwing his head back to do it properly.

She laughed. And so did Kyle and Jake. Luke tried to mimic him.

Sean moved to Elizabeth's side and faced Patrick. "This one—" He nodded at Elizabeth. "—refused to come in for free."

"We're not freeloaders," Elizabeth said. "Everyone has to make a living."

Patrick's gaze went to Sean. Sean had his hands in his pockets and a serene look on his face, but it was all a façade. He was too calm.

Luke tugged on Elizabeth's arm. "Can we get pretzels? I'm hungry."

"I'll take them," Kyle said.

She looked behind him to the concession stand and bit her lip. She pulled a twenty from her pocket. "Yeah, just..."

Patrick and Sean exchanged glances. Looked like she was stretching her funds being here.

Elizabeth sighed. "One pretzel each and no cotton candy."

Jake stepped forward. "Can I have cotton candy instead of a pretzel?"

Elizabeth shook her head. "No."

Patrick looked at him. "You don't want one, trust me. I saw a fly get wrapped up in one once." He was lying, but it was worth it to see Jake's face scrunch up.

"Yuck." Elizabeth handed a twenty to Kyle. "Thank you for that, Patrick."

Patrick shrugged.

Sean snatched the twenty from Kyle and handed it back to Elizabeth. "I've got this."

She took it and frowned. "No, Sean. You don't have to do that." She tried to give it back.

"I know, but if I do, then you'll owe me." Sean winked at her. "Sounds like a good deal."

"Ha ha." Elizabeth handed Sean the money, but he jumped back. He then draped an arm over Kyle's shoulders and led him away.

Patrick grinned. "Tim's working the stand; he'll load them up for free."

Luke started to follow, but Elizabeth grabbed the back of his shirt, stopping him.

"Not you," she said. "You stay with me."

"Awww, but I want a pretzel," Luke whined.

Sean yelled over his shoulder. "I'll get you one, buddy."

Tim waved a pretzel in the air. "This is for you, little guy."

Elizabeth grimaced.

"There. Now you owe me," Patrick said.

"No, I owe Tim."

"Lucky sod."

She rolled her eyes and faced him. "How are you?"

He frowned. "A little hurt, to be honest."

"Why? What's wrong?" Elizabeth's brow pinched together.

A tinge of pride unfurled. She was concerned for him. "I was expecting you to run into my arms like your brothers did, but you barely even said hello."

She fought back a smile. "Oh, please. I haven't run into your arms in years."

"Only two years, actually." He held up his thumb and index finger.

"Like I said."

"You were making it sound like it'd been decades."

She shook her head. "I'm grown up now. It'd be weird."

"Yeah, it'd be weird," Luke repeated, though Patrick wasn't sure he was really paying attention to the conversation.

"Well, that's an argument for never growing up, if ever I heard one." A good one. He wanted a hug.

"And we're back to Peter Pan again."

Patrick rolled back on his heels, then lurched forward and wrapped his arms around her.

"Oh, jeez!" She went stiff as a board.

He didn't let go. "If I'm Peter Pan, does that make you Wendy?"

She patted him on the back. "Sure."

Luke grabbed Elizabeth's arm and swung it back and forth. "I'm a Lost Boy. And so are Kyle and Jake."

As if startled to hear her little brother's voice, she yanked out of Patrick's grasp, her cheeks tinged with a lovely pink.

Patrick chortled, then grinned at Luke. "Sounds about right to me."

"Can we go to Neverland?" Luke asked.

Elizabeth dropped to a knee. "We're already there. Look around."

Luke spun as he took in the circus, seemingly seeing it for the very first time. The wonder there reminded Patrick of when Luke was two.

Luke pointed to a tent with a sign out front that read "World's Largest Crocodile." "It's the crocodile!"

Patrick pointed to one of the kinkers, who was performing a knife throw. "And we have pirates."

Luke's eyes grew wider. "And Sean's Captain Hook!"

Patrick laughed, pleased to hear a chuckle from Elizabeth as well.

Tilde and Jay came out of Maggie's tent wearing their costumes, Jay in his strongman outfit and Tilde in her American flag inspired trapeze one-piece that looked like a bathing suit with ruffles, and headed toward them through the crowd. Patrick pointed to them. "We even have natives."

Tilde waved. Luke glanced up at Elizabeth. He nodded and ran into Tilde's arms.

Elizabeth clasped her hands together and let out a giggle.

Patrick stepped closer to her. She'd always seemed so tiny to him, and even though she hadn't grown any taller than the five-feet-two-inches she'd been last time he'd seen her, she seemed bigger now. Somehow.

"I haven't seen him that excited since..." She breathed out, her smile falling. "Since the last time we came here."

"How's your dad?"

She went blank-faced. "About as can be expected."

Patrick turned to her.

She was still watching Luke with Tilde and Jay.

"I'm sorry about your mom," he said. "She was an amazing woman."

Elizabeth reached up and touched the crucifix around her neck.

He'd missed it until now. He'd seen that crucifix before on her mother.

"Yes. She was." She faced him. "Speaking of moms, any word on that front?"

"Maybe," Patrick said. So, she didn't want to talk about her mom or her dad. Which meant there was probably a story there she didn't want to discuss.

Two years after he'd first met her, the two of them and Sean had decided to go through the circus's haunted house. Someone had jumped out at them and had scared her. It'd taken her a minute to calm down, though she wouldn't admit she was afraid. Then, she'd run off by herself. He'd asked her why she'd done that later, and she'd told him she didn't need his help to get through, that she could do it on her own.

He'd since learned that was her pattern. If she was scared, she shut people out and handled it on her own. He was pretty sure it was a pride thing. It'd always been cute, but now, with her taking over as mom, he could imagine how debilitating that must be.

"Maybe? What does that mean?" Her eyes warmed with hope for him, fire lighting the golden flecks. "Did they find something?"

"Not sure," he said. "They're going to let me know."

Sean and the boys came back. Kyle and Jake were already halfway through their pretzels.

Crestfallen, she said, "Oh."

Sean handed Elizabeth a pretzel. "What did I miss?"

She grinned at him. "Luke's decided that you're Captain Hook."

Sean made his hand into the shape of a hook. "Excellent. I love Captain Hook."

"Might want to stay away from the crocodile tent," Patrick said.

"Thanks for the heads-up." Sean popped a piece of his pretzel in his mouth. "Now, where's me ship?"

Elizabeth chuckled. "Are they doing the trapeze act tonight? The boys would love to see that."

Patrick went into a deep bow and glanced up at her. "Just think a happy thought."

"And we can fly?" she asked, lifting her brows.

He stood and took her hand, tucking it around his elbow. "We can fly."

"We can fly." Luke ran back, his arms out as though he were flying.

Patrick took a deep breath as they made their way to the tent with the trapeze act. Sean narrowed his eyes for a split second at Elizabeth's hand on Patrick's arm. It caused a nervous pinching sensation in Patrick's gut.

CHAPTER SEVEN

"Pull another quarter out of my ear!" Luke grabbed Patrick's arm and tugged.

"Okay," Patrick said, "but this is the last one." He dropped to one knee by the ring toss game, bringing his two empty hands toward Luke's face, palms forward. When he got right up to Luke's face, Patrick shot his right hand forward toward Luke's ear and with a twist of his wrist, he made a quarter appear in his hand.

"Yay!" Luke grabbed the quarter. "I wonder how many I've got in there."

Elizabeth chuckled.

After the trapeze act, they'd gone on a few rides, and then Sean's competitive side had taken over. They'd spent the last hour playing games. Patrick stood as Sean paid Katelyn, the game master, and collected their rings.

"What's the score?" Sean handed Patrick his rings.

The boys crowded in around them in order from tallest to shortest: Kyle, Jake, and Luke.

Patrick glanced at Elizabeth out of the corner of his eyes and sighed. She'd leaned against the booth with her back to it and with a big stuffed elephant wrapped around her waist that she'd won at the shooting game. Neither he nor Sean had gotten close to beating her at that booth.

They'd been to nearly every booth in the last hour, and the boys weren't as enthusiastic now. Not that Patrick could blame them—it was ten. Elizabeth had lost interest a few games ago. It wasn't like Sean to not notice something like that.

This had to stop. "You won the dart throw and the strongman, which is worth two points. I won the ping-pong toss, the sticky tic-tac-toe, and the whack-a-mole. Three to three. We're tied."

"Two to three." Sean elbowed him. "I don't need your charity. I'll beat you fair and square."

Patrick flipped his rings around in his hand. "It's not charity. I live here. I play these games all the time. It's an unfair advantage."

"Yeah, Sean." Luke reached up to the purple elephant his sister held and rested his hand on its leg. "It's an unfair advantage." He yawned.

Sean glanced around at the group. His gaze stayed on Elizabeth a moment longer than it had on the boys.

She rested her head on the elephant. "I think we're ready to call it quits."

"Fine, I'll take the extra point," Sean said. "But I only get to throw two rings and you get three. And we only get points if the rings go around the red bottles."

Patrick stared at the red bottles in the sea of greens and blues. There were seven of them, and two were at the back.

He shrugged. "Fine. Go."

Sean went first. He took a deep breath and threw his first ring. It hit the neck of the red bottle and spun its way down.

Patrick quirked a brow. That was unexpected. "Something you want to tell me, Sean?"

"Nope." Sean smiled, grabbed his second ring, and kissed it. "See that red bottle in the very back?" he asked Jake.

Jake nodded.

"I'm calling it." Sean threw the ring. It, like the first, landed around the neck.

Kyle high-fived him. "Wow!"

Sean pushed his shoulders back. "Beat that."

Patrick threw the first ring, and it went around the neck of a blue bottle just to the right of one of the red bottles.

"Ouch," Jake said.

Patrick breathed out. "I've got two more." He took aim again and threw the second ring. It landed on the red bottle he'd missed the first-time, sliding down the neck.

"One more red or I win," Sean said.

"Thank you," Patrick said.

Luke grabbed Patrick's vest pocket. "Don't miss." His big honey-colored eyes were glossy.

Patrick winked at him. Poor kid needed to get to sleep. He took aim at another red bottle and threw. It bounced off the top and flew off the table.

Sean leaned his hip against the counter and crossed his arms. "So, what's the score now?"

Patrick rolled back on his heels and retrieved the silver coin from his vest pocket. He could've won and kept the coin for more than a few hours, but this had been an easy way to end it. He turned and offered Sean his hand, and the silver coin stashed there. "You have experience with the ring toss, don't you?"

Sean gripped his hand hard and took the coin with a grin. "I don't know what you're talking about." Sean's favorite thing was taking the coin from Patrick, though Patrick couldn't say he didn't enjoy taking it from Sean.

Elizabeth came over to them. "You're amazing. You're wonderful. You're the king."

Sean smiled at her, and Patrick furrowed his brow.

"Can you take us home now, please?" She slouched.

Patrick chuckled.

Sean nodded. "Love to."

~

ONCE THE BOYS were in the car, with Luke's pudgy little arms wrapped as far around the large stuffed elephant as possible, Elizabeth faced Patrick. "We had fun."

A small smile crossed Patrick's face that made her feel more than a little wary. Before she could react, he grabbed her and pulled her into a hug. Her arms went stiff at her sides again. Why did he always have to do stuff like this? He knew she wasn't a hugger. And why did she let it make her nervous? And why did he have to smell so good? Like chocolate. It was so ridiculous, yet her breath still hitched.

"We're here for five months, and you and I have plans," he whispered into her ear, sending chills up her spine. He pulled back. "Come again."

She narrowed her eyes at him while rolling a rock under her shoe. She wanted to ask what he'd meant by that, but she knew. He did remember their "date."

"We can't," she said. "But you can come see us."

He shook his head. "You're family. You don't have to pay to get in."

She chuckled. "I appreciate the sentiment, but—"

"Please, Elizabeth." He bent his knees, coming eye to eye with her.

His sea-green eyes bore into her. She hated it when he looked at her like that. He wasn't really a psychic, but sometimes when he looked at her like that, she felt like he was staring into her soul. It made her feel vulnerable, and now, more than before, that was something she didn't want to feel.

"We'll see." She ducked into the front seat of Sean's car. A small chuckle followed after her, and she clenched her jaw.

"You okay?" Sean rested his hand on the gear shift.

She nodded.

Patrick grabbed her seat belt, then leaned across her to buckle it.

Elizabeth kept her eyes on the glove box to avoid his gaze. His hand brushed over hers where it rested in her lap as he moved out of the car. A zing shot through her from head to toe.

"Let me know when you hear from Rafferty." Sean lurched the car forward a foot.

Patrick jumped back a step, and the door slammed shut, nearly catching Patrick's hand in the process. Then they were peeling out of the parking lot.

"Sean." Elizabeth grabbed the handle above her passenger window, leaning into the door, and glanced behind her at Patrick. He was staring after them. "You could have hurt him."

Sean looked out the rear-view mirror and smiled. "He's fine."

"Don't drive like a maniac." She felt something in her hoodie pocket.

"Of course not," Sean said.

She reached in and pulled out several bills—four twenties. The money she'd spent getting herself and the boys in. He must have put it there when he'd hugged her.

Argh, Patrick! She was going to beat him. Or kiss him. *No!* She shook the uncomfortable thought from her mind. Still, now they could go again. She smiled and put the money back.

CHAPTER EIGHT

Patrick jerked awake, the book he'd fallen asleep reading
toppling off his chest as his nightmare, a shadow of a man
stalking his mother, faded in the morning sunlight. He sucked in a
deep breath and dropped his head back to his pillow. His entire body
ached from his nightly chores. He stretched and rolled to his side, two
more books sliding off his bed and onto the floor of his trailer, from
the movement.

He normally did his chores between shows, but as he'd spent the
night with Sean and the Sheas, he hadn't done any shows and hadn't
gotten to his chores until eleven. He and Jay cleaned all the living
spaces of the animals and then put them away and fed them. After
that, Patrick helped the kinkers clean the large tent. When that was
all done, he'd had to put up the tent that he and his father used for
private readings.

Jay had offered to help, but the large man was tired after a long,
hard opening day. Patrick had sent him back to Tilde for the night. It
wasn't too hard setting up the tent alone, but Patrick hadn't gotten to
bed until past two.

After that he hadn't been able to sleep, remembering the way

Sean had lurched the car away. It'd made Patrick uneasy. Why had he done that?

The trailer door squeaked open and in clomped heavy, staggering footsteps. His dad groaned and stumbled into the kitchen counter. The water turned on, and Patrick, from his bed where the table stood during the day, peered at his dad as he splashed water on his face.

His shirt was untucked, and his vest unbuttoned. His unkempt hair stuck up in all directions, and he reeked of cigarette smoke and alcohol.

He turned toward Patrick, and Patrick closed his eyes again until his dad clunked and banged down the hall to his room. He slammed the door behind him. Patrick buried his head in his hands and groaned. Then he let loose a slurry of cuss words into his pillow.

"Trust me," his dad had said, and now he'd lost all their money. If he hadn't, he would've woken Patrick to show him his winnings and to gloat about what he was going to do with it. He might even have given Patrick a twenty. He hadn't done any of that. He'd lost their money, and with whatever measly change he'd had left, he'd drunken himself into a stupor.

Patrick had saved fifteen thousand for them over the last seven months. It made him sick to think what all his hard work had gone to. He'd known better. He should have hidden it.

Pushing himself off his comforter, Patrick went to the kitchen faucet and turned the water off. His phone vibrated from its spot on the floor. He picked it up, knocking over a stack of books in his hurry to answer it before his dad started yelling.

He looked at the caller ID. It was Rafferty. His heart leapt in his chest. Glaring at his dad's bedroom door, he went down the steps of the Airstream and answered the call.

"Rafferty?" He glanced around. It was still too early for most of the performers to be up, but Jay was probably feeding the animals.

"Did I wake you?" Rafferty asked.

Patrick plopped down on a lawn chair and ran a hand over his face. "No, long night is all."

"I've been reading through your mom's file."

Patrick sat up straight. "Found anything?"

"I've only had the file for an hour."

Patrick rested his head in his hand.

"I have some questions for you and your father and some of the folks at the circus. Can I come by tomorrow morning?"

"I guess, but I don't know why you'd want to talk to us. Everything we know is in that file."

The sound of shuffling papers came through the phone. "Just going over a few things. Looking at things from a different angle."

"You're the expert." The cold edge of the lawn chair pressed against Patrick's thigh. "We both had alibis for the night of her disappearance, if that's what you want to know."

The line went silent.

Patrick waited for a second for Rafferty to say something, but nothing came.

"Hello?" He ran a hand through his hair. "You still there?"

Rafferty cleared his throat. "Yes, still here. I'll call you tomorrow when I'm on my way." He hung up.

THE SMELL of fresh hay wafted over Patrick as he entered Maggie's tent. Jay stood beside her, his head only a few inches below her eyes. Jay handed her an apple and rubbed her trunk as she ate it. They both turned to Patrick. Maggie shifted her weight from her left foot to her right and back again as if deciding whether she should go to Patrick or get another apple.

Jay chuckled deep in his throat. "Looks like you have competition for Maggie's affection after all."

Patrick reached up to Maggie's ear, rubbing the soft spot there. She tilted her head into his hand and made a soft trumpeting sound.

Jay gave her another apple. "What are you doing up so early?"

He thought of all that money his dad had flushed down the toilet.

Then out of nowhere, he thought of Elizabeth and Sean. He scowled. Before Jay could get a good look at him, he rubbed his eyes with the palms of his hands.

"Couldn't sleep. Thought I'd come and give you a hand."

Jay walked to the back of the tent and grabbed a bale of hay like it weighed nothing. Patrick knew better than that. Each of them was a hundred pounds; Jay could carry one in each hand. It was only recently that Patrick had been able to carry one across the length of the park without having to stop to catch his breath in route.

Jay pulled a pocket knife from his jean pocket, flipped it open, and cut the bailing twine. "I saw your dad come home when I was leaving my trailer this morning. He looked drunk." He closed the pocket-knife.

"Hung over."

"He didn't win?" Jay leaned against the wood barrier between them and Maggie.

Burning fury threatened to burst from Patrick's chest. "Nope."

"How much did he lose?"

"Don't know for sure, but if I had to guess, I'd say all of it." So far he'd never guessed wrong concerning his dad's betting.

Jay hung his head and shook it back and forth.

Patrick hadn't had any grand schemes planned for that money, though the idea of college had come to mind a couple times. He could stop moving, get an apartment. He'd be close to Sean, and Elizabeth and the boys, and to the investigation into his mom's disappearance. Plus he'd never been to a proper school before.

He had to change the subject. "Sergeant Rafferty's coming by tomorrow."

Jay furrowed his brow. "How come?"

"He's looking into my mom's case."

Jay stood tall and smiled. "Well, that's good, innit? He's a sergeant. That's gotta be better than those detectives, right?"

"I hope so." Patrick faced Jay. "Listen, can you talk to everyone, please? Convince them not to give Rafferty a hard time and answer his questions?"

Jay rubbed his thick beard and sucked in a breath through his teeth. "I'll do what I can, but you know how these folk get 'round the po-lice."

It was exactly why Patrick had asked Jay to help. "I know, but once he gets what he needs from us, he can start investigating where he needs to."

"They're not gonna to like it," Jay said. "But I'll whip 'em in shape."

"Thanks. I better get started on my chores." He turned.

"Elizabeth looked good, I thought." There was a smile in Jay's tone.

Patrick smirked, reined it in, and looked back. "Compared to what?"

"All the girls you ever dated," Jay said.

Patrick grinned right out. "Below the belt."

"This is the circus. Low blows are how we roll." He grabbed a shovel from the tent wall.

Tilde, in her nightgown and robe, passed Patrick, holding a mug of steaming coffee. Patrick wrinkled his nose at the pungent smell. He was a hot chocolate man himself.

"What are you boys chattering about?" Tilde handed Jay the coffee and placed her hands on her hips.

"Nothing," Patrick said at the same time Jay said, "Elizabeth."

Tilde nodded. "She's grown into quite the stunning, young woman."

Patrick sucked in a breath and looked heavenward.

"If you're interested," Tilde continued, "you'd better say something toot sweet. You're not the only eligible, young man who has eyes for her."

Sean. Patrick frowned. That explained a lot.

"Now stop, Tilly, look what you're doin'." Jay pointed at Patrick. "You made Smiley frown."

She lifted a hand, palm up. "It ain't my fault he has competition. He needed to know."

"I'm leaving now." Patrick exited the tent to the sounds of soft chuckling from the two he left behind. But then he stopped in place.

Patrick headed toward his trailer again, moving slowly.

Sean had never shown the least bit of interest in Elizabeth. Last summer he'd dated at least three girls and not a one of them resembled Elizabeth in looks, temper, or heart. She had substance, and substance hadn't ever been in Sean's wheelhouse.

Sean liked her. Patrick hadn't noticed it because he hadn't wanted to. Sean was his best friend—he didn't want to fight with him, but Elizabeth wasn't just any girl. She hardly had any experience with boys. She'd never even dated due to a rule her parents had made about not dating until sixteen. And Sean, at nineteen, had lost count of his conquests.

Sean had probably been laying the ground-work with her for months.

Patrick pulled his phone out of his pocket and dialed Sean. It rang through to voicemail. He tried again. Sean answered on the third ring.

"This had better be good, Paddy." Sean's voice was gravelly from sleep.

"Are you going after Elizabeth?"

"What?"

"Don't mess around with me, Sean. Do you want her?"

The line was quiet a moment. "What if I did?"

Every protective and crazy instinct inside Patrick shot to the fore. "She's not one of your psychotic girlfriends that you can feel up in the back of your car."

"I know that." Sean's voice rose.

"You can't mess with this one, Sean. She's too good—"

"Too good for what?" Sean barked. "For me? Is that what you were going to say?"

He'd been about to say she was too good for *that*, but didn't correct Sean. Sean was his best friend—always would be. But Patrick knew too much about his exploits with women to be okay with him and Elizabeth. She deserved better than that. "Yes."

"Why? Because you love her?"

Patrick froze.

"You know what—*you're* not good enough for her." Sean's tone was cool and collected, much like what Patrick had heard from Mr. Jones in the cell. Normally that would've freaked Patrick, but this was Elizabeth, so he couldn't care. Not now.

Sean continued, "At least I have a home. You live in a trailer. I have money—lots of it. Your dad gambles away every cent you make. My dad's a judge. Yours probably killed your mom. If one of us isn't good enough for her, it's you."

Patrick took a deep breath before speaking. "Out of respect for our friendship, I'm going to forget you said that. You're mad at me, I get it, but Elizabeth isn't a conquest. You can't steamroll yourself into her life and then ditch her once you've got what you want."

"Let her decide." Sean disconnected.

Like she'd have all the information she'd need. Sean wasn't about to tell her he'd be done with her after she gave in. Patrick lifted his phone in the air to throw it when he thought better. Rafferty was calling him on that phone.

He had to stop this. Had to talk to Elizabeth.

He ran into the trailer and got his dad's keys and was off.

CHAPTER NINE

A s Elizabeth loaded Jake's and Luke's backpacks for school, her dad stood at the stove cooking scrambled eggs and bacon. He caught her staring and waved to her with his spatula. She smiled. He looked good today. Better than he had in months. She wasn't sure what brought on the change, but she wasn't one to second-guess a miracle.

"Boys," he yelled down the hall. "Breakfast is ready."

Jake and Luke came tearing into the dining room.

"Bacon!" Luke hopped all the way to his seat.

Jake took his place. "I don't want my food to touch."

Her dad plated the food. "The bacon and eggs are in their separate corners."

Elizabeth grabbed their bags and headed for the door. She set them down next to her backpack and turned. The doorbell rang. She glanced at the clock on the wall. *Who on earth?*

Opening the door, she came face-to-face with Patrick Daley in the same clothes he'd worn yesterday, only more rumpled. He looked like he'd just woken up. He had dark circles under his eyes, and his curly hair was a mess, but perfect. It kind of irritated her. He was a mess, and he still looked amazing. So not fair.

They locked gazes.

She waited, her grip tightening on the doorknob.

He blinked.

She shook her head, trying to rid herself of the strange fog that had descended. *Jeez. Snap out of it.* "Hey?"

He ran a hand through his hair. "You said I could come by anytime."

Uh... "Yeah, I did say that." She cleared her throat. "I guess, when I said it, it didn't occur to me that you'd be dropping by at a quarter to eight in the morning."

"Sorry," he said.

Was it perfect timing? No. Was it weird? Yeah. Did she mind? Not in the least. Though she knew she probably should. "It's okay. Just a surprise."

There was another awkward silence as he stared at her. She couldn't remember if she'd done her hair yet. It took all her will-power not to reach up to her head and check.

"You look great." His lips quirked.

Now she touched her head. *Whew, it's done.* "Thanks?"

"Who is it?" her dad called from the kitchen.

She turned. "Patrick Daley."

Her dad peeked around the corner. "Jeez Louise, it is!" He strode down the hall. "Invite him in."

She looked from her dad to Patrick and back again. *Okay.*

Patrick inched over the threshold like he was entering some strange new land.

"It's good to see you. Are you hungry?" Her dad shook Patrick's hand.

"I think he just wants to tell me something." Elizabeth's gaze went to Patrick.

Patrick stared at her for a moment, then grinned. "I'm famished."

"Great," her dad said. "I made too much."

Patrick followed her dad down the hall and into the kitchen.

"Patrick!" Jake and Luke yelled. Chairs scraped over the floor, and Elizabeth could just imagine them rushing out of their seats to hug him.

"Look." Luke pounded across the kitchen. "I drew a picture of Maggie!" He grabbed the picture he'd taped to the fridge this morning with an entire roll of scotch tape. She was surprised he'd been able to remove the drawing to show it to Patrick.

"Wow. It looks just like her. Great job," Patrick said.

"I know," Luke said. "You can have it."

Patrick chuckled. "Where's Kyle?"

"He left for the bus already," Jake said.

Elizabeth pulled her chin back. This was so... *weird*. She tried to school her expression as she headed to the kitchen. No, not weird. He was here for a reason.

She sucked in a nervous breath.

He wanted his date.

PATRICK PULLED over at the curb of Jake and Luke's elementary school. Elizabeth hopped out of the front seat and pushed it forward so the boys could climb out. The boys jumped down, gave side hugs to Elizabeth, and waved at Patrick before running off.

Elizabeth put her hands in a cup around her mouth and called after them, "I'll be here after school!"

They didn't respond, but she watched until they were lined up with their classes. Then she got back in. Patrick grinned when she grabbed the handle above the door to pull herself up.

Once in, she pulled her pack into her lap and wrapped her arms around it. She stared at him out of the corner of her eyes as he turned in to traffic.

He grinned. He had a good idea of what was going through her mind. She was sixteen now, and he *had* asked her for first date. But that wasn't the purpose of this visit.

Elizabeth breathed out long and slow. "It'd probably be better if you took me back to my house and I rode my bike. That way you won't have to pick me up from school."

"I don't mind. I'd like to." That way he could head off Sean.

They turned on a residential street.

She faced him, scratching over the duct tape holding the seat together.

He quirked a brow.

She narrowed her eyes. "All right, stop. Stop the car."

"What?"

"Pull over."

"Elizabeth—"

"Do it, or I'm bailing," she said.

He chuckled. "Yeah, right."

She opened her door.

He grabbed her arm. "All right, all right, I'm stopping." He pulled to the curb, and she shut her door again. "I can't believe you did that."

"Oh, please. I'm not stupid enough to jump out of a moving car." She reached over and pulled the keys from the ignition.

His jaw dropped. She tricked him. *Him.* The master of the con. She'd eased him into complacency with her by-the-book ways. He knew he should be upset, but he kind of liked that she'd just pulled a fast one on him.

She dangled the keys between them. "What's going on?"

He shrugged. "I woke up this morning and had an overwhelming desire to see you."

She pursed her lips and opened the door again. "The truth or I'm going to chuck your keys into those bushes—" She signaled to a yellow rose bush, thick with thorns, at a fence line by a house. "—and then I'm bailing."

He smiled and raised his hands in surrender. "All right, I'll tell you, but first you have to promise me something."

She lowered her hand. "What?"

"You have to play hooky with me today."

She lifted the keys again.

Focusing his gaze on the window behind her, he pointed. She turned to look, and he lurched across the seat. He grabbed the hand that held the keys and glanced down at her.

She scowled. "Get off me."

"These keys aren't mine." A little white lie to keep the keys out of the bushes wouldn't hurt. "You wouldn't want to throw Jay's keys away, now, would you?"

She blinked, then looked down. "Fine." She dropped the keys in his palm.

He pulled back, and she turned to get out of the cab.

"Wait, Elizabeth," he said. "I'm sorry. Please don't leave. I need to talk to you."

"I can't skip school," she said. "I have a test today."

He studied her face and grinned. "Liar."

She lifted her chin but didn't deny it.

"It's just one day, Elizabeth. I need you."

Her scowl was replaced with worry. Last night the look of worry had been for a different reason. Now it was there because she thought he was about to have a break-down or something. He didn't love that she thought that, but if it meant her spending the day with him, he'd deal.

She took a deep breath. "Okay, but this had better be good." She slammed the door. "And I want to go to the library first."

"The library? Why?" He turned the truck on.

"I need to get today's homework assignments." She straightened her spine. "And I should get them done now so that I'm not worried about them all day."

"You want to spend your day of hooky doing homework?" He didn't disguise the mock in his tone. She deserved it. She was an uber nerd.

She turned an icy glare on him. "Do you have a problem with that?"

"Nope. Library, here we come." He chuckled, but tried to hide it because he was still a little afraid she'd change her mind. Hey, if she wanted to study on her day off, who was he to judge? He made a U-turn. "I feel so naughty. The library."

"Patrick," she warned.

"Maybe I'll get a library card. 'I'm quite illiterate, but I read a lot.'"

She turned her head, but he could still see her cheek rise when she whispered, "*Catcher in the Rye*. I read that book, too, smart alec."

WALKING toward his trailer with a stack full of books balanced in his arms, Patrick swayed, nearly dropping the top two.

"Whoa." Elizabeth reached out and grabbed them. "Let me take a few of those."

"You're already carrying a bunch," he said. "And I need someone to open my trailer door for me anyway."

"Right." She rushed ahead to the door and opened it. "Why you felt the need to get this many books is beyond me."

"Thank you." He went up the stairs, and she followed. "I don't go to school, remember? And this circus stuff doesn't take as much time as you might think."

He placed his books in an empty chair across from the table. The table was loaded with the books he owned. At night they were either in the bed with him, or on the floor.

Elizabeth came to a halt at the top step, her eyes falling on his collection. "Whoa. You weren't kidding. How many books do you have?"

He shrugged and rushed over to her, taking the books she held. Two-hundred seventy-three. It wasn't as many as he'd like, but their trailer was small, so he had to be picky about what he kept and what he traded. This library card idea wasn't so bad after all.

She set the rest of his books in the chair, then went to the table and started browsing. "*Science and Human Behavior*, Edgar Allen Poe, *Jane Eyre*, *Adventures of Huckleberry Finn*, the *Happiness Hypothesis*, 1984... *Where the Sidewalk Ends*?" She grinned at him.

Patrick pointed to the last. "That's a classic."

"Quite a variety you have here." Her fingers trailed over several more books before she picked one up. He pretended not to notice what she had.

"*Moby Dick*? This is pretty well-worn for a..." She flipped to the back. "Eight-hundred-and-twenty-two page book."

He sucked in a breath. "Yes."

"Isn't it, I don't know, kind of depressing?"

"Yes."

She glanced at him through her thick lashes.

His breath hitched.

"Doesn't Ahab die?" she asked.

He nodded. "But he takes the whale with him."

She stared at him until he felt uneasy. Finally, she turned away and set the book down.

She glanced at her watch. "It's almost noon. Now, what are we going to do?"

He let a wide grin cross his face and enjoyed the split second's worth of panic on her face before she lifted her chin.

She. Was. Fun.

CHAPTER TEN

Patrick glanced over at Elizabeth as she took a big lick of her mint chocolate chip ice cream. It'd started to melt down the side of her cone and got on her chin. She chuckled and wiped at her mouth with the back of her hand.

Her eyes were fixed on her brothers. They ran ahead through the circus grounds toward the big tent, laughing as they went. They'd already finished their ice creams.

She shook her head. "I can't believe you got my dad to let Tilde pick up the boys."

Patrick licked his own rocky road ice cream, turning it around against his tongue to gather the drips. He hummed in his throat and swallowed. "You didn't actually think I could let your we-can't-come-back-to-the-circus act stand, did you?"

"Guess not." She took another lick of her cone. Her phone rang, and she pulled it from her pocket. He took a quick glimpse and saw Sean's name on her caller ID.

She hit end after two rings and shoved the phone back in her pocket. He sighed in relief.

"I've had a lot of fun today," she said. "Thank you."

He'd had fun too. When he woke up that morning, this was the last thing he'd expected to happen, and it had been just what he'd needed; even the studying in the library. It'd been the best day he'd had since his mom had disappeared. Just being with her and talking to her was relaxing.

She finished her ice cream and took a bite of her cone. "So, were you planning on telling me what this whole day has been about or not?"

He grinned at her. She was good. But what could he say? *I've come to save you from Sean?* He doubted she'd be impressed and frowned. He'd segue. "How was your birthday?"

Her spine went a little stiff, but she ignored the implication and played dumb. "So you don't want to tell me what today was about, then?"

"Patience, woman, you've got to have patience."

She shook her head. "Okay, fine." When she spoke again, it was in an overly cheery tone. "My birthday was great!"

"I don't appreciate the sarcasm, but I'll take what I can get," he said. "By the way, don't think I forgot that you promised me a date when you turned sixteen."

"You don't know when my birthday is. As far as you know, I'm still fifteen." She was trying really hard to avoid the whole "dating" part of the topic.

"It's June 26th."

Elizabeth glanced over at him. "Whoa, you do know my birthday."

He rolled his eyes. "Of course I do."

She pinched her brow together. "I don't remember telling you when it was."

Patrick finished his ice cream and started on his cone. "You told me the year we met. At my birthday party. We closed the park to the public that night, remember? Your family and Sean were the only towners invited. You were so excited about it that you asked my mom if you could have your birthday here."

She shook her head. "That was four years ago."

He continued, "She asked you when your birthday was, and you placed your hands on your hips and stuck your chin in the air and said, 'June 26th.'"

She finished her cone. "How do you remember that?"

He shrugged. That question always bothered him because he never knew how to answer it. He just remembered things, even things he'd rather not.

Her eyes lit up. "I do remember that party. Luke was two. He ran off, and everyone was looking for him." She stared into space as though she could see it. "We heard him giggling inside the big tent. Maggie was holding him with her trunk at the height of her eyes. He was kissing her trunk, and she was flipping her ears up and down."

That'd been a great moment in an even better night.

"My mom loved Maggie so much from that moment on." She faced him. "I don't know if your mom or Tilde and Jay ever told you, but my mom used to bring bags full of apples to Maggie every time you came to town."

His eyes went wide. "I didn't know that, but it makes sense. She always had way more apples than she needed. Of course, now she has to have at least one apple with every meal, or she won't eat at all. So thank you for that."

Elizabeth hid her head in her hands. "Oh no." She chuckled and peeked through her fingers. "Sorry."

"Maggie's worth it. And, I want my date—"

"I don't date." She said it like it was so normal, like she was saying grass was green or muscle cars were cool. Now she was playing with him.

He shook his head and took her in. She was incredible. He'd always known it, but it was more pronounced than in the past. In mid stride, he dropped a hand to her back and stopped.

She faced him. His hand slid down to her hip.

"We'll get back to the I-don't-date thing in a second." He kept his touch light and unobtrusive. "You wanted to know what today was about."

"Yeah."

"It's..." Behind her, something caught Patrick's eye. He glanced up, and his stomach did a somersault. "Sean?"

"Elizabeth," Sean hollered.

Elizabeth spun around in time to see Sean sprint up to them.

"Sean?" Elizabeth pulled her chin back.

Sean's eyes were bloodshot, one of his eyes was black, and his clothes and hair were rumpled. Patrick had never seen Sean rumpled before in his life.

"Are you okay?" Elizabeth stepped forward. "What happened to your eye?"

"Got in a fight at the gym."

"Sean?" Patrick moved forward, close enough that he could smell the Altoids in his mouth and the musky scent of too much cologne. He was drunk and trying to conceal the smell. Patrick had seen Sean do this before to fool his dad.

Sean ignored him. "Can I talk to you for a second?"

Elizabeth glanced back at Patrick and then nodded to Sean. "Sure."

SEAN TOOK her hand and walked away from Patrick. He'd take her all the way to the moon to get her away from Patrick if she'd let him.

She tugged on his hand to stop him. "What's going on?"

He turned on her. "Where have you been?"

She pulled her chin back. "Excuse me?"

He shook his head and fought for clarity through his alcohol-addled brain. It didn't help that he'd gone to the gym like this, unable to fight properly, and had gotten beaten down. He'd never been beaten down. "I went to your house. You weren't there."

"Did we have plans?" She placed her hands on her hips.

Sean glanced at Patrick over her head. Patrick had his eyes narrowed in on them and his hands in his pockets. Sean scowled. How dare Patrick do this? How dare he try and get between him and Elizabeth? Patrick had everything. Freedom, people who cared about him, and a will to succeed at anything, and now he wanted Elizabeth, too?

"Sean!" Elizabeth grabbed his shoulder and shook once. "Snap out of it."

He focused on her. "I'm sorry. It's been a rough day."

"Let us take you home." She turned toward Patrick, and Sean grabbed her arm.

"No, I came to tell you..."

She dropped her hand to where he held her. "Yeah?"

"I love you. I want you to be my girlfriend." He blinked at her, willing her to come into focus.

"What?" She froze. "Sean? You can't—"

"I can't what?" He tightened his grip on her arm. "Love you?"

"You're hurting me."

He loosened his grip, but didn't release her. "Just give me a chance. I could be good for you."

"Let me go." She yanked her arm from his grasp.

"I'm sorry. I didn't want to hurt you. Elizabeth, please?"

She took a step back. "Are you drunk?"

"Tell me you'll go out with me," Sean raised his voice.

She shook her head. "You need to go home and sober up. We'll take you."

Sean glared at her. "It's too late, isn't it? You've already chosen him." He signaled to Patrick, who rushed over.

"Sean, you're scaring me," Elizabeth said in a tone that was infuriatingly calm.

Sean stumbled back a step, and Patrick was there to catch him.

"Let me take you home," Patrick said.

Sean pulled away and narrowed his eyes at Patrick. "I wish I'd never met you." He turned and sprinted away.

"Sean," Patrick called after him. "Wait!"

CHAPTER ELEVEN

The old, family truck, creaky from years of towing Maggie and her trailer around, rumbled and groaned as Patrick pulled it over to the curb at the Shea's house. It was already close to ten, and the two youngest boys had fallen asleep in the back seat on the way home. The house was pitch-black inside, and Mr. Shea's car wasn't in the driveway.

"My dad's not here." Elizabeth bit her lip.

Patrick glanced over his shoulder at the boys in the back, all sleeping except Kyle. He spoke in a whisper. "What time does he normally get home?"

"He's supposed to be home around 3:30 in the afternoon," Kyle said, his tone derisive.

Elizabeth clenched her fists for just a moment, her gaze locked on the darkened house. She opened her door and jumped down.

Patrick exited and pulled his seat forward at the same time Elizabeth did to make room for the boys to get out. After Sean had run off, Patrick had felt ill, but he'd kept it to himself, making sure the Sheas had a good time. He was worried about Sean though. Had called him several times.

Patrick knew he should've stopped him. Should've kept him from driving. There was nothing he could do now, and he didn't want to worry Elizabeth anymore than she already was. She had enough on her plate as it was.

Kyle nudged Jake awake, then slid out and stretched over his head. Elizabeth took Jake's hand and encouraged him to slide over. He did, but it was slow going. He rubbed his eyes as he swayed back and forth exiting. Elizabeth had to catch him to keep him from falling onto the pavement.

Patrick lifted Luke and laid his head on his shoulder before shutting his door. When he reached the front of his truck, Elizabeth smiled at him over the hood, then turned to the house. Kyle was already halfway to the door. She wrapped an arm around Jake to help him.

Patrick felt a painful thud in his chest. Elizabeth was so young. His mom had vanished when he was sixteen, and it'd been horrible, but he'd only had to worry about himself.

He liked Mr. Shea, but Elizabeth needed more than this. She deserved more than this. She deserved to be a teenager and not have to worry about being a mom or about coming home to a parentless house alone with three brothers.

Patrick came around Jay's truck and marched up to the house, rubbing Luke's back as he went. There had to be something he could do, some way he could help her, some way to relieve a little of her burden.

She held the front door open for him. After locking up, she led him down the hall to Luke and Jake's room. He lay Luke down on the bed as she helped Jake climb under his own covers. Luke's head hit his pillow, and he rolled over. His eyes never opened. Patrick removed Luke's shoes and pulled his Spiderman blankets up over his shoulders.

When he turned, Elizabeth was tucking Jake's sheets around him. She rubbed a hand over his head in a very maternal fashion. She then turned to Patrick and crooked a finger at him as she went to exit.

Kyle had already gone into his room, shutting the door behind him. She knocked on his door.

"Yeah?" Kyle called from behind the door.

She pushed it open.

Patrick glanced in. Kyle was already in his bed with his eyes closed, but still clothed, and he hadn't turned off his bedside lamp.

"Going to bed already?" Elizabeth asked.

"Yeah, I'm pooped," he said.

"Okay, good night." She stepped out of the room.

Patrick leaned in and started to close the door, when Kyle opened his eyes and winked at him.

Patrick grinned. *Troublemaker.*

Kyle rolled over as Patrick shut the door. Elizabeth led him down the hall and stopped when it turned to the front door. She glanced at it.

He held his breath. Last thing he wanted to do was make her uncomfortable, so he waited to see what she might do, ask him to stay or leave. He shoved his hands in his pockets as the anticipation grew. He didn't want to leave. He wanted to stay here with her and the boys. He wanted to make sure they were safe until their dad got home.

Finally, she turned, her ponytail flipping over her shoulder. "Can I make you some hot chocolate?"

He tried not to smile. Really, he did. "What kind of hot chocolate? Not all hot chocolates are equal."

She screwed up her face and glanced at the ceiling. "I don't know. Maybe Stephen's?"

"Mint?"

She grinned. "Yeah, actually."

"I'd love a cup."

She motioned for him to follow her into the kitchen, shaking her head as they went. While she went to the pantry, he filled the kettle with water and started the burner.

She stepped out of the pantry with the hot chocolate.

"I don't suppose you have tea-cups, do you?" He opened a cupboard.

"No, sorry." She pointed to the cupboard next to the fridge. "Mugs are in there."

He pulled out two mismatched cups and sat them next to the stove. They didn't speak as she scooped the hot chocolate into the mugs and waited for the water to boil.

She kept glancing at the clock on the microwave.

When the kettle whistled, she grabbed it and poured. The room went silent as she stirred their cocoa.

Elizabeth tapped her fingers on her mug. "You think he's all right?"

"Your dad or Sean?"

She swallowed. "Sean."

Patrick had hit a nerve. She was worried about her dad but didn't want to talk about it.

He nodded. "Physically, I'm sure, but I doubt you're an easy one to get over."

She shook her head. "He never had me to get over."

Patrick stared at her. He had to know. "If he'd asked you out when he was sober, what would you have said?"

"I think I'm a little slow on the uptake," she said.

"I'm sorry, what?"

"I only saw him once in a while when you were gone," she said. "He didn't even come by when my mom died. But then I turned sixteen and all of a sudden he was here all the time. I thought he wanted to help us, and I was so grateful that I let it slide. He was buttering me up. I'm an idiot."

"So, you would've said yes?" Sounded like it.

"Why would you think that?"

"He likes you."

She scoffed. "So? Just because he likes me doesn't me he gets to have me."

Patrick shrugged. "Girls do tend to like him."

"They like you, too. This isn't a good argument. If I'd known how he felt, I'd have distanced myself. He's just not the guy for me." Her gaze flitted to his, and she blushed. She grabbed her spoon and gave her hot chocolate a good, forceful stir.

Patrick sucked in a breath. A part of him had always wondered if she liked him, and hoped she did, but now he knew for sure. It was equally exciting and overwhelming. He couldn't decide if he wanted to kiss her or run for the hills.

He glanced at the clock on the microwave. It was eleven now. Guess that meant he'd be running for the hills. "Do you know where your dad is?"

Elizabeth stared at her hands. "Last time he was out this late he was at a bar."

Patrick gritted his teeth. "You shouldn't have to do this."

She looked at him. "No, I shouldn't, but someone has to, and it might as well be me. My dad's a good man; he's just lost himself. He hasn't had to deal with anything without my mom for twenty years. She was the love of his life." She took a sip of her drink. "He'll figure it out."

Patrick sure hoped so.

"The guy who hit her—my mom. I used to hate him," she said. "I used to play out scenarios in my head where he'd done something different. What if he'd stayed home? What if he'd gotten a designated driver or a cab home? What if? What if?"

Hatred swelled inside Patrick; hatred for the man who'd T-boned Mrs. Shea's car, who'd robbed her kids of a life with their mom. He felt her loss deeply, almost as much as he felt his own mother's. "He deserves to die."

"I used to think that, too."

He set his cup down. "You don't anymore?"

She shook her head. "I saw him once. In court. He was a mess. He saw us and started crying. He couldn't even speak. I went in thinking that I'd hate him, but I didn't."

"He took your mother from you."

"Yeah, he did that." She cleared her throat. "It sucks. But I realized he didn't ruin my life. He made it a lot harder, for sure, but I get to choose how I react to this. I can do my best or I can let it control me. I know that my mom wanted the best things for me and my brothers in this life. I know that she wanted us to be happy, so that's what I chose. And most of the time I am. The only lives that man ruined were my mom's and his own. Truth be known, I feel sorry for him."

Patrick stared at her, astounded that only a little more than six months after her mom's death she had such a clear head about it. When his mom had gone missing, he'd become a recluse for six months, and after that, he'd had a string of bad behavior in his attempt to block it out. One night, he'd even gotten as drunk as Sean had been earlier. It'd been horrible. The hangover alone was enough to make him never want to drink again.

If it hadn't been for Tilde and Jay, he'd probably be in jail by now —or worse. He'd gotten better because of and for them. Not because of himself. And "better" was a relative term. On the outside, for the most part, he portrayed "well," but on the inside, he was still a seething mass of hatred and fear. His recurring nightmare about a shadow-man taking his mom was proof enough of that. The only time he felt normal was when he was with Elizabeth.

"How can you be so forgiving?" he asked.

Staring into space, she touched her mom's crucifix where it hung around her neck, and for the first time, he noticed a ring hanging there, too. It looked like a wedding band. "It's not easy, but it's better than the alternative."

He shook his head. "If I found the person responsible for my mom's... I'd kill him."

Her head whipped in his direction, her eyes wide. "You can't mean that."

He took a swig of his hot chocolate. "I do. Every word."

"You'd go to jail."

He nodded and set his drink down, the ceramic clinking against the granite counter-top. He thought of that when his mom had first gone missing, and nearly every day of the two years she'd been gone. The thing was, he just didn't care. "It'd be worth it."

Elizabeth pulled her chin back. "Don't say that."

He turned his gaze to her, and she swallowed hard. "Don't say what?"

"There are people who care about you, who would be devastated to hear you talking like that."

Well, that was an open invitation if ever he heard one. Now that he knew she didn't want Sean, maybe it was a good time to force the issue. So much for running for the hills. He didn't want to stay on this topic anyway. His revenge was his and his alone.

He took a step closer to her. "Like who, for example?"

She lifted her chin. "Tilde, Jay. Everyone at the circus, I'd imagine."

He took her mug, which she had clasped tight in both hands. "Only them?"

She flushed but refused to look away.

Stubborn. He grinned.

She stared at the clock on the microwave. "You know we'd be sad, too."

He reached up and took her chin lightly in his hand, encouraging her with just a little pressure to turn back to him.

She did.

He dropped his hand. "But *you*... you'd be sad?"

She set her jaw. "Don't mess with me, Patrick. I don't... I-I don't want to date you."

Stuttering was a good sign. "Liar."

She shook her head. "When I said I don't date, I didn't mean it as a challenge."

He took another step closer. "I didn't take it as one. I took it as an irritating impediment to the inevitable."

She guffawed. "Inevitable?" She unhooked her necklace and slid the ring off, then handed it to him. "That's my dad's wedding band. He took it off a month after my mom died, said that looking at it made his heart break. I won't go through that."

He rolled the ring around in his fingers. Then he glanced up at her and smiled. "You won't have to. I promise."

She narrowed her eyes at him, but a wicked spark seemed to ignite in their golden depths. "All right, let's say we do end up together—"

He chuckled and let the ring slide up his ring finger, just past the first knuckle. "I like where this is going."

She continued as if he'd said nothing. "I want to be a cop."

He furrowed his brow. Okay, he hadn't expected her to say that. Though, now that he thought about it, she'd make an excellent one. Her type A personality would make her formidable.

"And you just told me that you want to kill the person responsible for your mother's disappearance. And let's face it, you're just smart enough and stubborn enough to do it. Then what? I get to arrest my husband? Spend my life married to a man in jail?"

Husband? Married? Yikes. Yet, he kind of liked the sound of that. It was so normal and safe-sounding. He'd never had normal, and safe had abandoned ship with his mom. A future with Elizabeth? That thought sent a comfortable warmth through him. Maybe they'd even get a nice little bungalow and start a family of their own.

She snapped the fingers of her free hand in his face. "Stop grinning and focus."

Right. "Who says I'm not focusing?"

"If you are, then explain to me how you don't see the impasse we're in?"

"Impasse?" He furrowed his brow, even though he knew exactly what she meant.

"If you keep pursuing this course of action—" She signaled between the two of them. "—then this can never happen. Not now that I know what you'll do. So, yeah. Impasse."

This was fun. Their first ultimatum. "Okay, let me make sure I understand you correctly. You're saying that if I give up on revenge, then you'll give up your no-dating rule?"

She pulled her chin back and blinked several times. "That's not... I didn't—"

"I accept." He leaned forward as if to kiss her, though he wasn't going to. He just wanted to call her bluff. Okay, and kiss her if she'd let him.

Her hand shot up, landing on his chest, preventing him.

"Aw," he said. "Looks like you're not so willing after all."

He hated messing with her on this issue, but he'd been pretty positive about her reaction. He did want to date her, but not if it meant giving up on his mom. He wouldn't do that. Not for anyone or anything. His mom deserved better than that.

Good thing Elizabeth was so young and unwilling; it saved him from having to make a promise he couldn't keep. The plan now was to keep her on her toes, never let her doubt for a second what his feelings for her were, so that when he got his revenge, Elizabeth would be ready. If he didn't end up in jail.

Though, now that he'd confessed everything to her, he had a pretty strong motivation not to go to jail. He'd just have to be as clever and devious as the person responsible for his mom's disappearance. If they could get away with it, then so could he.

"You think you're so smart," she said.

He shrugged.

"You knew how I was going to react? You used your little mind games on me, didn't you?"

He shrugged again.

"Stop shrugging. It's irritating."

He chuckled. "Sorry."

"No, you're not." Her hand still rested on his chest. "You're still going all revenge-crazy, aren't you?"

He nodded.

Her jaw clenched, the muscles there pulsing under her skin. Boy, was he in for it now. What would she do? Slug him? No, she was too in control of herself for that. Her eyes narrowed, and he took a deep breath, preparing for the inevitable.

She grabbed the front of his vest where her hand rested and yanked him down to her in a kiss.

His eyes flew open. *Yowza!*

Okay, he hadn't seen that coming. His heart thudded in his rib cage as he wrapped his arms around her. She was inexperienced in this arena; regardless this was the best kiss he'd ever received.

He smiled against her lips, his giddiness increasing exponentially. Then the truth of it hit him. She was doing the same thing to him that he had done to her. Calling his bluff. He was in for it now.

She yanked away so suddenly that he nearly fell over, and turned her back to him.

"I shouldn't have done that," she said, her voice quivering. "I don't know what I was thinking."

He rested his hand on the counter, leaning his weight there. He wanted to be mad at her, it was a dirty trick, but it was kind of working. "What are you doing tomorrow night?"

She spun back around. "What?"

His gaze fell to her lips, slightly swollen and red from their kiss, and he felt inexplicably proud. "I'd like to take you to dinner. Say, at seven-thirty?"

She stared at him for a moment. "Do you mean...?"

He let out a shaky breath. How had he never noticed what a strong hold this girl had on him? "I'd be willing to reconsider my stance."

Okay, maybe he'd been a little drastic with the whole taking-revenge-into-his-own-hands plan. He could still find who was responsible and make sure they were punished to the fullest extent of the law without getting personally involved. Probably. Maybe.

A slow smile crossed her face. "Really?"

He nodded, his heart thudding in his chest for a different reason now. To see that smile every day and know he'd been the one to put it there, that was a dream. In a way, it'd be helping to fulfill her mother's wish that she be happy. He could do that, and he would.

CHAPTER TWELVE

A bright light shone through Sean's car window and into his closed eyes. The soft hum of traffic surrounded him. He lifted a hand to block the flashlight as he blinked, trying to get a look at the person behind the offending object.

"This is Officer Jacobs with the Sacramento Police Department. I need you to put your hands where I can see them."

Sean sat up, bringing his seat with him, and peered around, trying to clear his sleep and alcohol-fogged brain. His flask fell to the floor, emptied of all its contents. It was dark outside, and trees lined the busy street where he was parked. Where was he? "What time is it?"

"Sir, put your hands up."

Sean turned back to the officer and lifted his hands. Not because the officer had asked him to, but to block the light.

The cop pulled the door open. "Step out of the vehicle."

"What seems to be the problem, officer?" Sean got out of the car.

"Aside from the fact that you appear to be drunk and underage, the license plate number on this car is the same number as a car that out-ran an officer earlier tonight when he tried to pull it over for speeding."

Sean closed his eyes and breathed out his nose. He didn't remember being in a car chase, but he also didn't remember parking his car here and falling asleep. He was so in for it now. "I'd like to speak to an attorney."

The officer turned him to face his Jaguar and cuffed his hands behind his back as he read him his rights.

This was all Patrick's fault.

PATRICK WOKE the next morning to his cell phone buzzing on the floor next to him. He reached for it, feeling pleasantly groggy. No nightmares last night. He thought of the kiss Elizabeth had given him and smiled. When he picked up his phone, Elizabeth's dad's ring clinked against the glass. Her kiss had left him so surprised that he'd forgotten to give it back to her. He smiled as he thought of returning it to her tonight.

He glanced at the caller ID and frowned. All his happy feelings fled. He was going to have to deal with this sooner or later; might as well get it over with now.

"Sean?"

"Patrick, we have to talk," Sean said with an unmistakable urgency in his tone.

Patrick swallowed. "Look, I know you're mad at me, but we're not going to let this get between ten years of friendship, are we?"

"Shut up for once and listen to me. I know what happened to your mom."

Patrick sat bolt upright, wide awake. "That's not funny, Sean."

"I'm not joking, Patrick," Sean seethed under his breath. "While you were with Elizabeth last night, I was in a holding cell, and I heard something."

"What?" Patrick's voice rose in volume. "What did you hear?"

From the back of the trailer, his dad yelled, "Shut your trap, Rick. Your old man's trying to get some rest."

Patrick threw his covers off, throwing several books off his bed with several loud thuds. In his pajamas and bare feet, he rushed out of the trailer.

Sean lowered his voice. "I can't talk right now. Can you meet me?"

"Where?" His toes dug into the dewy grass.

"At my house—"

"I can be there in twenty," he said, even though it was a thirty-minute drive.

"No. Not now. Later. Tonight. Meet me there at eight," Sean said.

Patrick shook his head. "Eight? You want me to wait until eight?"

"I'm being watched. Eight tonight. I'll tell you everything."

WHEN ELIZABETH HAD KISSED Patrick last night, she wasn't sure who had been more surprised, her or Patrick. She still wasn't sure what had possessed her to do it. Her rational brain had turned off and didn't come back on until she was already kissing him—until it was already too late.

She'd been mortified. It was her first kiss, and she'd done it to make a point, though while it was happening, she couldn't recall what the point had been. It'd been her first kiss, and she'd done it to call Patrick on his bluff. Until he'd asked her out, she'd been sure she'd ruined it.

But he had asked her out. And the kiss had been enough to make him want to compromise with her on their... issues. She felt proud now. Her first kiss. Go her!

When he'd told her he'd reconsider his revenge scheme, her heart had been about to leap right out of her chest. The least she could do was reconsider her no-dating rule.

The next morning, all throughout the day, and as she'd been getting ready for their date tonight, she was surprised to discover that she was excited, despite her reservations about dating. Not that she had any intention of rushing things. She would take it slow.

Now, as she sat in the living room with her hair curled, and in her nicest Sunday dress, she wasn't so sure she'd made the right decision.

Kyle sat in the chair opposite her. "You look nice."

She stared out the front window to the street. "Thank you."

He followed her gaze. "What time is he supposed to be here?"

A lump formed in her throat. She swallowed and spoke over it. "He was supposed to be here at seven."

Kyle frowned. "Oh. Well, maybe he got a flat. Did you call him?"

"Twice," she said.

"Maybe his phone's on silent or—"

She lifted a hand in a staying motion. "Or he changed his mind." Forty-five minutes without so much as a text, let alone a call, certainly suggested that. She stood. "I think we should go to dinner. I didn't get all fancied up for nothing." She still had the money from the other night at the circus.

Kyle nodded, but he didn't look in the least bit pleased. "Are you sure?"

"Yep." She'd been a fool. It was just like she'd thought. Getting attached to someone only led to heartache. Just like it had for her dad. And she was not going to go down the same road he was. Not ever.

CHAPTER THIRTEEN

At seven-thirty, Patrick parked his dad's truck in front of Sean's palatial residence. All the windows were dark, except for the transom window above the door where a soft glow shone, probably from the kitchen. The house looked otherwise empty, and Sean's car wasn't in the driveway.

He'd wait for fifteen minutes, and then he'd go up and knock. Sean had to know Patrick couldn't wait until eight. All day, his mind had been playing over what Sean had said on the phone, and he still couldn't make sense of it.

The only thing he'd accomplished was making himself increasingly sick worrying about what he was about to learn. Sean hadn't been lying. Even over the phone, Patrick could call his bluff. Sean knew something. And it scared the living daylights out of Patrick.

For two years he'd fantasized about this moment. About learning what had happened to his mom. He'd played it up to be some earth-shaking, climactic moment that would forever change his life for better or worse. He'd eagerly anticipated it, now that it was here it was all he could do to keep from vomiting.

His phone rang from the seat next to him. Absently, he picked it up and glanced at the caller ID. It was Elizabeth again. He silenced his phone and chucked it onto the seat as guilt churned in his stomach. He couldn't talk to her; he'd end up telling her what he was doing. If anyone could change his mind, it'd be her, and that wasn't an option. He twisted her dad's ring on his ring finger, noticing a small indent in the ring he hadn't noticed until now.

What a difference only a few hours could make. Last night, he'd considered, even if only briefly, giving up this moment. He'd considered letting the cops take care of it. But now that he was so close to finding out who was responsible for his mom's disappearance, he knew he could never hand that person over to the police. He would kill them, just as he'd always said he would.

When fifteen minutes passed, he took a deep breath, stepped out of the car, and made his way to the house. He found the large double doors hanging open a crack. He stopped in his tracks, his heart thudding violently against his chest.

Sean had said he was being watched earlier before hanging up.

Patrick pushed the door open. If something happened to Sean, he'd never forgive himself. The front entry-way that led to the grand staircase was dark and empty. He took a tentative step inside and stopped.

"Sean, are you here?" he called out. "Hello? Mr. Jones? Mrs. Jones?"

When no one answered, he came in a little further, heading down the hall, his footsteps muffled by the red, decorative runner-carpet, until he reached the living room on the left. A lamp lay on the floor in the dark room, shattered into several pieces.

Patrick's breathing shallowed as he stepped back and into something solid, strong, and human.

He whirled around and came face-to-face with the man who'd kidnapped Sophie. "You."

"The name's Vadim." The man arched his arm back and smashed it into Patrick's face.

~

A THROBBING ache in Patrick's skull that far outdid the hangover he'd had last year woke him from a restless sleep. His brain felt suspiciously like liquid, way too soft and slushy. He moaned, then blinked, wondering what time it was. It had to be night because it was dark and the whir of a plane's engine hummed not far off.

Where was he?

He tried to raise a hand to his head and found them zip-tied behind his back. He yanked on them. Then it came crashing back. Sean's empty house, the broken lamp, the tall, muscular man with long, greasy, blond hair pulled back into a ponytail, and his fist slamming into his head. Vadim.

He jerked up, and the quick motion sent a wave of nausea through him.

"He's awake," Vadim said. "I was starting to worry I hit him too hard."

Bile rose up Patrick's throat, and it took every calming exercise he'd ever taught himself to keep from upchucking into what he now realized was a black, burlap sack covering his head. He breathed in and out for several seconds before he was able to calm his stomach.

"Where's Sean?" Patrick demanded. "What did you do to him?"

Vadim chuckled. "He's very loyal, this one, da? Not very bright."

"Take the sack off," Seans called from somewhere in front of him.

"Sean?" Patrick breathed a sigh of relief. "Are you all right? Did they hurt you?"

Vadim yanked the sack from his head, scraping its rough edges over his nose and eyes. His eyes watered. Patrick dropped his gaze as light streamed in from what seemed like everywhere. It was too bright, and he squinted.

Someone squatted in front of him. "Hey there, Paddy."

Sean.

Patrick's eyes began to adjust. He was in some sort of factory that looked like it'd been long abandoned. Dust particles floated through the bursts of sunbeams that were streaming in from big holes in the tin roof and through dirty, broken windows.

"Over here, pal," Sean said.

Patrick focused on his friend. He looked fine. Well-rested. No apparent injuries. No zip-ties on his hands. "What's going on?"

"You've been traded," Sean said, his tone cool and collected, though Patrick could read an underlying fury that he had never experienced in his friend before.

Patrick's gaze trailed to Vadim, who stood about ten feet back, leaning against a rusted, iron beam. He wore a wide smile, showcasing yellowing teeth.

The prickling fear that hid deep inside Patrick's psyche, the one he'd pushed back every morning after sleeping with nightmares, shoved its way forward, its wisps wrapping around his sanity. The nightmares where he saw his mother pulled into the dark by a faceless, nameless shadow.

"It seems you have a real skill at making enemies," Sean said.

"What did you do?"

Sean stood. "I wish I could say this was my idea, but all I really did was get you to my house." He nodded over his shoulder. "Vadim took care of the rest."

This had to be a dream, another nightmare. A nightmare like his others morphing into something far more terrible. That was it.

Sean stuck his hands in his pockets. "You're confused. How strange. Vadim, I think you did hit him too hard. Let me explain, Patrick. Vadim was given his freedom on the condition that he takes you out of the country and disposes of you. He agreed."

Leaning back just enough that he could touch the floor behind him, Patrick slowly started sweeping dirt into one palm with his other hand. "Who made the deal with him?"

Sean took a deep breath. "The man who killed your mother. Yes, she's dead."

Patrick's stomach sank.

"It seems the perfect murder can only be pulled off by a cop." Sean ran a hand through his hair. "Ironic, really."

A cop?

"Anyway," Sean continued, "I guess he decided he couldn't let you keep snooping into her case. Which is how we ended up here."

A lump caught in his throat. "Why, Sean? Why are you doing this to me? We're friends."

Sean squatted in front of him again. "We were."

"Why?" Patrick asked.

"You're a circus freak, and yet your life is perfect. Everything always goes your way. And without any effort you get Elizabeth... I shouldn't want to be you," Sean said.

From his kneeling position, Patrick jumped to his feet and swung his hands toward Sean's face, releasing the dirt. Sean cussed as it went into his eyes, and Patrick ran. Not two seconds later, Sean was on him, slamming him to the dirt-ridden floor.

Patrick struggled beneath his grasp.

"Stop struggling," Sean demanded, "or I'll break your arm."

He bucked one more time, and Sean slammed Patrick's head into the dirt. He placed his knee on Patrick's back and his forearm across the back of his neck. "I'm the winner here, Patrick. There's nothing you can do."

Patrick's head swam, the pain that had been there before now three-fold. Hot tears escaped his eyes. "Sean, please. Don't do this."

Sean moved a little above him, and a second later he lowered their silver coin to Patrick's line of sight. "I want you to have this. To remember better times."

Sean put the coin in Patrick's suit coat pocket, then yanked him to his feet and shoved him in Vadim's direction.

Vadim grabbed him and pulled him toward an exit at the back of the building.

"Wait," Sean called.

Vadim turned Patrick to face Sean.

Sean marched up to him. "Rafferty says hello."

CHAPTER FOURTEEN

The rolling of the waves on the open sea had been something Patrick had longed to experience since he could remember. He always thought that one day he'd buy a sail-boat and travel the world. See the seven wonders and all the other wonders that were left uncounted. He'd feel the wind in his hair, watch as it filled his sails, and he'd aim for the horizon.

He found it ironic that when he finally made it on to a boat that he was being held against his will and he was seasick.

Would anyone miss him? Would anyone care that he'd gone missing?

Yes. Jay and Tilde would. His mind wandered to Elizabeth, and a wicked pain pierced through his chest. Sharp and stabbing. It felt like a heart attack, but he knew better. He'd had panic attacks frequently after his mom vanished.

What would Elizabeth think? The very last time he was supposed to have seen her, he'd stood her up. And for what? A life sentence as, as a what? Was he to be sold as a slave? Or killed? Considering his company, either was likely. If only he'd kept his plans with Elizabeth.

Elizabeth...

The pain stabbed through him. He leaned forward on his knees, rocking himself back and forth on the hard metal floor. He was going to vomit. He could feel it building. He had to calm down. *Just breathe.*

The cramped, four-foot-by-four-foot room they'd locked him in didn't have any windows, and there were no furnishings. There was one small light in the corner, next to a bucket that he'd quickly learned was his bathroom. He'd long since lost track of when they'd left land. He wasn't even sure what land they'd left.

Vadim had put the burlap sack back over his head before leaving the factory and then had drugged him with chloroform right after that. Patrick remembered nothing before awakening on the ship.

His captors came once a day to bring him scraps of stale bread and water. Once in a while, they'd remove his bucket. Counting days by number of meals meant they'd been at sea for two weeks. They'd removed his toilet bucket six times in that period. The smell in his room was enough to make him sick without the concussion, the anxiety, and the unsteady sea.

He took several deep breaths, counting three seconds in and five seconds out. He couldn't throw up. It'd just make matters worse. So he kept counting until he'd gotten his upchuck reflex under control, until his heart rate slowed.

How was he going to get out of this mess? He'd always been able to get himself out of anything, but now, in his condition, lacking any kind of mental stimulation or human contact, all he could do was focus on not getting sick all over.

Was this their plan? To drive him mad before they arrived? Did they think he'd be easier to handle if he went insane? If that was their plan, they were sorely mistaken. He recalled his grandfather on his father's side losing his memory and soundness of mind in his later years. He hadn't lost the Daley cunning, or his ability to con people; what he'd lost was his reason for doing so. How did you reason with a crazy con man? You didn't.

Patrick let out a crazed laugh. His body convulsed painfully, but he didn't care. If he did go crazy, he hoped he'd be like his grandpa. They wouldn't know what hit them. His shaking increased until he could no longer hold himself up. He tilted to his side in the fetal position because there wasn't enough space for him to spread out.

How could Sean do this to him? And Rafferty. Patrick squeezed his eyes shut at the mere thought of the man's name. The man who'd sold him into slavery, who'd killed his mother. The one man he'd actually put his trust in to solve his mom's case. A lump swelled in his throat. Hot tears burned in his eyes that he refused to let fall. He should've known better than to trust him, to trust Sean, to trust anyone.

A creaking sound screeched through his prison. The door opened. He didn't think it was time for his measly crumbs, but time was so beyond him in here. Instead of the normal clunk of hard bread falling on the floor, footsteps crossed to him.

He didn't move.

A toe nudged him. "Up, get up." The man's accent was thick and Russian.

Drop dead. Patrick didn't bother to open his eyes.

Large hands grabbed him by his button-up and yanked him to his feet. He barely grabbed his suit coat before the man dragged him from the room.

"You have an audience," the man said.

That couldn't be good, but he was so tired, and the relatively fresher air of the dank, dark hall in the underbelly of the ship was confusing. What was happening? A little taste of freedom before even this reprieve was taken from him again?

He moved too slowly for the man who'd come to get him, but his physical strength was so depleted it was all he could do to stay standing. Several staggering minutes later, they entered a large room. It looked like a dining area with metal tables and benches, a kitchen window where food could be picked up, and a wash area.

Two men sat at a table, Vadim being one of them. A map and other papers were laid out.

The boat hit a wave, and Patrick stumbled into a nearby wall.

The new man turned when Patrick fell. A large smirk covered his face as he swung his legs out from the bench and approached Patrick.

"He's a very pretty boy, this one." He grabbed Patrick's head and tilted it back. "Yet you think we should not sell him?"

Vadim stood. "Maybe. Maybe not. He's clever, sometimes."

The new man shoved Patrick's head back, and it banged into the wall behind him.

Patrick cringed.

"He's the one who figured out your little code?"

Vadim crossed his arms and nodded.

"The code was not so hard, though?" the new man said.

Vadim shrugged. "Perhaps not. But definitely hard enough that the police couldn't figure it out. I'm told this one solved it in a couple minutes."

Patrick frowned. "Thirty seconds."

The new man faced him again. "What?"

A part of Patrick's brain, a very small part, warned him to keep his mouth shut. Yet... "It was thirty seconds. Not two minutes."

"He's cocky," the new man said.

"He's maybe not so wise, but his brain knows puzzles," Vadim said. "I say we let him look. If he can figure out, then—"

"We take him to Lazerev?" The new man placed his hands on his hips. He glanced at the guard who'd brought him up. "Help him to table."

The guard dragged Patrick to the table and pushed him into a seat.

The new man pointed at the guard and spoke in Russian. The guard nodded and headed back into the kitchen. A moment later he returned with a plate full of food: mashed potatoes with gravy, ham, and a roll. It smelled heavenly, and Patrick salivated. The guard set the plate down next to the new man and left.

The new man signaled to the food. "You are hungry?"

Patrick dragged his gaze from the food to the new man. He swallowed. Then swallowed again.

"Well?"

Patrick's stomach rumbled. Nothing had ever looked so delicious before in his life. He breathed in his nose, savoring the delicious aroma, and listed forward.

The man grabbed the plate and slid it away. Patrick kept his eyes on the food until the man placed something else in front of him.

"Tell me what this is, and you can have all the food you want."

Patrick blinked down at the sheet of paper in front of him. "What is it?"

Vadim laughed. "He's hungry."

"You tell me," New Man said, "and food is yours."

Patrick focused on the paper until he could read what was written there. He lifted his hands from his lap and settled his fingers at the edge of the paper. It was a cipher. His brain immediately started working, flipping through his memory bank. He knew this. He'd seen it before; he was sure he had.

"Well?" New Man said. "It's been thirty seconds."

"Shhh," Patrick said. "I'm working."

Vadim laughed again. "See, I told you, he—"

Patrick glared at him. Vadim immediately went silent. Patrick went back to work.

"He doesn't know what he's doing," New Man said. "This is waste of time."

"Give him minute," Vadim said.

Patrick grinned. "It's a bifid cipher."

"A what?" New Man peered down at it. "What does it say?"

Patrick slid the paper away. "Give me the food, and I'll tell you."

New Man stood and leaned over him. "You tell me now, or—"

"You'll what? Kidnap me? Starve me? Sell me into slavery? Go ahead. You were planning on doing those things anyway, so I find myself unmoved."

New Man turned his glare on Vadim.

Vadim smiled. "Oh, give him food. We need to know what this says."

BELLY FILLED, cipher decrypted, they took Patrick back to his cell, where for the first time in weeks he fell into a deep sleep. It didn't last as images of the faceless, shadow man from his nightmares returned full-bore. He jolted awake, gasping for breath, sweat dripping from every pore, and stomach roiling.

He hadn't dreamt of the shadow man since he'd been taken. He'd subsisted on very little sleep, his fear, nausea, and hunger too overwhelming to sleep through. He rolled on to his knees and lowered his head, trying to calm himself.

Why was the shadow man returning? Patrick knew who he was. Rafferty. Why couldn't he just dream about him? Granted, he didn't think Rafferty would be much of an improvement, but at least he had a face. At least he could name him.

He pushed those thoughts back and tried to remember why he'd woken so abruptly. It hadn't been the dream. It'd been something else. He'd been thinking about something. He took a deep breath and, to his relief, noticed the missing stench of his toilet bucket. They'd taken it. As far as he could tell, they weren't due to empty it for another day, at least.

He wiped his forehead and caught a glimpse of something by the door. He edged closer and found a plate of food with a banana, oatmeal, and orange juice. He grabbed the banana, peeled it and started cramming it in. He'd never really liked bananas, but this banana was like ambrosia. *So delicious.*

He wondered why they'd brought him more food when he remembered the thoughts that had pulled him from his nightmare. He dropped what was left of the banana back on the plate, then pushed himself as far away from the food as he could go.

They were rewarding him, setting him up to solve another code. The code he'd solved last night hadn't made much sense to him, it'd been coordinates, but it had made a lot of sense to Vadim and the new man, who he was told was called Bogdan. He had learned, however, that knowing what the cipher said had made them very happy.

The shadow man had come to him. Had laughed at him. Had made him see what he'd done. Patrick had helped the human traffickers. How could he have done that? He'd been so hungry, so hungry that he hadn't been thinking straight. But it wasn't an excuse.

What if he'd led them away from someone who could've rescued him? Or even worse, what if there were others on this ship that'd been kidnapped? Little girls like Sophie? What if by helping the traffickers, by solving their cipher, he'd kept them from being rescued?

He pulled his knees to his chest and dropped his head to them. He couldn't take these meals anymore. He wouldn't. He'd starve before he helped them again.

THE GUARD RETRIEVED him a day or so later. Once again, he was led to the dining room. Both Vadim and Bogdan waited for him, playing a game of cards. Patrick wanted those cards. A boon to his boredom and something physical to hold on to.

The guard took him straight to the table, forcing him to sit. Then he was gone.

Bogdan stared at the cards in his hands. "The guards tell me that you did not like fruit?"

Patrick glanced at Bogdan's hand. He had four jacks. "The fruit was fine. What I don't like is helping human traffickers." Patrick glanced at Vadim. "He has four of a kind."

Vadim's brows shot up, and Bogdan turned in his seat to look at Patrick. He laughed, then said something in Russian to Vadim.

"I like you." Bogdan pushed his cards into the middle of the table to Vadim.

"The feeling's not mutual," Patrick said.

Vadim shuffled the cards. "We have deal for you. And you should consider taking it. We give you food, a bathroom, a shower if you like, and in turn, all we ask is that you do a bit of decoding."

Patrick intentionally dropped his eyes to the cards in Vadim's hands as he shuffled, and rested his hands on the edge of the table.

Bogdan faced him. "What do you think? Is good deal, da?"

He made eye contact with Bogdan and then Vadim. "I think the deck is stacked against me. I think I have very little options in this matter." He made a sweeping motion toward the edge of the table. "And because of this fact, I think you think you can make me do whatever you want. Would you play against a stacked deck?"

Vadim stared at the cards. He shuffled and quickly stacked them and pushed them to the end of the table and out of the way.

It was all Patrick could do to keep from smiling. They sure took suggestion easily. Getting those cards would be easier than he thought.

"You do not have much choice in matter," Vadim said.

Patrick stood, resting his hands on the table. "I'll starve before I help you."

Both men tried to look amused, but they weren't—neither of their smiles reached their eyes. They needed him. Vadim called out in Russian, and the guard returned. As the guard pulled Patrick past Bogdan, Patrick bumped into Bogdan hard enough to make the table move, and while the men were focused there, he grabbed the stack of cards from the edge of the table before the guard pulled him away.

THE DAY after he'd stolen the cards, he sat in the corner of his small space and waited for them to come. Bogdan was the first to come, and when the door opened, Patrick whipped the pilfered playing cards at him one at a time.

Bogdan cussed in Russian as each card hit its mark. Several pelted his face, one hitting his eye before he slammed the door behind him.

Patrick had a good laughing fit from that even when Bogdan had sent several guards to rough him up a little and take the cards. The beating was nothing worse than the sparing matches he'd been in with Sean. The guards could never take his memory of Bogdan's face when he'd first got a card to the face... or, for that matter, the jack of hearts. That one he'd hidden in his sock.

For three days after that, they starved him, demanding he decode for them. When that didn't work, the real beatings came. First, they used their fists, and from there they graduated to brass knuckles, to a whip. But Patrick never gave in. He'd been rather proud of himself for that. For all the times in his life that he had tricked, conned, and cheated, he'd never felt as guilty as he had upon realizing what he'd done by solving that first code.

The beatings were nothing compared to that. Not even when the whip opened his flesh, leaving wounds he knew would never heal properly. Not that it mattered. His life was forfeited. It was hard for him to admit, but the chances he'd ever see home again were slim to none. Even if they didn't dispose of him like they were supposed to, no one knew where he was.

He lay on his side, staring at the wall when they came to get him for his daily beating. The guard pulled him to his feet and grabbed his shirt, vest, and jacket from the ground. They'd stripped him to his bare chest and torso the first time they'd whipped him. After that, he hadn't bothered to redress; the pain was too excruciating.

The guard shoved his clothes at him, then dragged him from the room. He led Patrick back to the dining hall and took him straight to the table where Vadim and Bogdan sat waiting. He was shoved into the seat next to Bogdan. He cringed in pain as the guard stormed off.

"Patrick," Vadim said. "Your time with us is at end."

"Shame," Patrick said, his voice barely a whisper. "I was just getting used to the beatings."

Bogdan and Vadim chuckled.

"So entertaining, this one," Bogdan said.

"What are you going to do with me?" A pang of panic shot through Patrick at the thought of what was to come. Would he be sold? Who would buy him? And what horrors would follow?

"Despite fact that you are stubborn man," said Vadim, "we believe you to be asset."

Patrick put on his best poker face. "I won't decrypt codes for you, not ever again."

They smiled.

"Oh, I believe you will. You wait." Bogdan signaled to Vadim. "Vadim and I have been thinking that we've been going about torture with you all wrong. You are man of the mind, and so that must be your torment. We send you to Lazarev, and they will deal with you there. You will decode—trust this if nothing else."

Bogdan rested a hand on his shoulder, his palm digging into a whip wound that had just barely started to scab. Patrick winced.

Vadim winked at him. "You wait."

CHAPTER FIFTEEN

Flat, barren, and snowy landscape was all Patrick could see for miles and miles. He sat in the back of an armored truck with ten other prisoners, several cans of gasoline crammed in amongst their legs, making it impossible to stretch. None of the men spoke a lick of English, so he'd taken to watching the depressing scene unfold. Outside the truck, he hadn't seen so much as a living animal in two days, let alone a person.

A hatch covered the back of the truck, and while the space was closed to the outside elements, it was still freezing even with all the extra men. None of these men had been on the ship with him. At least, he didn't think they had. He hadn't been conscious when they'd unloaded him. Apparently, they thought that keeping their victims drugged was the way to go.

From what Patrick could tell, the men were all from different countries and spoke several different languages. None of them were emaciated, though they were all thin. All of them either had a look of terror behind their eyes or nothing at all. Patrick wasn't sure which look bothered him most. They were all prisoners, and Patrick was willing to bet that they, like him, were merely men who someone wanted gone. Yet having this in common did nothing to create camaraderie. They all wanted to be left alone.

It was a weird feeling, being so secluded while surrounded by several people. It'd been close to three days since he'd left the ship, maybe four. He couldn't be entirely sure because they'd drugged him. However many days it'd been, no one had spoken to or even looked at him since he'd been loaded on the truck. And he attempted conversation.

No one had even glanced his direction when he'd belted out a slaughtered version of Ave Maria. In retrospect, that might have been a bad move. If they'd been put off by him before, they were downright cold now.

Perhaps Vadim and Bogdan were on to something when they'd said that his particular brand of torture would be of the mind.

On the ship, he'd been miserable... but this was the first time since they'd taken him that he felt the crushing sorrow of loneliness.

His eye-lids drooped, and he fought to keep them open. As much as he'd like to fall asleep, the truck was jostling them too much over the ice and dirt roads on which they traveled. His head constantly throbbed, and resting it against the side was a no-go. The last thing he wanted was to hit his head again. He wasn't entirely sure he didn't have another concussion from the last beating on the boat.

He played with Elizabeth's ring, spinning it round and around on his finger, feeling for the indent there. He supposed it was a win that he hadn't been sold into slavery, but the promise of some kind of mental torture now loomed in his future, and with desert waste-lands in every direction, he doubted he had any chance of escaping this. Just being secluded with men whom he couldn't speak to was torture enough. He could only imagine what was to come, and it filled him with a special kind of dread he could never have imagined.

He was well and truly trapped.

He wrapped his hand around the ring on his finger. The cold metal pressed against the palm of his skin until it warmed. He released it and spun it again.

He became instantly aware of the weight of the silver coin in his vest pocket. His mom had been taken from him. Elizabeth's mom had been taken from her. And now he was here. All because his best friend had been jealous of him.

He moved his hand from the ring and stuck it in his vest pocket. He grasped the coin. Somehow, he'd escape. One day this nightmare would be over. And then he'd get his revenge. Somehow.

HALFWAY THROUGH THEIR fourth day driving, the truck slowed. Each of them sat a little taller. They passed several mining structures, caves supported by 2x4s, and several wooden cranes. Whatever their destination, they'd arrived.

Another five or so minutes passed before the truck came to a full stop. Voices spoke from the front of the cab, and then they were driving into a compound marked only by a mix of three or four brick buildings that appeared to have been made in the seventies, and half a dozen smaller, much older edifices made of rock and concrete.

There wasn't a fence in sight.

The truck stopped outside a run-down, brick building that was two stories high. A satellite dish, about the size of the hood of a Toyota Corolla, sat atop the edifice.

Guards opened the back of the truck. The men hopped down from the bed. Patrick was the last one out and landed in an icy, mud puddle. All the paths were muddy, and a layer of snow covered the rest of the ground.

They left the bed of the truck open as he and the others trudged out of the way.

Several guards headed off into the red-brick building with the satellite dish, while two led the men toward the grouping of concrete structures that Patrick guessed were the living spaces.

Patrick started to follow when a guard came up and blocked him. He said something in Russian and pointed behind Patrick. A man, tall and lean with a crooked nose, straight white teeth, and a confident gait approached him. He wore an expensive suit with a knee-length wool coat over the top and an ushanka-hat with the ear-flaps tied up.

The man held a black cane in his hand with a silver tip. The tip was spotless, not even a dot of mud on it, which meant it was purely aesthetic. He pointed at Patrick, then let the cane slide through his hand. "You are the American?"

Patrick nodded. "Patrick Daley."

The man laughed. "That is sweet. You believe that I will remember your name? Such a childish notion." He pulled his black leather gloves up. "You will call me MacTep."

Patrick furrowed his brow, squinting in the sunlight that was twice as bright as it would be was it not bouncing off the snow. Patrick had zero childish notions of being treated as anything other than a slave. MacTep could call him whatever he wanted; it wouldn't change the situation. He was this man's prisoner.

The man swept a wide gesture toward the open land that surrounded them. "As you can see, we have no gates, no guard towers, nothing to keep you from running away. But know that if you attempt it, you will freeze to death before the night is over. In every direction is more of what you see here. You would not walk back from it."

This wasn't news. Driving in had made that point more than clear. The miles of land between here and civilization and subzero nightly temperatures were better deterrents than barbed-wire fences could ever hope to be.

MacTep made eye contact with him, his blue eyes as icy cold as their surroundings. "You are here to be our code breaker. If you do this, you will be rewarded. If you refuse to code, you will work in the mines. It's back-breaking work that you will be required to do for fourteen hours every day."

Patrick narrowed his eyes. Working in a mine didn't seem any worse than what he'd already been through.

"I can see from your eyes that you think you can handle the

mines, so before you make up your mind about which path you'd like to choose, we're going to start you in the mines and give you a real idea of what it'll be like. When you're not digging, you'll be secluded in your room. If months go by and you are still unmoved to decode for us, then you'll be sent back to Bogdan."

Patrick took a deep breath, and the cold prickled at the back of his throat and all the way into his lungs. If even breathing in this place was painful, he might be happy to go back to Bogdan. That would never happen though. MacTep was a horrible liar; he didn't even try to be convincing. Said things for the shock value alone. When Patrick had breathed in the painfully cold air, he'd unwittingly reacted in a way that made MacTep's eyes glow with excitement.

"So, young man," MacTep said, "you must decide where you want to spend the rest of your life. Here or in a deep, dark hole." Turning to a guard, he called out in Russian—then turned to Patrick. "This man will take you to your room for the evening. You will have a chance to decide what you want to do before the morning. At five you will be awakened to go down into the mine."

The guards that had gone into the building now exited with at least another dozen guards. They walked in pairs of two, carrying body bags. Patrick's eyes went wide. MacTep extended his cane in a whip-like motion into Patrick's chest, making him cringe with pain. Patrick stepped back to clear the way for the guards.

MacTep's speech was nearly giddy in its tonality. "Most of these corpses are men who died in the mines. One was a suicide. We were lucky to have found his body so far from camp."

The guards threw the bodies on the back of the truck, then returned to the building to get more until the truck was filled.

Patrick had never seen a body before, and now he'd just counted twenty. They watched until the guards dispersed, two getting in the cab.

When they were alone, MacTep turned from Patrick as if to go, then stopped and planted his feet. "Oh, and one more thing, slave."

He spun around and, with a fierce blow, back-handed Patrick across the face.

Patrick fell face-down in the icy mud, his head once again spinning and throbbing with pain. Liquid dripped from his temple. Red covered the vision in his right eye. He blinked as the world spun.

MacTep pulled his feet together and bent toward him at the waist. "This is Lazerev, but don't let the name fool you. Here you are a dead man, and you will never rise again." He swirled his cane through the air, then strutted back to the brick building.

Watching him go, a chill run up Patrick's spine that had nothing to do with the cold and everything to do with MacTep. He was an evil man, even more than Vadim and Bogdan. He wasn't doing this for whatever money he was making. He was doing it because he enjoyed it.

CHAPTER SIXTEEN

NINE YEARS LATER

"What case are you looking at, Shea?" Detective Lee asked.

Elizabeth Shea glanced up from her file folder and at her partner. When had he come in? He sat at the desk across from hers, reading Kerouac. His dark eyes seemed to be glaring holes into the pages.

She twisted her face in confusion, remembering a year ago when they'd arrested a man who'd answered all of their questions with Kerouac quotes. "I thought you hated Kerouac?"

"I do." He set the book down, keeping his face perfectly straight.

She grinned. That explained the glare.

In their years working together, they'd formed a tight bond that came from being dubbed "the binky squad." Now that they'd been promoted to serious crimes, the days of being undervalued and underappreciated were mostly over with only an occasional taunt.

Lee stood, came around by her chair, and leaned over to look at the file she held. His black hair fell over his forehead. "Patrick Daley. Who's he?"

Shea swallowed. "No one."

He stood. "Is that the same file you were looking at when you got back from lunch yesterday?"

She took a deep breath. She hated lying, especially to Lee, but this was an *unusual* situation. Ever since her violent and sudden headache at lunch yesterday, a lunch she couldn't remember going to, she hadn't been able to stop thinking about Patrick Daley. It'd taken her years to push him to the back of her mind, to not worry about what had happened to him.

Lee furrowed his brow and turned to leave, but she stopped him with a hand on his arm. He stared down at her, dark brows raised as he waited for her to explain.

She glanced around the bullpen, and when she was sure no one could hear her, she grabbed the chair from the desk behind her and yanked it over for him. She handed him a picture of Patrick that had been taken almost ten years ago. It was a poster from the circus of his psychic act with his dad. Apparently, it was the only photo Patrick's dad had had of him.

"Who's this?" Lee leaned against the armrest closest to her as he stared at the photo he held, his large arm muscles invading the space between them enough that she had to sit back.

"A cold case. The victim vanished without a trace. All his friends and family were interviewed, his face was posted on the local news, and as far as they found, no one saw anything, heard anything, knew anything." It still gave her the willies.

Lee picked up a few documents from the file and started reading. "How's the time-line for the day leading up to his disappearance?"

"Thorough."

"Do we know who the last person to see him was?"

She took a deep breath. "Some of the people he worked with at the circus saw him leave the day he disappeared. The last person to talk to him was me."

Lee whipped his gaze to her. "What?"

She gripped the edge of her metal desk. "He was a friend."

"I've been your partner for three years, and I've never heard of him. Why are you only bringing this up now?"

"I thought of him yesterday, for probably the first time in who knows how many years, and now I can't get him out of my mind." She also couldn't figure out why it'd never occurred to her before yesterday to look into his case file. She couldn't get it or him out of her mind.

She hadn't slept last night, she'd shampooed her hair twice this morning, and she still couldn't remember if she'd eaten breakfast.

"This was Brown's case?" Lee said, noticing their boss's signature on some of the paperwork. "Did Brown give you permission for this?"

She shook her head. "He's been in meetings all morning, and we don't have a case right now. I can't see it being a problem."

Lee nodded. "How can I help?"

It was on the tip of her tongue to tell him he didn't need to help her; to tell him that this was personal and she didn't want to drag him into it. But then she thought that if this were the other way around, and Lee was the one with the missing friend, she'd want to help.

"There's not a lot to go on. I've been through the file twice today."

"You want me to go through it? See if you missed something?" He extended a hand.

She handed the file to him. "Thanks."

AT A QUARTER to five in the morning, Patrick knelt in his small stone room near the radiator that clanked every thirteen seconds. He counted the quiet between clanks many times. It only put out heat within a foot of it. His room was lit by the moon bouncing off the snow-covered ground and shinning through his shoe-box-sized window. It made sleeping hard—that, and the creature from his nightmares. The faceless shadow man. Rafferty.

To calm himself, he quoted verses from books he'd read in the past, an exercise that also helped to keep his mind sharp. Today it was

Don Quixote. "'The scariest dragons and the fiercest giants usually turn out to be no more than windmills.'" He took a deep breath. "Just a windmill."

The only time it was dark was between six and seven in the morning. When the moon had set and the sun had yet to rise. Patrick was always down in the mines by then.

He stared at the gold band on his ring finger and twisted it around, allowing his finger to run over the small indent on the top. He wondered how it got there. If Elizabeth knew?

The very thought of her name filled him with hope. Even if only a little. He thought of her pale skin, rose bud lips, and honey-hued eyes. What was Elizabeth doing? Was she safe? Happy? How were her brothers? Did she miss him?

A sharp pain exploded in his chest. He reached up and pushed against his rib cage with one arm, while his other went to the wall to steady him. *Breathe. In, one two. Out, three four. In, one two, out three four.* He counted until the pain faded, until he could breathe normally again. Then he wiped the sweat from his forehead. Why he still had panic attacks after all this time, he wasn't sure. It was a weakness he hated.

He took a deep breath and removed the ring. It was close to work time. Crawling to the corner of his room, he removed a rock he'd dug up on his first day here and placed the ring down in the space next to his silver coin and playing card, careful not to look at them. He replaced the rock and brushed dirt over it.

Within the first week of being here, he'd learned a few things very quickly. Only workers were allowed personal items. Patrick had seen a man stripped of his wedding ring, and his wallet, which held only one thing the man had begged for—a picture of his daughter. They'd crumpled the photo in front of him. A week later, Patrick had seen the man's ring on one of the guards.

He'd also learned that the only person who spoke English was MacTep.

If his count was right, Patrick had been imprisoned for three thousand two hundred and twenty-eight days. Or four hundred and sixty-four weeks. Almost nine years.

He stood and crossed the space to his clothes, which he'd folded and placed on a chair. He took his pants and slid them on, then grabbed the rope he'd pilfered from the mine and slid it through the loops of his pants. He tied the robe and pushed the bunches of fabric from the waist band down flat.

A light knock sounded at his door.

"I'll, I'm—just give, uh... I'll be there." He stumbled over the words and, in frustration, rested a hand against the wall. He couldn't recall the last time he'd had a real conversation. He could talk to himself easily enough.

Really, it shouldn't matter to him. The person who had knocked wouldn't understand him anyway, and he didn't think he'd ever speak to someone again except for MacTep on their yearly meeting—the meeting in which MacTep would ask if Patrick was ready to start decoding. Patrick would then say the one word he'd gotten to practice often. "No."

He smirked at the thought. Any opportunity to harass MacTep was a good one. Of course, that would be followed by a beating, a week of longer hours in the mine, and half his rations. Two more weeks and he'd get to go through it again. Would the fun never end?

Maybe one day soon, he'd walk out of here and into the sweet oblivion of death. Maybe MacTep would let him, but he doubted it. Patrick was too closely watched to think for one second that they would let him freeze to death. Nine years and they still saw him as a potential asset. He didn't get it.

He grabbed his shirt and slid it on over his tight and weary muscles. He didn't bother tucking it in anymore. Any semblance of humanity dwindled to nothing as his clothes slowly became rags and his body shrank too much to fit them. Not that he wasn't grateful for them. Better rags than nothing. And they were his. The one thing no one would take from him.

After buttoning the last button, he faced the door to see a man standing in the shadows. Like everyone here, the man was rail-thin and had a long beard.

"Hello," the man said.

Patrick jolted back. "Who are—" He swallowed against the dryness in his throat. "—are you?" He'd never seen this man before, which didn't make sense because he knew everyone in the camp. Or at least he thought he did. Not being able to talk to anyone gave a man a lot of time to crowd-watch.

The man stepped back into the darkness and Patrick stumbled to the door, but by the time he reached it, the stranger was gone.

CHAPTER SEVENTEEN

Getting off the elevator on the second floor after lunch, Shea saw Sergeant Brown's door propped open. She made her way over and knocked; the blinds clinked against the glass.

"Boss?"

He glanced up from his computer and waved her in.

She stepped into his office, stopping just to the side of his desk. "How were your meetings?"

"Long." He leaned back in his chair. "Have a seat."

She sat on the edge of the chair opposite his. "I know you're busy. I don't need a lot of your time."

"Shoot."

"There's a cold case that grabbed my attention, and I wanted to make sure you were okay with me looking into it."

He threaded his fingers and rested his hands on his lap. "You don't normally ask me if you can work on a cold case. What makes this one different?"

"It was yours."

He narrowed his gaze. "Which case?"

"It's from nine years ago. An eighteen-year-old boy named—"

"Patrick Daley?"

She pulled her chin back. "You remember him?"

Brown leaned forward on his desk. "He's a hard one to forget. A bit of a troublemaker-kid. His mom went missing two years before he did. My partner and I worked both cases."

"Your partner was Steven Benson, right?" Brown talked about Benson all the time. The two men had dinner with their families nearly every week. "Where's he working these days?"

"You've been through the case file, I see." His tone sounded amused. "Benson's with the 23rd precinct now. There's more to this than you're telling me. Out with it."

She scrunched her nose. "Patrick Daley and I were sort of... friends at the time he went missing."

Brown's eyes widened. "That was you?"

She nodded. He was referring to the night he and Detective Benson had interviewed her. The interview had been relatively short, and while she'd seen Benson a year after Patrick's disappearance for a quick follow-up, it'd been four years after that when she'd met Brown again. She'd been a rookie at the time, and clearly Brown hadn't recognized her.

She'd remembered him, though.

He and Benson, seeing her distress and the fear from her brothers the night they'd interviewed her, had been kind. After they'd left, they'd bought hamburgers and shakes for her and her brothers and had dropped them off. She'd been grateful for more reasons than one.

"Wow," Brown said. "I can't believe I never put that together."

"Can I have a go at it?"

He furrowed his brow. "He was a circus kid, always traveling, and never enrolled in any school. How'd you happen to meet him?"

She didn't want to talk about this. Not with Brown, not with anyone. It felt too personal. "My family met him at the circus."

Brown ran a hand over his balding head. "And you made friends with a circus kid?"

She shrugged. "I guess."

He chuckled. "Okay, I get it. You don't want to talk about it. But one day, I'd like to know how a nice kid, like you *were*, could end up friends with a boy like that."

She blinked at him. "What do you mean 'a boy like that'?"

He folded his arms. "Like I said, he was a troublemaker. He caused me tons of grief with his mom's case before he went missing. He stole my badge, conned an officer, broke into the archives, and nearly sabotaging a kidnapping case with a little girl. Knowing your personality, I guess it surprises me that you'd be friends with a kid like that." He leaned back. "Benson liked him well enough."

She frowned. Why hadn't anyone told her Patrick had done all those things? None of it surprised her, but still. "He was very determined, and a good friend."

He nodded. "Then you have my blessing. If you have any questions, let me know." He turned back to his computer. "I'll have Benson call you if he has any insights."

She took that as her cue to leave.

There was clearly more to his story, but for now, she didn't want to ask. The last thing she wanted was him invoking quid pro quo. Patrick had been gone nine years, his mom eleven. She really didn't expect that either of them would ever come back, and the last thing she wanted to do was talk about that with her boss. Especially if her boss didn't like them.

~

"IS THIS SPOT TAKEN?"

Sitting in the poorly lit, busy lunch room, Patrick stared at his food, pushing it around his plate—a mish-mash of stew and vegetables that never got thrown out but was only added to every day. It took all his strength to swallow it down. Years of eating the same thing didn't help.

MacTep's laughter sounded from across the cafeteria where he was harassing a group of prisoners. Today, he was making three of the men jump up and down while patting their heads and rubbing their bellies. If they lasted for a minute, he'd let them have their rations. Last week, he'd made two men do a hundred push-ups. One of the men was an older gentleman who'd passed out from the exertion.

Patrick jabbed at his bowl, clinking his spoon against it.

Someone slid onto the bench next to him. "I asked if this spot was taken."

Patrick froze, and slowly turned his gaze to the man next to him. The man was staring straight ahead.

"Don't look at me," the man said.

It took Patrick a moment to register what was being said. He turned back to his mush, but probably not soon enough for one of the guards not to have noticed.

The man sighed. "Too late. They've seen us. Ah well."

Somewhere in the dark corners of Patrick's brain, a voice that sounded vaguely familiar, a voice that had probably been *his* once, told him to speak to this stranger. The voice told him he might not get another chance to speak English with someone other than MacTep. But the real him didn't know what to say.

"I wanted to apologize for scaring you this morning." The man rested his intertwined fingers on the table.

Patrick thought back, searching for the face of the man at his door. It was definitely this guy—though he could see him better now. His hair was dark, and his beard was graying. He was tan with wrinkly skin and had brown eyes.

The man cleared his throat. "I heard you speak when I was going by. I thought I was the only one here who spoke English. Was that *Don Quixote?*"

Patrick held his wood spoon just above his bowl, suspended as if time had stopped. His brownish gray mush blurred behind it. The man knew Don Quixote?

"You do speak English, don't you?" He had an accent underlying his English, but it was barely noticeable and hard to distinguish.

Patrick swallowed hard.

The man took a deep breath, his expression becoming disappointed. "Then again, maybe I'm going crazy." He placed his hands on the table and pushed himself up. "Too bad."

Panic swirled in Patrick's chest. He had to say something now or might forever lose his chance. "Pea-pease... pease."

The man stared down at him, brow quirked.

Patrick closed his eyes and tried again. "Pease porridge in-in the pot, nine days old."

The man chuckled and sat down again. "It appears you haven't lost your sense of the absurd." He clapped his hands together and started singing loudly and off-key. "'Pease porridge hot, pease porridge cold. Pease porridge in a pot, nine days old!'"

Startled, Patrick dropped his spoon on the table and leaned away. Everyone in the cafeteria quieted as they turned to look at the stranger. Their faces held as much surprise as Patrick was sure he had on his own.

"An oldie, but a goodie," the man said upon finishing.

Patrick picked up his spoon. "'*The* pot.' Not '*a* pot.'"

A guard yelled at them.

The man raised his hands and nodded his head as if in apology, then dropped his hands to his knees. "They do hate it when I sing. Which is why I do it." He laughed again. "They may lock me up, but they can't take my bad pitch from me."

Patrick frowned. "Who you—who are you?"

The man's eyes gleamed. Patrick didn't know that was possible in a place like this for anyone but MacTep.

"Westkeys," he said. "I'm a bishop."

Patrick cleared his throat. "Bishop? A... holy title?"

The man nodded. "Indeed."

"I don't believe in God." It was the first full sentence he'd said aloud to another person without faltering or stuttering in who knew how long.

"Free will gives you the right to not."

Patrick stared back at his food. "There is no free will here, and there is no God."

"Are you sure about that?" The man sat again. "I've seen men walk out into the desert, only to return if the guards happen upon their bodies. Is that not free will? Is not your choice to stay and live free will? Does it not also give our captors the ability to hold us against our will? If you were only a little stronger, a little less outnumbered, would you not take back your freedom?"

Great, the first person he talked to in years wanted to have a theological debate. *Perfect.* Patrick dropped his spoon and folded his arms.

"Freedom and free will are two different things," the bishop said. "They do not negate one another but coexist. Just as people choosing to use their God-given free will to do bad things or to not believe in him, does not negate His existence."

Patrick faced the man. "I don't need a sermon."

"But you need a friend, I think." The older man smiled and stood once more. He scratched his chin and faced Patrick. "Can you tell me who won the World Series?"

Patrick thought back through his addled brain. "Which year?"

"Does it matter?" the bishop chortled.

Patrick scrunched his brow. "Red Sox?"

"Aw, too bad. Thank you, young man." He started off.

A lump formed in Patrick's throat and angry tears burned in his eyes. "Wait, don't leave." He didn't have much left, and now he'd just given this man, this stranger, his pride by begging. Yet he couldn't bring himself to care.

The man signaled around with his hand, then leaned down. "Where would I go? Especially if I *choose* to live?" He winked.

Patrick stared at the ground.

"We've drawn too much attention for now. I'll find you later." With that, he marched to the cafeteria line and got his own bowl of mush. He nodded to the cook, and even from his table, Patrick heard him say, "Thank you."

Patrick noticed with some envy how the bishop held his head high and his posture straight. That he still walked like a man who was free. Not even the mine workers were able to do that. Though many of the workers nodded to him in passing, and one man even bowed his head and crossed himself. Word of a clergyman spread fast. Not that it would matter. This place spared no one, not even a man of God. One day, the bishop would be just like the rest of them.

CHAPTER EIGHTEEN

Outside her apartment door, Shea struggled with her key and several grocery bags. One of her neighbors nodded as they passed. She nearly dropped her bags. Finally getting the right key in the lock, she opened the door.

"Luke?" She crossed the living room into the kitchen and set the groceries down. She picked up the milk and put it away, smiling reflexively at the picture of Maggie that Luke had drawn when he was six—laminated in too much tape. "Luke? Are you here? You'd better be."

She went back into the living room as she headed to his room, removing her leather jacket and tossing it on her plush cream couch. She turned down the hall, went to the first door on the left, and knocked before pushing in.

The blue flannel blankets on his bed were bunched and messy, a basket of clean clothes sat by his closet, and his dirty clothes littered the floor. Against the wall, covered by two or three jackets, was Mags, the elephant she'd won for him at the circus when he was a kid. But no Luke.

A headache formed behind her brow, and she pinched the bridge of her nose to relieve some of the pressure. Pulling her phone from her pants pocket, she lifted it. An arm went around her waist. She sucked in a breath.

On reflex, she threw her elbow back, but missed as her target jumped out of the way. She turned, fists up.

"Whoa!" Sean held up his hands. "Elizabeth, it's me."

"Sean?" She dropped her hands. "What are you doing? I could have hurt you."

He chuckled. "I think I can take care of myself."

Feeling her hackles rise, she pushed past him out of Luke's room and headed back to the kitchen. "How did you get in here?" She'd told him repeatedly that she didn't like to be sneaked up on, but that never stopped him. One day she would punch him, and she couldn't say she'd feel all that bad about it. Though, she'd hate to damage his handsome face. Then again a black eye my accent the deep blue of his eyes. *Something to consider.*

"Luke let me in on his way out," he said.

Great, and now her brother was AWOL again too. She faced Sean. "Did he say where he was going?"

"Library. He'll be back for dinner."

She stared at the floor. Luke had been acting strangely for months. Three months ago, he would never have left without calling to tell her where he was going.

Sean rested his hands on her shoulders. "You're worried about him."

"I'm sure he's fine." She was always worried about him. Becoming parent by proxy for her brothers when she was barely nineteen-years-old after her father had drunk himself to death meant she was always worried about them. Kyle had graduated college a year ago and had moved to San Diego to take a job there. Jake was in his first year of college in Oakland. She still worried about them all the time. Sometimes worry felt like a full-time job.

Sean chuckled. "You're a horrible liar. You don't need to be worried. He's a fifteen-year-old boy. He's just growing up, is all. Remember, both Kyle and Jake did the same thing."

She nodded, then pulled away from him and started unloading the groceries. She didn't find that comforting.

Sean leaned on the counter. "You're not wearing your ring."

She froze with her head in the fridge, then closed her eyes briefly before pulling back. Guilt enveloped her, guilt for not wearing it and for being confused. Sean was a great guy, he'd always been there for her, and he loved her, but she still wasn't sure she was making the right decision. She faced him as he slid her engagement ring across the counter. She'd left it on her dresser.

"Do you not like it? Is that why you won't wear it?"

She shook her head. "You know perfectly well it's stunning." It was—a four-carat cushion diamond with accent diamonds on the band. It wasn't a ring she would have picked for herself, especially in her line of work. For a cop, it was too gauche. "It's not practical for work."

"Are you sure it's not because you're having second thoughts?"

Taking a deep breath, she crossed the kitchen to him and wrapped her arms around his waist. "I'm not." She planted a kiss on his lips, then pulled away and rested her head on his shoulder. Telling him the truth wouldn't help. Sean didn't take disappointment well. She had to figure this out on her own, and the last thing she wanted to do was hurt him.

He pulled back from the embrace and lifted the ring. "Prove it."

Shaking her head, she took the ring. "Fine, I'll wear it." She slipped it on, careful not to look at it, and went back to the groceries. She'd take the pestering at work to reassure him.

LYING on the dirt floor of his room with his eyes closed, Patrick hummed the tune of "Pease Porridge Hot."

"That's the spirit of it," the bishop said.

Patrick jerked back, opening his eyes in the process. The bishop knelt in front of him, hands on his knees, cocky smile on his face. That smile was irritating.

"We must keep our heads about us." The bishop chuckled, leaning back as though he'd said something completely hilarious.

"You find this situation funny?"

The bishop raised a finger. "A kidnap victim, sitting in a dark, dirty room in the middle of Siberia, humming "Pease Porridge Hot." Against all expectations. Against all odds. I find it liberating."

Patrick sat up. Okay, so the bishop was crazy. That was his deal.

A tight knot of anger slowly loosened inside Patrick's chest, morphing into something different and just as awful. Was this what hopelessness was? Being trapped in a place that drove men mad?

Tears once again brimmed at the corners of his eyes, and then, though he willed them not to, they spilled over. He sobbed then, dropping his head to his hands. Great wracking spasms shot through his body. This was his life. His forever torment. And now, maybe because God wanted to amuse himself, he'd thrown in a crazy man to show him his future?

When the sobs subsided, and heaviness crept over his limbs, the bishop grasped his shoulder. "Look at me."

Patrick did.

"I've been where you are. It passes. It's not until one reaches rock bottom that they can truly find their way."

Into Looneyville? Great. At that Patrick chuckled and then laughed. It felt good. And strangely, so had the crying. It'd been so long since he'd done either. In a weird way, he felt as though a huge burden had been lifted.

"You feel better now," the bishop said. "Don't you?"

Patrick nodded and wiped at his wet cheek with the back of his hand.

"'One man scorned and covered in scars still strove with his last ounce of courage to reach the unreachable stars; and the world was better for this.'"

The bishop did know Don Quixote.

"Now," the bishop said, "what is it you want more than anything else in the world?"

Patrick thought of Sean, of MacTep, Vadim and Bogdan, and of Rafferty. "Revenge."

The bishop's smile fell just a little, almost imperceptibly, before he nodded. "I can give you that."

Patrick pushed the bishop's hand from his shoulder. "Not unless you can get us out of here, old man. And seeing as you're still here—"

"I can get us out of here," the bishop said. "With your help. MacTep tells me you can solve ciphers."

Patrick jumped to his feet. "You're with him?"

The bishop stayed on his knees. "Look at me." He signaled to his person; bushy brows rose to his hairline. "Does my appearance somehow suggest that MacTep is my friend?"

He looked just like everyone else here: dirty, skinny, bruised, with a long beard, and rags for clothes. Though, he had made an attempt to pull his hair back and tie it. The whites of his eyes were even a bit yellow, which suggested he wasn't receiving visits from the doctor like MacTep and the guards did. Fine, he didn't work with MacTep.

"Then you're a fool." Patrick turned partially away. "I won't help human traffickers for any reason."

"You know what your problem is? You've lost faith in mankind."

Patrick wasn't sure he'd ever had faith. "Can you blame me?"

The bishop shook his head. "That's very noble of you. But, if I may, what exactly do you think you are helping them to do by decoding their ciphers?"

Patrick turned halfway away from him. Did it matter? Help was help.

"The ciphers they want decoded are from their competition," the bishop said. "Other traffickers. Yes, it does help them, but by putting other traffickers out of business."

Patrick clenched his fist. "By giving them a monopoly on the market?"

"One organization is easier to bring down than many. How long have you been here?"

Patrick crossed his arms and hung his head. "Why does it matter?"

"Appease me."

He breathed out. "Almost nine years." In his peripheral vision, the bishop nodded.

"And for all time, you've refused to help them. Was that decision made from pride or—"

"It was the right thing to do." Patrick faced him dead-on. "I've seen one of the girls these men took. I know who their victims are."

"Altruism." The bishop's smile returned. "You say you want revenge, but what if I could give you more than that? What if I could help bring down this ring, as well?"

"You can't do that."

The bishop leaned back and opened his arms. "If that's the case, then you better not take me up on my offer."

Patrick appraised him again—searching his eyes for deceit. He'd always been able to spot a liar, and this man was lying. He had to be. Then Patrick thought back to the cafeteria and the way the bishop had held himself as he'd walked off. Head high, posture strong despite his emaciated body. The bishop had told him not to look at him, and how quickly he'd disappeared in the hall outside his room that morning despite the fact that he was getting on in years.

"Were you a military man?"

The bishop's smile grew wider. "Something like that."

"Where are you from?"

"The US, but I was born and raised in France." He let that sink in. "Do we have a deal?"

There was more to the bishop than he was letting on. Much more. He was cunning. And if anyone could get Patrick out of here, it would be him. "What's the plan?"

The bishop clapped his hands together. He stood and went to the window, pointing to the large satellite over the two-story brick building. "While we're receiving and breaking codes for them, we'll be doing a little hacking of our own."

CHAPTER NINETEEN

Patrick and the bishop worked on the second floor of the redbrick building in a room crammed with dusty, old office furniture. The warm, musky air was a comfortable reprieve from their sleeping quarters, and Patrick remembered the first time he'd sat in one of the padded swivel chairs; he'd never felt anything so wonderful.

The bishop lay under a desk next to where Patrick sat by the window and fiddled with their computer. "Patrick." The bishop's hand came out from under the chair. "Screw-driver, please. The flathead."

Reaching over the cipher Patrick was currently working on, he grabbed the flat-head and dropped it into the bishop's hand. He stood and peered out the window behind his desk. A passenger truck pulled up and let new workers off. Patrick wondered how many bodies they'd be taking with them when they left this time.

Under the desk, the bishop murmured to himself. "Soviet Era piece of junk."

Patrick chuckled. "I'm pretty certain this computer wasn't made in the 1920s."

A banging came from under the table, and the old box screen on the desk next to Patrick flickered, then flashed to life.

The bishop sat up from under the desk. "Exactly, so you see my frustration."

"Yes, but you always fix it." Patrick caught sight of MacTep coming out to greet two guards carrying a body.

The warden stopped the guards and opened the body bag. He reached in and grabbed the man's left hand, then proceeded to remove the man's wedding band. MacTep held the ring up to the light, then grimaced and chucked it into the snow covered ground as the guards loaded his body on the truck.

Patrick gritted his teeth. Apparently, it wasn't enough that MacTep took these men's lives from them; he had to steal and disrespect what little they had that the men found value in. This was why Patrick had hidden his valuables.

The bishop pushed himself to his feet and turned to the computer as it flickered to life. "Aw, there she is."

Patrick furrowed his brow. All he saw was rows and rows of numbers.

The bishop sat in his red-upholstered swivel chair with a mysterious black spot on the edge, and without taking his eyes off the small computer screen, pointed at Patrick. "How many times do I have to tell you not to solve those things so fast?"

Patrick glanced down at the cipher the bishop had intercepted and printed off for him twenty minutes ago before the computer screen had gone black.

Patrick lifted his hands, palms up. "What? It's easy."

"But they're not to know that." He signaled over his shoulder to the door.

When they'd first brought them into the brick building with the satellite dish, he'd been too overwhelmed and addle-brained to solve any of the ciphers quickly. He'd been too many years removed from the practice, and it'd taken him a couple weeks to figure things out again. The bishop had been impressed, but Patrick had been annoyed with himself.

A month into their little venture and he was almost back to a hundred percent. No closer to escaping.

The bishop scrolled through different files. A mechanical whirring from outside the building directly above them indicated the bishop was moving the dish.

"No luck?" Patrick looked down at the truck again. They were loading bodies now, only three this time. MacTep glanced up at the building as the guards dispersed, leaving him there alone. The truck drove away. Patrick took his seat again.

The bishop began frantically typing and ignored him all together. Their dish was good, but not great. Certainly not large enough to send an SOS to the US unless he could hack into satellites in orbit around the earth, and apparently that wasn't a process that the bishop thought he could accomplish with the equipment he had access to.

At this point, the plan was simply to shoot out SOS messages in every direction and hope to get lucky that it would be found by good people, willing to help... who understood Morse code. Patrick had figured out fast that it could take years, if it worked. A couple months with the bishop, and he soon found he didn't care as much anymore. Just having someone to talk with had improved his life considerably.

A clicking against the metal frame of the door drew Patrick's attention. MacTep stood in the frame, the tip of his cane tapping against it.

Patrick reached over to the bishop and tapped his shoulder.

"Not, now Patrick."

"Bishop," Patrick said.

"I'm almost—"

"Bishop!"

The bishop faced him, then quickly followed his gaze to the door.

MacTep kept his excited, beady little eyes on him.

Patrick swallowed, fear clenching his stomach muscles. He forced himself to relax.

The bishop stood. "Have you come to see our progress? Patrick has just decoded another cipher for you."

The warden stepped into the room and pointed his cane at Patrick. "Has it really been nine years, slave? Isn't it amazing how time flies?"

Patrick didn't understand. It was a month after his anniversary. He was decoding the ciphers. He was doing what they'd wanted him to do since he'd come here. Why would MacTep do this?

Four guards rushed in and grabbed Patrick. He didn't fight them. It was what the warden wanted, and Patrick wouldn't give him the satisfaction.

"Wait," the bishop called out as Patrick was removed from the room. "I need him. Beating him will only put your schedule back. MacTep. MacTep!"

HANGING FROM HIS WRISTS, the weight of his entire body pulling at his sockets, Patrick tried to lift his head. The guards untied his hand from the loop on the ceiling of his room, and let him drop to the compacted dirt and rock floor. He landed on his stomach. Drool came from the side of his mouth, wetting the dirt there. He closed his eyes and sucked in ragged breaths.

MacTep went to one knee next to him. "Look at me."

Patrick opened his eyes, afraid that refusing would be seen as resistance and would get him twenty more lashings. He lifted his cane for Patrick to see. Blood splattered the dark wood and the silver tip. He'd never used his cane before, only a flogger.

"You got blood on my cane, but I would say it was worth it, would you not?" He raised the cane as though he were going to bring it down on Patrick's head. Patrick flinched away, and his tormentor laughed. "Yes. Worth it. Definitely. Now you know how much worse the beatings can be, you will not think to quit solving ciphers for us?"

That's what this was about? They'd had a taste of what he could do and beat him to assure he'd keep at it? Some logic.

"Yes?" MacTep asked in a sickly-sweet tone as he used the tip of his cane to brush Patrick's long hair off his face.

Patrick nodded. "Yes."

"Good." MacTep stood. "You will return to your post tomorrow."

STARING INTO SPACE, Patrick clenched his teeth to keep from crying out while the bishop cleaned his wounds with warm water.

"He does this to you often?" The bishop dipped the cloth in the water and wrung out the excess.

"Beats me?" Patrick closed his eyes as the cloth went to an open wound. "Once a year. This is the first time he's drawn blood."

"You have old scars."

He nodded, his cheek scratched against the dirt floor. "Those are from the men who took me when I was eighteen."

The bishop shook his head. "You were just a boy."

"A lot older than other children they took. Beatings are nothing to what they've suffered." He shook in anger. "Where is your God in all of this?"

"You cannot see him because you do not want to, but I can. And now I finally understand my purpose here." The bishop's tone was as soft as his healing touch.

It was on the tip of Patrick's tongue to ask what that purpose was, to perhaps gain some higher understanding possessed by the bishop, but he couldn't. Not now.

The bishop started to hum a song. It was a song he often hummed, and while Patrick had recognized it, it'd taken hearing the tune half a dozen times before he could put a name to it: A Poor Wayfaring Man of Grief.

He swallowed the lump in his throat. "How did you become a man of God?"

The bishop stopped humming and quirked a brow. "I don't believe it is a story you wish to hear."

Shame washed over Patrick. He didn't believe in God—how could he, after all of this?—but taking his anger out on the bishop wasn't fair either. "I'm sorry. I didn't mean it."

"Yes, you did, but I forgive you." He smiled. "You were beaten. If that's not an excuse for a bad attitude, then I'm not sure what is."

Warmth filled him, and they stayed silent for several minutes.

"When I was young," the bishop spoke in a whisper, "I became a part of something that I thought was good, something that was supposed to work for the greater good, and for it, I became a spy. It wasn't until many years later that I learned what the expression 'the road to hell is paved with good intentions' really meant. I was sent to a village and ordered to become part of the community and report back on it. They were good people, just trying to defend themselves."

Patrick sucked in a breath, trying not to cause any interruption.

"When I reported that very information, I was transferred, and the next day, the town was bombed."

"That wasn't your fault," Patrick whispered. "You couldn't have known."

"I knew. Another spy, and good friend of mine was in the town with me. He begged me not to file my report and refused to leave with me. I knew something was wrong but was too blinded to see clearly. So I did nothing. And that is something I will have to live with for the rest of my life. Men, women, children, the elderly, and my friend all died because I refused to see the truth. Refused to trust my friend."

Patrick swallowed hard.

"After that, I came to the US, and for years I had no direction or purpose. I worked as an accountant, and that was my life. I had only one friend, my boss. When he died, I was even more lost than before. I moved around and ended up in Florida. After several months, I met a neighbor who invited me to church.

"For months I declined, and for months they kept asking until I finally gave in. In their chapel, for the first time in years, I felt peace. I learned about their religion. I learned about forgiveness, namely how to forgive myself, and was eventually baptized. And then, many years later, I became a bishop. Of course, the title is no longer mine, but I had it when I left, and it brings me much comfort, and comfort to others here, I think. The men like thinking there's a clergyman here, even if they can't talk to him."

"How did you end up in here?" Patrick asked.

"The man that I worked for was a weapons manufacturer and distributer through the United States Government, though apart from them, and worked namely with the United States Military. He was a good man, but he was a solitary man. He never had a family, and like me, he had no friends. His life was his work. When he died, he died very wealthy. I was taken and brought here because I was his accountant."

"They think you have his money?"

"When he died, his money was never accounted for. It wasn't distributed, so now it is hanging out in a bank account somewhere with no one to claim it. There are many bad men in this world who were brought down by weapons manufactured by my friend's business, and many who feel that his money would be the perfect recompense for their 'suffering.'"

"How much money are we talking here?" It just popped out.

"Rockefeller comes to mind."

Patrick's eyes bugged out of his head. What money Rockefeller had upon his death would today equal near three-hundred and forty billion dollars.

The bishop chuckled. "He was an expert investor."

"Sounds like an understatement." Patrick shifted his weight from one side of his stomach to the other.

"Even if I knew where the money was, I would not give it to them."

Patrick could understand that. "How long have you been here?" He wasn't sure why he hadn't thought to ask sooner.

"Fifteen years."

Cringing, Patrick rolled on his side and looked into the old man's eyes. "Fifteen years? How have I never seen you?"

"They've kept me hidden, afraid that a billion-dollar bribe to the workers might cause a riot. Fifteen years in, and they no longer believe I can get them the money. The only thing they think I'm good for is finding ciphers for you to decode. It's given me some leeway, just as decoding ciphers has given you some." His eyes twinkled in the light coming from the window. "Won't they be surprised in the end?"

"How can you be so calm? So rational after all this?"

The bishop gave a sad smile. "Simple." He pointed up.

Patrick looked, then closed his eyes and shook his head as though he'd been duped.

When he faced the bishop again, the man was smiling. "Now, it's your turn. How did you end up here?"

Patrick pulled himself into a cross-legged position, though it made the pain in his back worse. He sucked it up and told the bishop about Sean, and the human traffickers, and Rafferty.

The bishop stared into space, rubbing his long beard. "Ultimately, you weren't surprised by Sean's actions, am I right?"

"No." Patrick's answer was instantaneous. Sean always had a bit of a cruel streak, but he was charming and fun, so it could be hard to see as long as you were on his good side. He wanted things his way, and if he didn't get it, he went nuts. Patrick hadn't been surprised; he'd been hurt.

"But you were surprised by Rafferty's part?"

Patrick stared at his hands interlaced in his lap. "Yes." He'd always trusted Rafferty and losing that had hurt almost worse than Sean's betrayal.

"You're a very observant man, Patrick. How did you miss it?"

"I don't know. I've played it over and over again in my head, and no matter what scenario I choose, it doesn't make sense. He played me. He tricked me into thinking he cared. Into thinking that he really wanted to help me find out what happened to my mother, when all along he was responsible for her death."

"According to Sean—the known liar," the bishop said.

Patrick narrowed his eyes. "Yes, but it makes sense."

"You just said it didn't make sense."

Patrick took a deep breath. "It didn't make sense from a cold read of his behavior—"

"A cold read? What is that?"

Patrick signaled to him with his hand. "When I first met you, I could tell you were former military. Also, you were way too cheery, which suggested that you have had experience and/or training with demoralizing situations. Either that or you were crazy."

The bishop leaned back and chuckled under his breath. "Very good."

"The guards didn't like you, but they more or less left you alone. So once my initial shock of having met you wore off, I knew you could be trusted."

"And your cold read of Rafferty said he could be trusted?"

He nodded. "But he had access to my mom's case and took an interest in me. Two characteristics of a predator."

"And of a good man."

Patrick glanced up.

"Let's say, as an alternative theory, that your good friend Sean lied to you, perhaps because he wanted to be cruel. Let's say that you put your trust in the wrong man. Who would be the next most likely suspect to have killed your mother?"

"You mean another cop?"

The bishop nodded. "It seems likely. Vadim didn't just walk out of prison. Someone had to let him go. If it wasn't Rafferty, then who?"

Patrick scrubbed a hand down his face. "I don't... I don't know." He thought of Detectives Brown and Benson and immediately counted them out. Brown didn't like Patrick and vice versa, but that didn't make him a killer, and he wasn't the one who closed the case. That had been...

"Captain Wright."

"Captain Wright?" The bishop leaned forward.

"He closed my mom's case. He had access to all the files. He knew everything that was happening with her case at all times, and he's a slug. He presents well, but he's like Sean in that respect. Charming on the surface and—"

"Corrupt underneath? Why would he want you to disappear? Why not just have you killed back in Sacramento?"

Patrick thought hard. "Only a few months after my mother went missing, he was promoted to captain. My mom's case was all over the news for months; it was bad publicity for his newly-minted position. Then it went cold fast, and interest died off enough that while I was gone with the circus, he was able to have it closed, and no one said a thing until I got back and started stirring up interest again.

"And getting Rafferty involved." That was it. "Rafferty is the best at what he does. Benson told Sean that Rafferty should have had Wright's job. Two days after Rafferty said he'd look into my case, I was taken. I was digging up things Wright wanted to stay hidden and siccing Rafferty on him. He had to get rid of me. Having me killed in Sacramento would've just brought the spotlight back on my mom again. Whereas disappearing me could be explained away.

"'A troubled, circus kid, who lost his mother too soon, with a loser father and no family. He probably ran away.'" He said this as though quoting Wright. "And no one from the circus would go to the cops. They don't trust them. I might not have even been reported missing."

The bishop started clapping. "Bravo, Patrick. Bravo."

All this time, Patrick had wished ill will on Rafferty, a man who'd been so kind to him, who'd been better to him than even his own father. Patrick stood and kicked the pan across his room, sending water splashing against the wall. He clenched his fists as adrenaline shot through him, then turned and pointed at the bishop. "You, you know how to fight."

The bishop said nothing.

"Teach me."

"No, I won't. All of this, everything you put yourself through, it's been so much more than revenge. It's been justice. I won't teach you to—"

"Then you can escape without me." If Patrick didn't decode the ciphers, there would be no reason to have someone looking for them, and if they didn't have someone looking for the ciphers, then the bishop couldn't use the satellite.

The bishop sat in silence for a moment.

The silence was almost more than Patrick could stand.

Finally, the bishop looked up. He seemed resigned. "All right, I'll teach you. As soon as your back heals."

Patrick nodded.

The bishop turned to the empty water pan and frowned. "You know how hard it was to get that warm water? And might I say you could've used it. You're rather pungent."

Patrick furrowed his brow. "And you smell of roses, fresh laundry, and sunbeams?"

The bishop stood and headed for the door. "I know."

CHAPTER TWENTY

"Luke." Shea shoved his lunch into a brown paper bag. "We've got to go, or you'll be late for school."

"Okay, okay, I'm coming." Dragging his backpack behind him, Luke slumped into the kitchen and sat on a stool at the counter. He looked nice but tired. His raven hair was parted and combed nicely, and he wore a green shirt that made his golden eyes pop by contrast.

She smiled as she reached his lunch across to him, then pointed to his bag. "Is your homework in there?"

He gave her an oh-please look. "Of course."

She turned to the fridge and opened it, knocking into his drawing of Maggie. The magnet holding it fell, and the picture drifted to the floor. She grabbed it and the magnet, and stuck it back on the fridge before she tossed Luke a Go-Gurt.

"Why don't you just throw that away?" Luke ripped open the plastic wrapping with his teeth.

"Your drawing?" Her heart sank a little. She loved that drawing.

He nodded. His eyes were droopy with exhaustion.

She smiled. He'd stayed up late studying last night, even though she'd told him not to, and now he was grumpy. "I like it. Why, are you too grown-up for it? Because if you are, I could always get rid of your stuffed elephant, too?"

He pointed the end of the Go-Gurt at her, yogurt hung precariously from the top, threatening to drip over. "Don't you dare."

She raised her hands. "Just checking."

She went to the door and slid her shoes on. "You ready?"

"Yep."

"You're not going to disappear after school again today without telling me, are you?" She grabbed her black leather jacket and put it on. "I hate it when you do that."

He jumped off his stool and grabbed his backpack. "Okay. I wasn't supposed to tell you, but Sean's been paying me to go to the library once a week to do my homework so he could hang out with you alone."

"Wait, what?" That was so not okay! Why would Sean do that, especially without asking her first?

Luke smiled. "Twenty bucks each time. It's awesome."

"How long has he been doing this?"

He shrugged. "I don't know. A year. Since you got engaged."

She clenched her jaw. "Was it before or after I put on the ring?"

His eyes strayed to her rock, and he scrunched his face. "I don't know. Maybe a couple months before that."

"I'm going to kill him."

"See, this is why he asked me not to tell you. Now he's going to know I ratted him out. Come on, El, it's only once a week for a couple hours." He slipped his backpack on.

Boxing champ or not, she was taking Sean down.

Her phone rang, and she answered. "Shea."

"We have a homicide," Lee said.

"Can you send me the address? I'm taking Luke to school."

"Sent. Hurry."

"Why, what's wrong?" She waved her brother from the apartment and locked the door behind them. A tinge of panic made her move faster. Something in Lee's tone was wrong.

"It's Steve Benson."

She froze. "As in Steve Benson, Brown's former partner?"

"Yes," Lee said.

She covered her mouth with her hand. After months of trying to get him to meet up with her to talk about the Daleys, he'd finally agreed. They'd had an appointment for Friday. "Does Brown know?"

"Not yet. He's been in a meeting, and we haven't been able to get a hold of him."

She closed her eyes and breathed out. "What happened to him?"

"It's not good," Lee said.

She hung up.

Luke turned to her. "Everything okay?"

She smiled and guided him down the hall with a hand to his back. "Nothing you need to worry about."

"Isn't Steve Benson one of the cops who was trying to find Patrick Daley?"

She turned to Luke. "You remember Patrick?"

"Of course I do." Luke tossed his head, sending his raven hair off his forehead and out of his eyes. He needed a haircut. "I was six-years-old, not a baby. I gave that drawing of Maggie to him. And Benson and Brown brought us those burgers that one time. Those were good."

She blinked. "You never talk about him."

He shrugged. "I figured you didn't want to." He headed down the stairs.

For years she'd been under the assumption that Luke remembered nothing and for some reason the idea that he remembered Patrick all this time plowed into her like a Mack truck full of emotions. She was so glad Luke remembered Patrick but panicked at the same time. Had Luke had nightmares like she had? Had he spent nights awake and worried? She should've asked.

～

PATRICK LAY PINNED to the floor of his room, his face smashed into the dirt and his arm twisted behind his back.

"Come on, Patrick. I've taught you better than this."

He had. For months the older man had taught him everything he knew which had turned out to be substantially more than Patrick had thought possible. They focused primarily on the weakest parts of the body, and what kinds of hits could take a man down in seconds, but they also wrestled and sparred as well.

"And you're forty years younger than me," the bishop goaded. When they'd started, Patrick had been worried about the age difference, worried he'd hurt the bishop, but the bishop had quickly laid those fears to rest.

The bishop's skill set was so specific that anyone who was trained properly could use it effectively against an opponent younger, stronger, or with any kind of perceived advantage. His skills were easy to learn and deadly, but even some of the most elite soldiers in the world knew nothing of the likes of them.

"You know this. How do you get me off?" the bishop asked.

Patrick popped his hips up and brought his knees under him in the process. The bishop's grip on his arm loosened, and then he let go and wrapped his arms around Patrick's waist. Once this happened, Patrick moved his legs out from under him and sat on his butt, wrapping his arms tight over the bishop's arms so he couldn't pull away. Patrick dropped into a roll, bringing the bishop under him, and slammed an elbow into his face and then his gut. The bishop released him, and Patrick jumped to his feet.

Seconds later, the bishop was up. "Well done." He threw a jab.

Patrick blocked it.

The bishop threw a right hook, hitting him in the ribs, but Patrick saw it coming and dropped his arms into the punch, making it glance off. It still hurt, but not as much as it could've.

They continued to throw punches and kicks, to block, to attack and retreat until finally, Patrick flipped them, both landing painfully on the ground on their backs. One of Patrick's legs and one of his arms part lay part-way over the bishop. Neither moved, just fought for breath.

Then the bishop asked, "What's the most important thing I learned in the—"

Patrick lifted his head and looked down at his mentor. "Milieu? DGSE? Stasi? The IRA?"

"Special forces." The bishop glanced over at Patrick as he shoved one his legs aside so he could stand. "The IRA?"

Patrick collapsed back again. "I gave it a shot."

"I'm French."

"Westkeys isn't a very French last name, and the Stasi are German." Patrick raised his brows and waited.

"I thought you were supposed to be good at guessing." The bishop stood and reached a hand down to Patrick.

"So did I." His gaze strayed to the many bruises covering the bishop's arm as he pulled him to his feet. The old man had bruises everywhere. Sure, they fought often, but the bishop gave as well as he got, and until recently he had overpowered him in nearly every fight. Patrick wasn't sure, but wondered if a person just bruised a lot more when they got older. A lot more.

The bishop moved his hand. "You haven't answered my question."

Patrick rested his hands on his knees and hunched over, trying to catch his breath. "What's the most important thing you learned in the 'special forces'?" He made air quotes.

The bishop nodded.

"How to dance?" Patrick chuckled.

The bishop rested his hands on his hips and looked down his nose at Patrick. "That's the next thing we learn. Perhaps a nice waltz and the fox-trot? Try again."

Patrick stood tall. "Situational awareness."

The bishop lurched forward and threw a punch into Patrick's face, knocking him flat.

Patrick groaned and grasped his nose. "What was that for?" He lifted his head and glared.

The bishop stood over him. "Define situational awareness. You don't appear to have a grasp on it."

"Being aware of what's happening around you, I get it," he snapped.

"Do you? You think you notice things others don't, but you missed me setting up that punch. You missed the signs that Wright was involved in your mom's death, that your friend was a psychopath, and the night you were kidnapped, you missed a man sneaking up on you in a completely empty house."

Patrick dropped his head again, grinding his teeth so hard it hurt.

"Do you really want to beat these men, or is this just a game to you?"

"Yes!" Patrick jumped to his feet.

"You're out-numbered, out-trained, and up against something a lot bigger than you could have ever imagined. And on top of all that, you're angry."

"Yeah, I'm angry," Patrick barked. "They stole my life."

"And that's why you'll lose."

Patrick froze, surprised.

"You have an emotional investment in this that they don't. One that's fogging your vision. You're good, Patrick. You are. But good isn't going to get you there. Righteous anger will get you nowhere. You want to win? You've got to learn to control your anger. You've got to learn to be extraordinary." He clapped. "Go again."

CHAPTER TWENTY-ONE

Kneeling in front of his secret spot, Patrick glanced over his shoulder, making sure he was alone. The hall was dark. He reached down and wiggled the rock until it gave way, then set it aside. A slight shine bounced off the ring and coin, which sat atop the playing card, and Patrick's heart swelled.

He dropped his fingers, letting them skim over both briefly before he removed the ring, and slid it on. He immediately traced it with the tips of his fingers, going to the dent, the one that reassured him that this ring was hers.

It'd been months since he'd last pulled his treasures out. At first, it'd been because the bishop had been around all the time, and he wasn't sure if he entirely trusted him yet, and then it was because he'd been so busy.

The bishop had heard about the coin, even though he'd never seen it, or had reason to believe that Patrick still carried it with him, but he knew nothing about the ring, and Patrick just had no clue how to broach it or if he even wanted to.

Patrick lifted the coin and wiped the dirt from it. He flipped it over and over as he took in the image. On one side there was an eagle and on the other a woman walking before the sun. For so long it'd been a symbol of his capture, but it looked different to him now. Both images were so symbolic of freedom.

"That's the coin?" the bishop called from behind him.

He momentarily froze, then nodded.

The bishop knelt next to him and placed a hand on his shoulder. "You're a different man than you were a year ago, Patrick. The change has been obvious to everyone. Life is coming back to you; happiness isn't so foreign. And now—" He nodded to the coin. "—even you can feel it, can't you?"

Patrick took a deep breath and glanced at the bishop. "Yes."

"You shouldn't keep those here," the bishop said. "You should keep them on your person at all times. One day we'll be leaving this place, and I doubt you'll have time to come back for them."

"I don't want the guards to steal them."

"We can sew them into the lining of your pants," the bishop said. "They'll be safe there."

"You can sew?" Patrick tried to picture the bishop with a needle and thread. It made him smile.

"The women in my church would often hold activities; one of them was a sewing class. I became quite proficient, I'll have you know." He rested his hands on his hips.

Patrick lifted his hands, palms forward. "Okay, okay."

For a moment, they were silent, and then the bishop spoke. "Now, tell me about the ring."

Patrick glanced down at his hand and at the ring. How could he explain it? Explain the ring and the person he got it from? All he had left were his memories, and he felt suddenly so inadequate to the task of doing them justice.

He glanced over at the bishop.

The bishop's eyes lit with joy. "It's got something to do with a girl?"

Patrick nodded.

"I love stories with a romantic twist." The bishop clasped his hands together. "And let's face it: your story could use a little romance in it. Now, tell me all about her."

YELLOW POLICE TAPE sectioned off the tree line by I-80 where Benson's body was found. Shea pulled to the side of the road behind several police vehicles, an ambulance, and a fire truck.

Making her way to the cordoned-off area, she reached her left thumb over to her ring finger and turned Sean's ring upside down, hiding the diamond in her palm. Most the time it kept the diamond from being so noticeable.

She crossed the yellow tape and headed toward Lee and the coroner, Carol Jenkins, who were huddled around the body. Lee stood when he saw her.

Benson had been severely beaten, and he had three large bullet holes to the chest. His dirty blond hair was matted with blood.

Shea took a ragged breath and absently reached for her crucifix. On the way, she tried to prepare herself for this, but he was her boss's best friend. She took comfort in knowing Benson was in a better place now, but for those left behind...

She glanced over at Lee who stood with his hands on his hips. The expression on his typically stoic face said the same thing she was thinking. *Poor Brown.* She couldn't imagine what it'd be like to lose Lee but especially not in such a horrific manner.

"We won't be sure about cause of death until the autopsy," Lee said. "But looks like he was shot here."

She glanced around. There were no drag marks, so yeah, shot here, and a large surface of the ground had been trampled.

"He put up a fight," Shea said.

"That he certainly did," said Carol Jenkins, the coroner. She pointed to Benson. "He has defensive marks all over his arms and hands."

"He was a prize-fighter, wasn't he?" Lee faced Shea.

Shea nodded. At least, that's what Brown had said. Apparently, he was one of the best prize-fighters out there, too. "Which means whoever he fought, knew what he was doing."

"And probably got as good as he gave." Carol shook her head. "I always liked Benson. He was a good cop and good person."

Shea nodded, then bent down to get a better look at him. Her gaze trailed down to one of his hands, clenched around something. She glanced up at Lee, who handed her a latex glove from his back pocket. With some effort, she pried Benson's hand open and removed a quarter.

"What's that?" Lee asked.

Her eyes went wide as she held the coin up for him. "I've seen this before."

"What?"

"My first year with the department. A man named Frank Miller." She swallowed thickly at the thought of pulling up on a homicide by herself. "I was giving speeding tickets when someone called in gunshots from a wooded area off the freeway. I was closest, so I went. With Miller, there were no signs of a fight, but he'd been shot in the chest and had a coin in his hand. A nickel."

Frank Miller had long jet-black hair that had been pulled back into a ponytail, he wore a shiny, salesman-type suit, he had a crescent-shaped scar on his cheek reaching from under his left eye down to his jaw line, and he was missing his pinky and ring fingers from his left hand. She'd found out later he'd lost them as a child.

He'd been a private banker or more like a legal loan shark, and while they'd felt certain at the time that his client list would lead to the killer, they'd never been able to get their hands on it. Miller had taken too many precautions for them to even find the general location of it.

Lee placed his hands on his hips. "It could be a coincidence. There are enough differences."

"The possible drugging, lack of defensive wounds, and a nickel instead of a quarter?" She nodded. "It could be different, or the killer's getting smarter."

AROUND SEVEN-THIRTY AT NIGHT, Sean stood in his kitchen washing his hands. His front door opened, followed by several footsteps heading in his direction. He turned off his faucet and grabbed a kitchen towel to dry his hands, then rolled his sleeves back down and fastened them at the cuffs. In his peripheral vision, Elizabeth stopped in the entryway to the kitchen and leaned against the archway.

He tossed the towel on the counter and faced her. "You're early."

Elizabeth's hands were crossed over her chest, and she was scowling.

"And grouchy."

"I've had a rough day." She pulled away from the arch and walked forward. "And you are in for it."

He grinned. "In for it? That sounds like fun."

"You've been bribing my brother into giving us alone time?" Her eyes flared.

He threw his hands up. "Oh, that? Yeah, for like a year now. Luke was threatening to raise his prices, so I'm kind of relieved it's out in the open."

"You can't do that." She stepped in front of him.

"Sure, I can. I did it." He took a step closer and reached for her, but she flinched back. "You're really mad about this? It was only for a couple hours once a week—for date night."

"If you wanted to be alone with me, you should have talked to me, not paid Luke off." She looked away and placed her hands on her hips.

He studied her for a moment, the tense crease between her brows and pursed lips. "There's something else going on. What is it?"

"No—"

"Please, Elizabeth. It's me." He took her shoulders in his hands. "I've known you forever. I think I know when you're worried about something. This isn't just about your brother. If it is, it's a major overreaction, which you're not prone to."

She took a deep breath and nodded. "Don't do that again. I'm not okay with it."

"I promise," he said. "What is it? What's got you so fired up?"

"Just a tough case at work today. It's nothing."

Ah, now he was curious. "Tell me?" he cajoled, reaching for her again. He pulled her into his arms, and she didn't protest. "You'll feel better."

"I don't think it's a good idea."

How intriguing. He moved back from her a little to get a look at her face and plastered a confused look on his own. "What is it?" When she looked anywhere but him, he tried a severe tone. "Elizabeth, what is it?"

She sucked in a deep breath. "Detective Benson, the man who worked with Brown on the Daley's cases, was murdered."

He forced a frown. "What happened?"

"We don't know yet."

He stepped back again, releasing her. "Why would you keep this from me?"

"I was... worried that it would dredge up old emotions."

"You mean Patrick?"

She nodded and shoved her hands into her front pant pockets. She swallowed hard once, then twice, and her eyes glistened a little. "He was your best friend."

All these years later and she still cared enough to get this emotional about it? Fury stabbed at him, and it was all he could do to not lash out at her. Instead, he turned away. "Can we cancel our dinner plans for tonight?"

"Sean." Her tone dripped with pity.

"It's okay, Elizabeth. It's not about Patrick. I got a new case load today, and I need to get started. A lawsuit that will make Hanson,

Jackson, and Jones a lot of money." He schooled his expression and glanced over his shoulder. "I'll see you tomorrow?"

A tear slid down her cheek. She nodded, then wiped the tear away. "Okay."

When the front door shut, he grabbed the nearest object on the counter, a vase of sunflowers, and threw them across the room. Would she ever stop caring? Could he make her? He dropped his hands to the edge of the counter and stared at the floor.

A few deep breaths later, and it hit him. It was time to make her pick a date. Once they were married, she'd forget Patrick.

CHAPTER TWENTY-TWO

The electronic buzz of the satellite made Patrick glance over to the bishop from the current cipher he was working on. "Where are you trying today?"

The bishop's lips quirked up at the corners. "43.2798 degrees north and 5.3251 degrees east."

"Uh-huh." He scratched his head with his pencil, then went to their list and marked off the coordinates. *Only a billion more to go.*

The bishop yawned and sank down in his swivel chair.

It was still early, and the bishop seemed more tired than usual. Come to think of it, he'd hardly slept and seemed to have lost his appetite over the last few days as well. He had dark circles under his eyes, and his face looked more drawn than usual.

Patrick frowned. "Think we'll get any bites?"

"Not likely," the bishop said with a wink. "It has to be heard first."

"How encouraging."

"Stop your whining, and tell me the proper procedure for assuming a new identity." The bishop fidgeted in his chair, his hand going to his abdomen, as it had so many times over the last few weeks.

Patrick sat his pencil down and pushed the cipher back. "You change everything. The way you look, your mannerisms, your clothes, the way you talk, everything."

"What are your major tells?" the bishop asked, and let out a little groan.

"You okay?"

"Yes, just a little belly-ache." He rested his head on the back of his chair. "Your tells?"

Patrick breathed out. "My hair. My wardrobe. The way I roll back on my heels. My love of hot chocolate." He thought of Elizabeth and smiled. "My smile."

"How will... how will you hide these-these—" The bishop let out another groan and clasped his side.

Patrick turned in his chair. "Bishop?"

The bishop fell from his chair. He released a moan of pure agony.

Patrick bolted out of his seat and dropped to his knees beside him.

"What is it? What's wrong?"

Large drops of sweat dripped down the bishop's face, and through his thin clothes, his body trembled. "Something happened. Something's not right."

"I'll get help." Patrick went to stand.

The bishop grabbed his arm. "No, no. They cannot help me." He grasped Patrick's hand.

"Please, let me help."

He grabbed the right side of his abdomen, his face twisted in agony. "I'm going to be sick."

Patrick grabbed the little dust bin from under the bishop's desk and handed it over but not fast enough. The bishop threw up, only part of it going into the bin. He breathed heavily, his face pale and covered in a sweaty sheen.

"I'm dying," the bishop said, but his tone was calm.

Patrick closed his eyes and shook his head. The bishop couldn't die. He couldn't be left here alone all over again. He'd never survive it a second time.

"Listen to me," the bishop groaned. "Listen. I have the money."

Patrick's eyes filled with tears. "You lied?"

A small smile crossed his friend's pain-racked face. "I am a bishop, not a saint. Well..." He shrugged then, a tiny chortle escaping his lips. "It's yours now. You'll need it if you're to get your justice."

"You can't give me this money." Patrick shook his head. "I won't seek justice; I'll seek revenge. You know I will."

The bishop closed his eyes, and his body twitched. Under his breath, he quoted, "'The flesh was weak; my blood ran chill...'" He opened his eyes and made eye contact. A tear slid down his cheek, carving a mark in the dirt encrusted there. "You will do the right thing, Patrick. Just learn to trust people. That's always your weakness. Trust. Do good, and don't give up on God."

"Why not? He gave up on me." Tears streamed down his cheeks.

"No, my dear boy. And he never will." The bishop's eyes darkened.

Patrick nodded. "Don't—don't quit on me."

"Remember. Account # 13, 14, 20, 5, 3, 18, 19, 20, 15." His eyes flitted opened and closed. "Pin number 2734."

"I can't, it's—"

"'But my free spirit cried, I will.'" The bishop blinked slowly and then closed his eyes.

Patrick pulled him into his lap and wrapped his arms around him. "Bishop, please. Don't leave me." He felt for a pulse. It was still there but just barely.

He couldn't let this happen. Patrick jumped to his feet and rushed down to find the guards.

～

PATRICK STOOD at the back of the passenger truck next to MacTep as the guards loaded it with this month's bodies. Why was he out here? He should be inside with the bishop and with MacTep's physician.

MacTep smiled at him. Patrick quickly turned his gaze to the ground. He had to be respectful, obedient, fall absolutely a hundred percent in line, for the bishop.

The sun set. The guards dispersed. Two went inside as the physician came out and to MacTep. They conversed in Russian, and Patrick caught the words "sick," and "alive." He hadn't learned much Russian, but those words were common enough. The two men came to some agreement, and the physician retreated inside once again.

"It was lucky the truck was here today," MacTep said. "I hate keeping bodies all month."

Patrick waited. MacTep wanted to torture him, wanted to worry him, wanted to put him in his place, and he'd let him, as long as it meant they'd help the bishop.

MacTep faced him. "The doctor believes that the bishop's appendix has burst."

That wasn't good, but it was fixable, wasn't it?

The doors to the building opened, and out came the guards with another body bag. Patrick's stomach knotted as the bag got closer. The men stopped in front of MacTep. MacTep unzipped the bag, revealing the bishop's face.

Patrick stepped forward. "You said you would help him!" He was dead? No, he couldn't be. He just couldn't. Patrick needed him. Could never survive this place without him.

"We tried. It's a shame really. He's been such an asset, but there's nothing we can do here." MacTep zipped up the bag again and nodded to the guards. "He's as good as dead."

Patrick kept his eyes on the gray bag with his friend, piled up with eight other bodies. *Good as dead?* He shook his head, and then dread seeped through him. "He's alive?"

"Not for long," MacTep said.

Patrick faced him, the man's cold glare shined back with amusement. Patrick fisted his hands as a black oozing hatred seeped through his veins, through every pore. He made and held eye contact until MacTep took a step back. Patrick knew what MacTep saw in his eyes. It was what every man here had seen in MacTep.

MacTep lifted his chin, but the fear in his eyes was unmistakable.

"Don't look at me." MacTep lifted his cane, bringing it down toward Patrick's head.

Patrick caught the cane in his hand and ripped it from his grasp. "He dies, you die."

"How dare you?" MacTep growled and reached for the cane. "You'll pay for this."

Patrick punched him in the face, knocking him to his hands and knees.

The truck roared to life.

Patrick lifted the cane.

MacTep stared, blinking.

Bending at the waist, Patrick said, "I am Lazerev." He brought the handle of the cane down.

MacTep dropped. Patrick grabbed him, pulling him through the mud, and lifted him into the truck. The truck pulled away, and he dove into it.

The account number flashed across Patrick's mind, as did everything the bishop had taught him in their time together. Patrick was the bishop's legacy. He rolled MacTep, unconscious and bleeding from his nose, away, and unzipped the bishop's body bag. He pulled the bishop into his lap and placed his fingers on the bishop's pulse point.

Patrick found the thready beat and repeated, "Account # 13, 14, 20, 5, 3, 18, 19, 20, 15."

~

THEY DROVE straight through the night. The back was still open to keep the bodies from getting warm, so Patrick huddled between MacTep and the bishop. Near dawn, when the moon had set, and the sun hadn't started to rise quite yet, when it was at its darkest, the bishop's pulse stopped for good. Patrick wrapped him in a hug as tears ran down his cheeks.

A moan came from beside Patrick. MacTep's eyes blinked open.

Patrick knelt and pulled the man up by his lapels. "You killed him."

When MacTep got his bearings, he started cursing in Russian. Before he could yell, Patrick put a hand over his mouth. MacTep struggled against Patrick's grasp.

Patrick stood, bringing MacTep to his feet. "Walk back from this, you worthless sack of dung." He kicked him out of the truck and watched him fly backwards, eyes wide, and into the night. Snow poofed up around him as he rolled to a stop. MacTep pushed himself up on his hands before vanishing into the darkness.

NEARING the end of the day, the truck slowed to a stop. It was time for them to refill the tank. Patrick squirmed his way under the bodies as best he could, hoping that they wouldn't notice that there was someone not in a body bag.

Their doors opened, and they immediately started yelling in Russian. What was going on? Then other voices, voices not with their party, yelled in return. It wasn't minutes later when gun fire filled the air.

Patrick's breathing accelerated as footsteps approached the back and opened the hatch. Voices yelled back and forth, and then they started pulling bodies from the truck. Patrick braced himself. As soon as they pulled the last body from him, he'd have to come out swinging.

He didn't expect that he had much of a shot at surviving this, but death was better than going back to Lazerev.

They yanked the last body from him. Patrick sat up and jumped from the truck and at the man closest to him. The man screamed in surprise and Patrick threw an uppercut that knocked the man backward to the snow, then turned and kicked the feet out from the next man in his sight. Another ran at him, and within seconds he had him down, too.

More yelling sounded around him, footsteps thudded in his direction, and Elizabeth's face popped into his mind. He threw a fist knocking someone in their jaw. A blow hit him in his back, sending pain shooting through him, but he kept struggling. Kept fighting. He didn't even see faces anymore, just one big mass of attackers. It didn't matter.

He'd spent too many years of his life being passive, letting things happen to him and doing nothing to stop them. Not anymore. If he died now, at least he'd go down fighting. At least he could have this one last glorious moment.

He gave one last punch, throwing it into a man who'd just tried and failed to kidney-punch him. Then a sharp pain exploded at the back of his skull, and everything went bright white.

"I'm sorry, bishop. I tried."

Right before he lost consciousness, he saw the bishop standing in the distance—a smile on his lips and in his eyes.

CHAPTER TWENTY-THREE

S hea sat at her desk with her desk phone held between her ear and shoulder. On the other end of the line was a coin collector, John Wilson, she'd found online who was an expert in all American coins. On her keyboard, in two separate evidence baggies, sat the dime and quarter found in Miller's and Benson's hands at the scenes of their murders.

"I don't suppose you could send me the actual coins?" Wilson asked. "It'd be easier to give you an appraisal."

Shea had sent him photos of the fronts and backs of each in an email earlier today. "No can do. They're evidence."

Wilson sniffed and blew his nose.

Shea scrunched her face until he finished.

He cleared his throat. "Nasty cold. Okay, we've got a 1944 Mercury dime and a 1946 quarter, and from the photos, they appear uncirculated."

"If they're uncirculated, that could mean they came from the same person?"

"Could be, but not just that. Both of these coins are worth a lot more than their printed value."

"How come?"

"From the year they were distributed, we know they're both at least 90 percent silver. The quarter could be anywhere from three dollars to ten, and that mercury could be worth between ten and 70 dollars."

"Seventy dollars for a dime?" She picked it up. *Wow!*

"Like I said, it's hard to know for sure unless I could look at them, but from what I'm seeing in these photos, they could definitely be uncirculated. You have a collector with a good eye on your hands."

"Would it be possible to find out who owned these coins?"

"If it were a silver dollar, possibly, but with dimes and quarters I'd say it's a slim chance." He breathed into the phone. "What did you say this information was for again?"

"I didn't." Shea glanced across her desk at Lee. He was reading some paperwork. "Thanks for your help, Wilson. It's appreciated."

She hung up and stared at the coins. It wasn't much, but it was more than they had before.

"Shea! Lee!" Brown's voice boomed across the bullpen.

Shea jumped in her seat and glanced up at her boss as Lee turned in his seat. Even from her desk, the circles under his eyes and their redness were noticeable. Brown hadn't taken the news of his partner well, and she doubted he'd slept since they'd found him three nights ago.

"They got him," Brown said. "They found the SOB."

Benson's killer? For three days they'd found nothing, and now they had him? Three days of zero leads, zero witnesses, and of zero prints on the body or the coin found in his hand, and they had him?

"Which precinct?" Lee asked.

"Twelve." Brown zipped up his dark, navy blue sports coat.

Twelve was Benson's. Benson had died in her jurisdiction, so whoever they had in custody was their witness. Shea just hoped they got to the man before Benson's colleagues got to him.

"How'd they find him?" Shea placed the coins in her desk drawer and locked it.

"He turned himself in." Brown marched off and pulled keys from his pocket as he went. "Let's go!"

Jumping to their feet, Shea and Lee ran after him.

PATRICK WOKE IN A LOW-LIT ROOM, on a too-soft mattress. For a moment, he thought he was dreaming. When they'd first taken him to Lazerev, he'd had many nights where he'd dreamed of being in a bed. Though, in those dreams, he'd never had a needle in his arm attached to a drip.

He sat bolt upright and reached for the offending object, ready to yank it out.

"I wouldn't do that if I were you," a male voice said.

Patrick kept his hand on the needle, but he glanced around the room, which appeared to be part of a log cabin, until he found a man sitting in a corner desk. The man's face was turned from him, and a lamp back-lit him, making it hard to get any real indication of his appearance.

It didn't help that Patrick's vision was blurred. He reached up and rubbed his eyes with his palms, then looked again. The man was tall, muscular, and Patrick thought he had dark hair, but with the low lighting, it could be lighter. He was also writing something. When the man finished, he turned in his chair to face Patrick.

It was still too difficult to see his facial features, but Patrick was now certain the man was wearing a red and black plaid shirt. "You were severely dehydrated." The man pointed to the IV. "It's an isotonic crystalloid solution to rehydrate you."

Patrick tried to speak, but his throat was dry. He swallowed hard, and it hurt. "Who are you?" He was still alive, which seemed miraculous. It also made him wary.

"My name is Zakhar." He had a Russian accent, but only a slight one.

Patrick scooted back and leaned against the headboard. His

entire body ached, but he was pretty sure it had more to do with the softness of the bed than anything else. "Zakhar?"

The man nodded.

"Who are you?" Patrick dropped his hand back to the IV.

"Perhaps you should tell me who you are first?" Zakhar rested his elbows on his knees. "We know you came from the work camp." His English was perfect.

The only person who'd wanted to know who he was since he'd been taken was the bishop. A lump formed in his throat at the thought of his mentor. What had they done with his body? Would he receive a proper burial, or be thrown in a nameless grave? "Patrick Daley."

Zakhar stood and moved across the room to him. He stopped at the small bedside table that Patrick had missed until now. On it sat a glass and a pitcher of water. Zakhar filled the glass and handed it to him.

Patrick swallowed the water in three gulps.

Zakhar refilled it, and Patrick got a better look at him. He had short, dirty blond hair, a curve to his nose, and large hands.

Patrick reclaimed his glass and took another swallow. "I was a hostage and prisoner in Lazarev." He tried to push himself up a little more, but his energy was depleted. "How long have I been out?"

"Two days," Zakhar said.

"Are you a slaver?" If they were, Patrick needed to know. The one and a half days of freedom he'd had in the back of that truck with the bodies had been enough to cement in his mind that he would never be going back, that he would be a free man or die trying.

Zakhar's lips pursed. "No."

"Then what are you?"

Grabbing the wood chair at his desk, he dragged it back to the bed. He sat down and leaned back. "That is a difficult question to answer."

"I'm a quick study," Patrick said.

"Let's say that I am a... supplier." Zakhar's eyes crinkled at the corners as the conversation went on, his tone gaining a cheery lilt.

"Of what? Drugs?"

Zakhar nodded and shrugged. He put his hands in front of him, palms up, and circled them a little. "Eh. Yes and no. Liquor and cigarettes, sure. Aspirin, and other medicines, yes. Anything harder, no."

"What else do you *supply*?"

Zakhar scooted forward in his chair. "Oh, anything, anything. Anything a person could need or want. If you want it and have the money to pay for it, I will make it yours."

Patrick closed his eyes and chuckled. "You're a pirate." *Figures.*

Zakhar tipped his head back and laughed out loud. "I like that. Pirate. Sounds much better than smuggler. Don't you think?"

"Can a zebra change its stripes?" Patrick didn't think so.

Zakhar slapped his knee. "Well put. I am what I am. You are a funny man. I like you."

"Thanks." Patrick took another drink. "Why am I here? And where *is* here?"

"You are in my home-town of Podnyalsya, and you are here because I brought you here."

"Why?"

"Why not?" Zakhar's eyes lit with amusement.

Why not? Really? "I came out of the back of that truck swinging. I floored at least three of your men, maybe more."

Zakhar nodded. "After I knocked you out, I had one of the best laughs that I've had in years. You have spirit—fire. For a prisoner of Lazerev, it's most surprising and refreshing. Not even the free men who come out of there can lay claim to that."

Patrick scrubbed a hand down his face. He was so tired. "You thought that was funny?"

With his hand, Zakhar signaled up and down Patrick's frame. "Look at you. You are a twig. A twig with some muscles, yes, but I still think a stiff breeze could tip you over. My men are well fed, and were armed."

"I took them by surprise."

Zakhar pointed a finger at him. "And you have been trained."

Patrick finished his second glass of water and felt the need to pee. A pinching in the groin that reminded him of being a kid when they moved the circus around and he get a desperate need for the bathroom with no rest stops in sight or, just as likely, a father unwilling to lose time.

"Where did you learn to fight like that?"

"Is that why I'm here? You want me to fight someone? Or fight for you?"

"Ah, you *are* a quick study." Zakhar folded his arms. "I wish it if you do. I have no interest in men who don't want to be here. If you want to go, we'll drop you in the nearest big city, and you can find your way home."

Patrick's stomach somersaulted. *Home.* "Out of the goodness of your heart, you kept me alive, gave me medical attention, and are willing to set me free?"

"Yes."

"I don't buy it," he said.

"You are a wise man, Patrick." He tapped his foot on the ground. "There is something I need."

Of course. Patrick suddenly couldn't care, his own desperation taking precedence, and swung his legs off the bed. "Yeah, yeah—I need a bathroom."

Zakhar smiled and came to his feet. "Follow me."

Patrick pulled the IV from his hand and stood. He staggered on his first step, and Zakhar steadied him with a hand on his arm.

"I'm fine," Patrick said.

Zakhar opened the door of the room and led Patrick down a darkly lit, but well-decorated hallway. The cabin wasn't large, but it wasn't exactly small either. Patrick counted five doors, including the one they'd just come from. They hall wasn't anywhere near as uninviting as his room had been, and had several impressionistic paintings decorating the walls.

One at the end of the hall caught his eye, and he stopped. It was lit with an overhead lamp. A painting of a bridge in mostly blue and some brown shades. It was signed by Claude Monet.

Zakhar pushed open a door, which Patrick assumed was the bathroom.

"Is that..." He stepped forward. "Waterloo?"

Zakhar glanced over his shoulder and smiled. "Ah, you know your art. Impressive. It's a beautiful copy, no?"

Patrick squinted at the brush marks. "It's real." What was the real copy doing here? "I thought it was hanging in a museum in Rotterdam?"

Zakhar smiled. "Was it?"

This didn't make sense. He was a smuggler. "You could get a lot more money for this than anything else you sell."

Patrick passed Zakhar, pulling the dark wood door closed behind him.

As Patrick lifted the lid on the toilet, there was a thud of someone leaning against the door.

"It's not money that we need here in Podnyalsya but services," Zakhar said. "Without those, many in our town would not survive. Which is why you were such a lucky find. You will make it possible for me and my men to do what we do."

"Exactly how will I accomplish this?" Patrick flushed the toilet and went to the sink. He did a double take when he caught sight of the bearded, dirt-covered, emaciated, older man staring back at him from the mirror. He'd had the image of himself as an eighteen-year-old in his mind.

He turned on the hot water and watched it flow—its crystal-like shine mesmerized him. He inched his hands under the water and closed his eyes at the overwhelming feeling of warmth.

"I told you already. You will fight him."

Patrick quickly soaped up his hands and rinsed them. He then opened the door. There had to be some way he could play this "fight" to his advantage. "Who is this man?"

Zakhar faced him. "Come, I'll take you to meet him now."

Patrick lifted his hand, running his thumb over the side of his index finger.

Zakhar's gaze fell to Patrick's hands, and his eyes widened. The contrast of Patrick's pale, clean hands to the rest of him was striking.

"You are filthy." Zakhar made eye contact. "When was the last time you bathed?"

Patrick thought back. He was pretty sure the last time he'd showered was the day before he'd cleaned out Maggie's area of her dung. His heart clenched at the thought of his elephant. "Ten years, give or take a few months."

Zakhar took a step back, his blue eyes growing larger in his head until they appeared unnatural. "Okay, shower first. There are towels in the cupboard above the toilet. I'll get you clean clothes." He headed down the hall. "And maybe I'll burn your sheets while I'm at it."

CHAPTER TWENTY-FOUR

"That's him?" Shea glanced away from the suspect to Lee and Brown who stood to her right. Lee's arms were folded across his chest, and Brown had a hand up on the one-way glass that overlooked the interrogation room.

Caleb Yance was the last person Shea would've pegged for the murder of Benson. Aside from the fact that he was five feet seven with platforms on his shoes, weighed a buck fifty soaking wet, and had a broken hand, he was also hunched over, shaking, and stuttering.

Perhaps he was normally more confident than now, but she'd imagined it'd be hard to maintain confidence after getting worked over by several officers. Fortunately, he only appeared to be sporting what would tomorrow be a black eye, and a swollen lip. He was also cradling his broken hand to his chest, but it was already in a cast, so she wouldn't blame the officers for it.

The whole thing disgusted her. Sure, she'd wanted to deck suspects before, and even had once, but the guy she'd hit had been evading arrest. He wasn't someone who'd turned himself in. If Yance did kill Benson, she wanted him to pay, but not like this.

"That can't be him," she said.

"He knew he was beaten, he knew about the coin. He works in the area, he had opportunity, and he admitted to it." Brown ran a hand over the back of his head.

"You don't think this guy could beat Benson in hand to hand combat?" Lee jumped in. "And even if he somehow could, his hand is broken."

"Yance was in the military. He's had training." Brown cleared his throat. "Besides, I've seen teenagers lift cars off people. I saw a marine lift a helicopter off a fellow soldier before. People can do incredible things in moments of extreme stress," Brown said.

Shea shook her head. This wasn't right. "What about Frank Miller?" Their murders were connected. She was sure of it.

"Coincidence," Brown said.

"No—"

"He's our man." Brown raised his voice, then lowered it again when he drew the attention of other officers. "You've heard him. Only someone who had been there, who had committed this crime, could've given the evidence of guilt that he has."

She pulled her chin back. He was right, of course. He had to have been the one to do it. She looked at him through the one-way mirror and stared at his eyes. Despite his total lack of confidence in his body language and way of speaking, there was a hardness in his gaze—a determination that she couldn't deny. Weirder things had been known to happen. But...

"It's getting late." Brown turned to Lee. "You two go on home. There's nothing more you can do."

Once they were outside, Lee asked, "Do you think he did it?"

"No," she said.

"Me either."

~

"BEFORE YOU BATHED, I thought you were a brunet, but your hair is even blonder than mine, Trup," Zakhar said.

"Trup?"

Zakhar grinned. "It means corpse."

Patrick sat in a chair in the living room in a brand-new pair of jeans that were an inch or two too short for him, but fit him around the waist, and a white, cotton T-shirt that hung loosely on him, while Zakhar's wife, Valeriya, cut his hair. "Because I'm skinny?"

Zakhar shrugged. "You are not skinny. You are a dead man walking."

Large chunks of wavy hair fell around him on a sheet that had been placed on the wood floor as Valeriya combed through and cut his mane. Valeriya was gentle with him and gave him a bit of a scalp message as she worked. It would've been relaxing, had he not been so worked up over what was supposedly coming.

After he'd showered and changed, he'd asked that they go meet the man he was to fight right away, but Valeriya had taken one look at him and had insisted that he eat and get a haircut. At least, that's what he'd inferred from her interaction with Zakhar, which had been in Russian. Patrick had only caught random words here and there, but their body language spoke volumes.

"My wife doesn't speak English," Zakhar had said. "And neither do my children. All of my business takes place in English because she doesn't want the children to know."

Zakhar's children, a five-year-old girl named Sylvia and a six-year-old boy named Andrei, sat with him on the large, overstuffed couch watching as Patrick's hair got shorter and shorter. Zakhar's daughter said something in Russian that made Zakhar and Valeriya laugh.

"She says your hair is angel hair," Zakhar explained.

It made Patrick smile. He quirked a finger at the girl, and she glanced at her father. He nudged her with his elbow, and she slid off the couch and came to him, stopping two feet away.

He held his two hands out to her palms up, then twisted his fingers in and wrists around. When he opened them again, two pieces of Russian caramels, each individually wrapped in yellow paper, sat in his palm. He'd taken several from a bowl in the middle of the kitchen counter during dinner.

Sylvia clapped her hands over her mouth and giggled. Her brother, Andrei, leaned to the side from his spot on the couch to get a better look. Patrick tossed one of the candies to him and handed the other to Sylvia. She took it and rushed back to the couch.

Valeriya muttered above him, and Zakhar chortled. Patrick caught the word "stop."

"My wife wants you to stop moving. She says your cut will be uneven if you don't. Also, she likes your trick."

Patrick rubbed his beard. He'd trimmed it after his shower but hadn't shaved it. "Are you sure she's not mad at me for giving them candy?"

Zakhar laughed again. "How'd you know?"

"Lucky guess." Seemed more likely she'd mutter "stop" over the candy than his hair.

Valeriya finished her cut and removed the towel she'd wrapped around Patrick's neck. "Sdelannyy."

"You're done," Zakhar said. "Ready to go?"

Patrick stood, ran a hand through his now-weightless hair, and nodded.

The trip to town was quick across the barren, snow-covered terrain and it wasn't long before Patrick could see what Zakhar had meant when he'd said the town needed services. There were close to fifty homes, but only one small grocery store and one gas station. No other businesses, not even a post office or police station, were anywhere in sight.

Zakhar pulled his jeep into the gas station. "You are wondering how we survive out here with so few amenities."

Patrick knew how. "Smuggling."

"Yes, but in order to do that, we must pay heavy fines."

"Fines?"

Zakhar nodded. "To Sokolov. He blackmails us, and in return we pay him huge fees, and every year our fees rise. Pretty soon, we won't be able to continue our work at all. Everything this town has, everything the ten neighboring towns have, we bring in."

"Like jeans and T-shirts?" Patrick had noted the Calvin Klein tags in his pants and his shirt and doubted that was something that came into this place legally.

Zakhar faced him. "Like medicine for sick children, clothes to keep warm, and food. Not a month ago, a bottle of children's Aspirin saved my niece's life."

"But you don't make money off children's medicines." Patrick held Zakhar's gaze.

Zakhar's lips twitched up at the corners. "No."

"I won't kill him." He wasn't a killer for hire.

Zakhar raised his hands. "That's not what we want. I'm an honest man. If Sokolov needs to die, I will kill him myself. But first, we'll try our luck with you. Sokolov loves sport. Every year he challenges one of my men to a fight. If we win, he lowers his fee."

"If he wins?"

"He raises it, and this time, it will put us out of business."

Patrick tapped his lip. "Doesn't he need your services too? Why not call his bluff?"

Zakhar shook his head. "He has a reliable vehicle and easy access to the only gas station in town as he owns the station. He can get what he needs without us—maybe not best quality or prices, but he doesn't seem to care if it means getting what he wants."

"How often do your men win against him in his fights?"

The door to the gas station opened and out stepped a man well over six feet, with bulging muscles, a box-shaped head, and a sneer. He leaned against the door and saluted Zakhar with two fingers.

Zakhar lifted a hand to him. "What do you think? Not only is he built like a gladiator, but he's also the best fighter I've ever seen."

Patrick breathed out slowly through his nose. "You don't get out much, do you?"

Zakhar let out a roar of laughter. "It would be a shame if he killed you; you are too much fun."

Patrick turned in his seat and faced Zakhar. "If I do this and win, I want something in return."

"Anything."

Patrick smiled and offered Zakhar his hand.

Zakhar took it.

"When do I fight?"

SHEA SAT AT HER DESK, staring blindly at her computer screen. After Yance's official arrest, things had slowed down and left them with lots of paperwork, but she couldn't focus. Her mind kept jumping between Benson and Yance and... Patrick. There was a connection here, between them all. The mere thought of his name made her fall into a dark pit of confusion and terror. What had happened to him? To his mom? People didn't just vanish off the face of the planet.

For so long she'd blocked out memories of him, more often with success than not. Of course, there'd always been the occasional night when she woke in cold sweats after having a nightmare about his disappearance, but those had come less and less frequently as she'd gotten older.

Not anymore. Now she couldn't shake him. He was there all the time, pounding down the barriers she'd built in her mind to keep the horror at bay.

"You're doing it again," Lee said.

She jumped and glanced across her desk at Lee. *Jeez!* He was reading documents.

"Doing what?"

He made eye contact. "Staring into space. What is it?"

He hadn't even looked up and knew she was stuck in her mind. It was comforting, the idea that he'd always be there to bring her back. She pulled Patrick's file out of her drawer and dropped it on top of the desk. "It's my friend."

He breathed out through his nose. "Patrick?"

She nodded. "I can't help but think that Benson's death was related. I have no reason to believe that. Maybe if I could find a connection between Benson and Miller, I could figure it out, but I've got nothing."

"I've been thinking the same thing." He closed his file and looked at her.

"You have?" She sat a little taller.

"That's why, while you were staring at your computer screen for the last hour, I went down to records and pulled Samantha Daley's file." He stood, grabbing the file he'd been looking at, and came around to her desk.

She shook her head a little. He went to records? Oh man, she *was* out of it. But that was brilliant. She should've pulled Patrick's mom's file when she'd first remembered him a year ago.

Lee pulled up a chair. "I'll look through Patrick's, and you go through his mom's. Maybe fresh eyes will help."

With a smile, she took Mrs. Daley's file. "Thank you."

"One question," Lee said. "Were you in love with him?"

She sat back. "Why would you ask me that?"

"I know more about you than anyone here, but it was nearly a year of partnership before I knew you had brothers and that Luke lived with you. It was even longer before I found out about your parents, from Brown no less. I didn't even know you were dating someone until you showed up with that small boulder on your finger—"

Shea fidgeted with her ring and frowned.

"—but Patrick, he's always on your mind. That says love to me."

She swallowed the lump in her throat. A small, indignant part of her wanted to remind him that he was just as guilty of keeping his personal life private as she was, but he was asking her. He wanted to know, and if she couldn't tell Lee, who could she tell? Certainly not Sean.

"My mom was killed in a car accident; my dad drank himself to death. I grieved for them and moved on, but Patrick.... He was a kind, sunny, mischievous kid. He made me and my brothers laugh when all we wanted to do was cry. In a way, he was like family. Maybe I had a crush on him, but it was so long ago. It's hard to know. I did care about him very much. The salient point is that one day he was there and the next he was gone. Vanished off the face of the earth, as far as anyone knows. I don't know what happened to him, and that terrifies me. How do I move on from that?" Ignoring it wasn't working anymore, that was for darn sure.

Lee nodded, opened Patrick's file, and started reading.

THE FIGHT WAS SET at Zakhar's factory just out of town. The building was two stories high and held large shipping containers and crates from floor to ceiling. A large space was cleared out in front of the office, and all of Zakhar's men, about twenty of them, had circled around to watch the fight.

Sokolov stood in the corner with a dozen or so men of his own. They pointed at Patrick and laughed. Patrick guessed it was because he was so skinny, but he'd already put on five pounds since he'd arrived two weeks ago. Valeriya was very insistent he eat—a lot.

While Sokolov jumped around, stomped his feet, and pounded his fists into his palms, Patrick sat in a metal folding chair and waited for them to get on with it.

Zakhar stood next to Patrick, chattering on about Sokolov's most-used punches. "If he hits you in the head, you'll go down for good. See this bend in my nose? Courtesy of Sokolov..." and "You don't want him to go into body blows. Last man on the receiving end of that had to be taken to the hospital and almost died before we got him there..." and "Protect your ears; you don't want him to go Mike Tyson on you—he's done that before, too."

Patrick twisted Elizabeth's ring on his finger, then slowly slid it off and slipped it into his pocket.

"Trup." Zakhar dropped to a knee beside him. "Are you listening to me at all?"

Patrick smiled and patted him on the arm. "It's going to be fine, Zakhar."

A man from Sokolov's camp came to the middle of the floor and lifted a hand. The raucous chatter of the crowd dropped to whispers.

Zakhar rubbed the back of his neck. "I should never have signed you up for this. He's going to kill you."

Patrick stood. "Relax, my friend."

Zakhar's blue eyes wrinkled with worry.

"What's he saying?" Patrick asked of the man in the ring.

"He's saying there's no eye gouging, biting, hooking, or hair pulling. Everything else goes."

The man yelled, "Bor'ba!" then dropped his arm in a quick cutting motion. Patrick knew what that meant, and stepped onto the floor.

Sokolov moved forward with a sneer on his lips. The crowd cheered from all around them, clapping, whistling, and shouting things in Russian that Patrick couldn't understand but thought he could make a fairly accurate guess at.

Before Sokolov was ready for it, Patrick darted forward. Sokolov threw a fist at his head, more from instinct than skill, but Patrick side-stepped it, throwing a hook into his kidney.

Sokolov arched to the side and forward, bringing his head down. He cried out in agony and surprise for a split second before Patrick brought his elbow down, with the whole weight of his body, on the back of Sokolov's neck.

The large man dropped in a heap, and the room fell immediately silent. Patrick went to a knee by Sokolov's head. The man's big brown eyes reflected the agony he was in, but also awareness, which was all Patrick needed.

"That pain you're feeling right now... I'm guessing it's new to you?"

Sokolov muttered.

Patrick nodded. "That's what I thought. Your days of blackmailing Zakhar are over. Not just for the year but forever. If I hear you've started up again, I will come back and introduce you to several more different kinds of pain. Do you understand?"

Sokolov's eyes darted back and forth.

"A simple nod will suffice."

Sokolov moved his chin slowly toward his chest.

"Nice doing business with you."

Patrick stood, and turned to face Zakhar. The man's eyes were once again wide, the look of shock on his face mirroring that of the silent crowd around him.

"I need fake IDs—good ones," Patrick said. "I need passage to Florida and some cash to get me started. And I need hair dye."

Zakhar blinked. "Hair dye?"

"A nice chestnut, I think." Patrick reached into his pocket, removed Elizabeth's ring, and slid it back onto his finger.

CHAPTER TWENTY-FIVE

FOUR MONTHS LATER

The open-air café, where Patrick sat with Zakhar looked out over Miami Beach. His thin, Hawaiian-print button-up clung to him, and sweat formed at the back of his neck. He tilted his face up to the sun, glad that the red umbrella on his table was closed, and let warm rays seep through his skin. He'd never get enough of it, would never be too warm.

"So, did you get the money or not?" Zakhar asked.

Keeping his eyes closed, Patrick nodded. The tart scent of a pineapple chicken sandwich wafted over to him on the salty breeze.

"How?"

"With the IDs you provided." They'd been the best money could buy and hadn't been cheap, but that wasn't what Zakhar was asking. He wanted to know how he'd found where the money was.

When Patrick had arrived, the first thing he'd done was find out who the bishop really was. It hadn't been hard, as not many bishops had gone missing the year he had. In fact, it'd only been him. After he knew his real name, the IDs were ordered. Then it had only been a matter of locating the bank.

It wasn't hard to figure out that Westkeys was really Key West.

After that, Patrick had simply called around until he'd found the bishop's credit union.

Zakhar shook his head. "You are the richest man I've ever met, and you still look like a bum. This outfit cost you, what? Twenty dollars? And your apartment—pathetic."

In fairness, Patrick didn't love his clothes. He longed for his three-piece suits, for their familiarity and numerous pockets, but that's what the old him would wear, and so he couldn't. It was the same reason he'd dyed his hair.

Patrick chuckled and ran his thumb over his forefinger. "I have to keep a low profile, especially while I'm consulting with the police here."

Zakhar lifted his strawberry daiquiri and, with his nose, pushed the little yellow umbrella out of the way before taking a sip. "This is a mystery to me as well. Why are you working for them?"

"It's all part of the plan." A plan he'd spent ten years fantasizing about and the last four months perfecting. He'd gained the trust and respect of the Miami PD, had helped them solve a dozen cases, and with his résumé now in place, he was ready to go to Sacramento.

A group of women passed their table on the way to the door, and Zakhar followed their progression. He leaned forward. "Those women were checking you out."

"Were they?" Patrick had seen it, but he didn't care.

Zakhar sat his drink down. "Why not find a woman to love, get married, have a dozen babies, and settle down? You are happy here, my friend. And now that you are no longer skin and bones, you don't look half so bad."

Patrick rubbed his thumb over Elizabeth's ring on his ring finger.

"Why waste your time on revenge? If you must have it, you could always send someone to take care of it for you," Zakhar asked.

Since getting back to the states, Patrick had learned a lot about what had happened while he'd been gone and it increased his lust for revenge ten-fold. Patrick shook his head. "Wright is the chief of

police now, is running for mayor, and will probably win. And Sean..."
His jaw clenched at the mere thought of his former friend.

"I know, Trup—"

"No, you don't. The circus I grew up in has disbanded. My friends have scattered to who knows where. I don't know what happened to Maggie, my father ran away, one of the officers on my mother's missing person case was murdered, and the one officer I actually trusted quit and moved away shortly after I was taken." He hoped Rafferty was all right. He still felt guilty for thinking poorly of him.

"And what about the girl?"

Patrick stared at the beach. "I don't know."

He hadn't found much on Elizabeth, except that her father died three years after he was taken and that she'd become a cop. He remembered her threat from years ago. If he did this, she'd arrest him. He couldn't hope for anything of her because of that. He cleared his throat. "Revenge is mine and mine alone. It's time for me to go home."

Zakhar took a deep breath, then nodded. "I know."

"I'm going to need your help." Patrick pulled out his wallet and dropped a hundred dollars on the red-checkered tablecloth.

Zakhar came to his feet. "And you will have it."

The men embraced and patted each other on the back. Pulling away, Patrick dropped a hand to his friend's shoulder. "Thank you."

PULLING up to the trailer park, Shea parked her car and stared out her front window. It was a long shot, coming here. After Patrick disappeared she didn't want to come back, and a few years later, even if she'd wanted to, she couldn't have because the circus had closed.

She supposed it was a weird thing to feel guilty about it now, but she did. Tilde and Jay had always been kind to her, and they'd loved Patrick. She wished she'd checked on them, just once.

Now, she wasn't even sure they still lived here. This was their last known address, so she decided to give it a try—go over what Benson and Brown had talked to them about, see if they remembered anything else.

It was a cloudy day, which made the already cement property with its gray and dirty white trailers seem even dingier and depressing. She didn't remember it like this when she was a kid. They used to have trees everywhere, and when the tents were up; it was magical. Now it reminded her of a scene from a horror film.

She pulled her keys from her ignition and got out. She passed the one spot that she remembered well, where Patrick's Airstream used to be and stopped. The spot was now taken by a dingy old motor home. She glanced around, thinking back to where the tents used to be and which trailer had been closest to Maggie's.

Once the scene was fully mapped out in her head, her gaze landed on the cleanest trailer in the park. That seemed about right. If they were still here, Shea was certain that Tilde would want to keep her home spotless inside and out. She breathed in, crossed to the trailer, and knocked.

The trailer rocked slightly from movement inside, and the door swung open. It was Jay. He seemed taller than she remembered.

"Yes?" He pushed the screen open and stepped down to the bottom step.

"Jay?" She wasn't sure why it came out like a question. It was him. Ten years hadn't changed his appearance all that much.

"That's me," he said.

He didn't remember her. Of course he didn't. Last time he'd seen her, she'd been sixteen, and she had changed a bit since then.

"Who is it, Jay?" Tilde's voice called from inside the small home.

"Don't know," he said.

She swallowed the lump in her throat. "I'm—"

Tilde appeared in the door. She hadn't aged a day, from her mop of tight, curly brown hair to her toned athlete's build.

"She's po-lice, is what she is." Tilde turned her back on Shea.

"Wait, Tilde," Elizabeth said. "I'm Elizabeth Shea. I was friends with Patrick."

Jay stepped out of the trailer, and Tilde glanced over her shoulder.

"Elizabeth?" A smile spread across Jay's face. "By golly, it is. It's Elizabeth Shea."

A shadow crossed Tilde's face. Elizabeth didn't have time to really see it before Jay had scooped her into a bear hug. Her feet dangled in the air, and she went stiff in his grasp.

He set her down. "How have you been? Aside from selling out to the dark side?"

She caught her balance, then smiled up at the giant of a man. "The police aren't the dark side." She shook her head. "Aside from that, or that included, I'm good."

Then Tilde was there, the dark shadow gone, replaced by true delight. "Better than good, by the looks of that ring."

Shea glanced down at the engagement ring and immediately turned it upside down with her thumb out of habit. Tilde quirked a brow at her.

"You're engaged?" Jay's enthusiasm was heartening. "That's wonderful!"

"Yeah?" There she was, asking questions again that were really answers.

"Are you asking us?" Tilde smiled.

She shook her head. "Uh, no. I am. Engaged. To Sean..."

Tilde and Jay glanced at one another.

Tilde reached out a hand to her. "Now that's a story I want to hear all about. Come on in."

Shea followed Tilde inside with Jay behind and took a seat at their table. Tilde sat across from her. Jay sat in a recliner across from them and stretched his long legs out.

"Now," Tilde said, "you and Sean, how'd that happen?"

Shea took a deep breath. The last thing she wanted was to talk about Sean with the two people who were the closest thing to family Patrick had. For some reason, it made her feel guilty.

"I'm actually here to ask you some questions about Patrick."

"The po-lice didn't care enough about that boy to ask us any questions when he first went missing. Why on earth would they care now?" Tilde kept her tone light, but the underlying anger was clear.

"No, that's not... Detectives Brown and Benson came. I have the documents in Patrick's case file. They talked to you."

Tilde folded her arms and stared down her nose at Shea.

Jay pulled his legs in and leaned forward, resting his elbows on his knees. "We never met no Benson or Brown. The only officer we saw 'round here was that Rafferty fellow. Came the morning after the last day we saw Patrick. Asked around if anyone had seen him. He said he had an appointment with him. Of course, he wasn't here, and we didn't know he was gone yet, so we sent him on his way. But, like I said, it was the only time we ever saw a cop here."

Shea shook her head, trying to clear it. "They would've been in street clothes. Maybe you didn't recognize them?"

"We didn't recognize you just now," Tilde said, "except that you were a cop. You po-lice always think you're so inconspicuous, but you're not. Y'all stand out like an elephant among giraffes."

It didn't make sense. Benson and Brown were good cops—great cops. What had they been up to? And why was there paperwork saying they'd come here?

"Though we did get a visit from the one fellow," Jay said. "The one who talked to Alexander, Patrick's dad, before he skipped town. The bum."

Tilde glanced at her husband. "The one with the scar?"

"Wait, who?" Shea came out of her shock. "What happened?"

Tilde faced Shea. "About a month after Patrick... you know, a man came and talked to Alexander. The next morning, before we even woke, Alexander was gone."

"What did the man look like?" Shea asked.

"Black hair, sleazy." Tilde lifted a hand to her left cheek. "He had a crescent scar that ran down his cheek—"

Shea sucked in a breath. "Was he missing two fingers?"

"I only saw him across the path at Alex's trailer." Tilde shook her head.

Jay nodded. "Yeah. I saw him leaving after I fed Maggie that morning, walked right past him. At first, I thought his fingers were just bent up into his palm, but I glanced back after I walked by him, and sure enough, his ring and pinky finger was gone."

It was Frank Miller; it had to be. What was going on here? "Did you go to the police?"

"Why would we be doin' a thing like that?" Tilde leaned forward. "They ain't never done us any favors, and they sure didn't do that boy any good, either."

Shea closed her eyes and breathed out. She needed to talk to Brown. If Frank Miller was here and was killed after talking to Patrick's dad, then that was enough to connect him to Benson's death. There was a link, just as she'd suspected. Brown would have to listen to her now, especially when the wrong man was being held for Benson's murder.

She scooted out from the table and stood. "I'm sorry, but I have to go."

Jay stood and gave her another hug. "You'll come back and see us again?"

She nodded. "I'd love to. I'll bring Luke. You wouldn't believe how big he is now."

Tilde smiled. "Aw, my baby. I bet he's grown up all handsome—just like his big sis."

Jay walked Shea to the door. "Come back soon, Elizabeth."

Shea crossed back through the park with a sense of unease tightening around her like a python. A lump grew in her throat. When she got in her car, she called Lee.

CHAPTER TWENTY-SIX

Pushing into Brown's office, Shea spoke before he could. "Frank Miller went to see Alexander Daley after Patrick's disappearance, and shortly after that, Alexander packed up and got out of Dodge."

Lee stopped at her side.

Brown's initial glare faded to shock. "Are you sure?"

She nodded. "I have two witnesses who described him down to the crescent-shaped scar on his cheek and his two missing fingers."

"Who?"

She clenched her jaw. "Jay and Tilde Swan. They worked with the circus."

Lee pulled a document from Patrick's file that he held and set it in front of Brown. "That's not all. This document says that you and Benson went and interviewed them, along with several others with the circus, only you never did."

Brown's gaze darted between Lee and Shea. He stood and came around to close his door. He signaled to the chairs in front of his desk. "Please, sit."

"I'd rather stand," Shea said.

Brown nodded and went back to his desk. "It's not what it looks like."

"We're listening," she said.

Brown scrubbed his hands down his face. "After Patrick's disappearance, a lot of heat came down on Sergeant Rafferty."

Shea glanced at Lee, then back to Brown. She'd never met the man, but she'd heard of him, not only from Tilde and Jay but from other cops. He'd been an outstanding cop until one day he up and quit—moved out of Sacramento. "What do you mean?"

"He was helping Patrick with his mother's case before the kid went missing," Brown said.

"So?" Lee folded his arms.

"The day before the kid went missing, a man named Vadim Mikhail was arrested for human trafficking. Patrick was responsible for his arrest," Brown said.

Shea furrowed her brow. "How is that possible? He was a kid, barely eighteen-years-old."

Brown waved a hand as though brushing the comment off. "He decoded a cipher that led to the rescue of a little girl who'd been kidnapped. The next day, despite sufficient evidence against Mikhail, we had to let him go. Rafferty had wanted to be certain that everything was handled properly, and filled out all the paperwork himself." Brown breathed out. "He did something wrong, filed something wrong, and Mikhail's attorney got him released on a technicality. Mikhail and Patrick went missing the same day."

"You covered for Rafferty?" Bile began to rise in her throat. "The man screwed up, got a human trafficker released, who probably kidnapped Patrick and did who knows what with him."

"There was more to it," Brown said.

Heat flushed over her. She needed air. Now. "What?"

"You don't know Rafferty." He rested his palms on his desk and shook his head. "He never messed up a single document in his life.

He was organized, methodical to a fault. He swore he did everything right, and Benson and I believed him. We didn't go to speak to Patrick's folk because Rafferty went there the day after looking for him and no one knew he was missing. We got rid of any evidence suggesting he'd been there and doctored that document saying we had."

"Why didn't you go anyway?" Lee asked. "Double-check?"

"Rafferty was sure no one there knew what happened to Patrick. He was sure that Mikhail had taken him. We didn't think it'd be an effective use of our time to go back," Brown said.

"Why'd you get rid of the documents showing that Rafferty had gone?" Lee asked.

"Because with him being held responsible for Mikhail's release, going to Patrick's home the day after looked suspicious. Rafferty was already taking the fall for Mikhail, I've never seen anything like it. It was a blessing they let him retire, though they only allowed that to try and keep his story out of the news. Not that it worked. His wife left him, too. The last thing we wanted was for him to be connected to the kidnapping in any way."

Shea pinched the bridge of her nose to relieve some of the pressure there. "And for years we've been clueless as to Frank Miller's connection to this because you didn't go."

Brown sat in his chair. "Look, Shea, I am certain that Vadim was responsible for Patrick's disappearance. Miller's visit won't change that, but it is compelling enough evidence for me to ask Wright to reopen the case." He cleared his throat. "Hindsight is twenty-twenty, but you have to remember we'd just lost our boss, a man we knew to be innocent of any wrong doing or error, a good friend who was being smeared. And if he was innocent, it meant that there was a cop on the inside who intentionally sabotaged him. It was a hard time, and we did the best we could, considering the circumstances."

She nodded. "Don't tell Wright what we've found if you can avoid it. He's taken to sharing too much with the media since he decided to run for office."

"You noticed that too?" Brown frowned. "I'll keep the details to a minimum."

Lee rested his hands on his hips. "We should keep details between the three of us. I think it's safe to assume there may still be crooked cops involved."

"The four of us," Shea said.

Both men turned to her.

"Rafferty," she said. "We need to know what he knows. Maybe he has some insight into this that we've missed." And if he did, she was going to get it.

PATRICK STARED at the door to his new office in downtown Sacramento and smiled. The title of his company was written in large block letters: Westkeys Investigations. It was a lot nicer than the one in Miami, by design of course. He pulled the door closed and locked it. His phone rang from his blazer pocket. The number was one he'd memorized upon arriving: the office of the Chief of Police.

After arriving, he'd immediately started throwing money around. He rented an office space in a prime location, purchased a mansion, hired interior designers, and had crashed a couple high-society parties. Looked like word was finally getting around about the wealthy PI.

On his way to the elevator, he answered. "Hello?"

"Mr. Westkeys?" came a friendly female voice.

"Yes." He hit the elevator's down button, then fiddled with his tie, which he wore loose fitting. He was glad to have new clothes, clean clothes that fit, but he wasn't sure he'd ever get used to jeans all the time, or ties, which is why he'd picked them in the first place. He decided to go with button-ups and blazers, which was closer to his old three-piece suits.

"This is Kelly calling from Police Chief Wright's office."

"Hello, Kelly. How are you today?"

The line went quiet. "Oh, uh... I-I'm good?"

The elevator opened, and he stepped in. "Excellent. How may I help you?"

Kelly cleared her throat. "Yes, Police Chief Wright asked me to invite you to his fundraiser tonight."

Patrick leaned against the back of the elevator. "How flattering. I'm curious; how did he know I was in town? I've only been here for a week. I'm barely moved in."

"I'm not sure, sir, but you must be quite distinguished if he's asking you to his fundraiser. It's very important to him."

Patrick chuckled. "How diplomatic of you, Kelly. I'd be delighted to come. Where is it being held?"

"Do you have something to write with?"

He put his free hand in his pocket. "Yep."

She gave him the address. "We're trying to keep this as low-key as possible, which hasn't been so easy since he announced his run for mayor. So, if anyone asks—"

The elevator stopped. "Mum's the word." Patrick hung up as he crossed the lobby.

Wright didn't want paparazzi at his fundraiser. He guessed that made sense—the man was still looking for donors for his mayoral run, and this would be a perfect opportunity to enlist them without the pressure of the press.

But Patrick was fond of pressure. He'd spent the last ten years of his life under pressure and decided it was time to pass it on.

SAUNTERING THROUGH MARSEILLES GALLERY, Patrick grabbed a glass of red wine from the bar. Men and women dressed in tuxes and cocktail dresses filled the well-lit, high-ceilinged open space. Waiters rushed around with trays of drinks and appetizers and a band played from a small stage.

Several people stared at Patrick as he passed by. Apparently, he was the mystery man of the party—the unknown element. He had to admit that his tuxedo made him feel the part.

Still, being a mystery guest wasn't enough to keep people from gossiping about what was happening right out the front doors of the gallery. He held back a smile as words like "paparazzi," "unprofessional," "foolish," and "Wright" floated about him.

Wright stood on the far side of the gallery near a back exit. He was speaking with two other men, trying to keep a pleasant expression on his face as he gave orders. He stopped briefly when a man approached him to shake his hand and commenced his quiet rant once the man had left.

Patrick went to one of the tall tables standing in the middle of the room and grabbed a small napkin that had an M embossed in it. He removed a pen from his pocket and scrawled the message "Samantha Daley will be avenged" on it, then pressed his thumb down hard on the corner before shoving the note in his jacket pocket.

Turning on the charm, he approached two women who stood in front of a large painting that was clearly the centerpiece of the exhibit. The younger of the two looked to be in her early thirties, and the older was at least twenty years older than that. Both of them were dressed to the nines and decorated in fine jewelry.

He stopped behind them and stared up at the painting of a castle rising off a cliff with the ocean below and a cloudy gray sky above. He cleared his throat.

The women jumped and turned to face him.

Without taking his eyes off the painting, he said, "It's true what they say about beauty lighting a room."

The older woman spoke, her gaze flitting to the younger. "You like the painting?"

"It's..." He spread his arms wide as if trying to encompass the work. "...a masterpiece." He faced her. "But of course I was speaking of the beauty of you charming ladies."

The women laughed, and from his peripheral vision, Patrick noticed Wright look at them.

"Aren't you the flatterer?" The older woman pushed back a stray lock of silver hair from her face.

"To flatter wasn't my intention, but if that's what I achieved, I am happy to have done it. Now, which of you lovely ladies painted the other beauty that will be hanging in my home?"

The older woman grabbed the arm of the younger woman. "Haydee painted it, my daughter."

Patrick turned to Haydee, who kept her face down and stared up at him through her lashes, not out of an attempt to flirt, but because she was nervous. He immediately liked her—so different than most of the people in the room. He reached a hand out to her, and hesitantly she took it.

"What a pleasure to meet such a talented artist," he said.

Her cheeks flushed with pleasure, and she bit her bottom lip to keep from smiling.

"Alexander Westkeys?" a male voice spoke from his right.

He glanced over as Wright approached. His stomach muscles clenched as though he'd just taken a blow to the gut. He straightened his posture and smiled, taking the proffered hand of the man who'd murdered his mother.

Patrick smiled and reached into his pocket. He wrapped his fingers around the napkin. "I'm sorry, have we been introduced?"

From across the room, Patrick had been able to hold his anger at bay, but now that the man was so close, he couldn't help but think how easy it'd be to close the space between them and snap his neck. But no. That wasn't enough. It'd be too easy. He deserved to suffer, and Patrick would do whatever necessary to see that that happened.

"The name's Robert Wright." He pointed to the older woman. "And this is my wife, Helen, and my daughter, Haydee."

Patrick kept his poker face, despite discovering that Wright had a family. And a family he'd taken an instant liking, too. He felt bad for Helen and Haydee and for the future he was hurling their way.

"Aw, yes. I thought I recognized you; your picture is all over the city. Running for mayor?" Patrick took a sip of his beverage. "Thank you for inviting me to your little shindig."

"You're enjoying yourself?" Wright asked.

"And the company." He signaled to the ladies, then leaned in next to Wright and spoke in a stage whisper. "Perhaps a little too much. I'm buying this painting."

The ladies laughed again, and he slipped the napkin into Wright's jacket as he backed away again.

"Wonderful, wonderful," Wright said. "All proceeds go to charity."

"Yes, I heard a spokesman telling the reporters that as I came in," Patrick said.

A shadow fell over Wright's face. "Yes, well, it became necessary. The reporters weren't supposed to be here. I hope it wasn't an inconvenience for you?"

Patrick shook his head. "Not at all. I haven't felt that interesting in at least ten years." He'd actually come in a side door. The last thing he needed was a picture of himself in the media. "Though, I wondered. One of the reporters was asking about a case involving an officer named Benson?"

Wright's smile fell. "They did?"

Patrick lifted his glass. "They wondered if it was entirely appropriate for you to be holding this kind of function, in lieu of new evidence. Reporters certainly have a way of prying into a man's personal life." He laid the bait but couldn't help but to push. He smiled. "I hope you don't have any skeletons in your closet, mayor."

A faint giggle came from Haydee. "My dad, with hidden skeletons? Well, I suppose he likes to indulge on fudge ice cream."

"But only a gallon at a time," Helen said.

Wright winked at his family and mimed zipping his lips. Haydee and Helen laughed.

Patrick clenched his jaw.

Wright faced him. "Thank you for telling me about the reporters, Alex. I apologize you had to hear that."

"Sounded pretty serious."

Wright dropped his chin a little. "Yes. Well, a death of an officer always is, but I can assure you that we have our best men working the case."

"I think you've misunderstood my motives," Patrick said. "I don't ask for reassurances, but to offer my services."

Wright furrowed his brow, then made an *aha!* face. "That's right; you're a private investigator."

"You sure do your research." Patrick's phone rang, and he pulled it from his pocket. The number on the caller ID was Russian. He wasn't expecting a call from Zakhar. "If you'll excuse me, I must take this." He answered it, but kept it down and kept talking to Wright. "Ask around about me. I worked in Miami last. You have my number if you decide you want my help."

Wright seemed puzzled. "Of course."

"It was a pleasure to meet you," Haydee said.

Patrick nodded to her. "The pleasure was all mine."

When far enough away, he lifted the phone. "Zakhar? What is it? What's wrong?"

"Nothing, Trup. I'm calling to see how it's going?"

Patrick closed his eyes and breathed out his nose. "It's going as expected." He turned back around as Wright moved to another party. He shook hands and said something that made the group laugh.

"Have you found your girl yet?" Zakhar asked.

Patrick furrowed his brow. "I'm not here for a girl."

Zakhar laughed. "Right, right. Just revenge. I know."

Wright stuck his hand in his jacket pocket, then glanced down as he pulled out the napkin. He was about to deposit the napkin on the tray of a passing waiter when he saw the note. His face drained of color.

"I need to go." Patrick squeezed the phone tight.

"Okay, okay. I'll call again tomorrow."

Patrick thought to argue, but then Wright was making his excuses to the group he was with. He said something in passing to Helen and Haydee, then went to the two men he'd been ordering about earlier. He was then promptly escorted out the back door.

Zakhar spoke again. "Patrick?"

Patrick smiled. "He bought it."

CHAPTER TWENTY-SEVEN

Chimes wafted through Sean's mansion. He grabbed the remote and muted *Dragnet*, Elizabeth's choice, and faced her. "Doorbell."

She sat to the right of him, her legs pulled up under her. "You expecting someone?" She grabbed a handful of popcorn out of the bowl in her lap.

He shook his head and stood. "At nine-thirty? No." Whoever it was, it had better be good; he hadn't had much time alone with Elizabeth in months. Not since she'd found out he'd been paying Luke to skedaddle once a week for date night. "I'll be right back."

"Okay," she said. When he turned in to the hall, she called out after him. "Ask who's there before you answer the door."

Reaching the door, he yanked it open to find Wright standing on his porch wearing a tuxedo and a frown. Sean quickly glanced over his shoulder, then stepped out and pulled the door closed behind him.

"What are you doing here?" Sean hissed. Sure, they'd seen each other in public on several occasions since the night they'd made their deal ten years ago, but they'd never come to one another's houses.

Wright lifted the napkin. "Is Patrick Daley dead?"

Sean took it, examining it.

"Is he dead?"

Sean shushed him. "My girlfriend is here, and in case you've forgotten, she's a detective. If she heard what you just said—"

"It'd be your problem to deal with." He lowered his voice. "Is he dead?"

Sean lifted his chin. "Yes."

"You saw it handled?"

"No, but he is. Vadim told me he was."

Wright snatched the napkin back and pointed a finger at Sean's face. "He'd better be. If I go down, I'm taking you with me." He marched back down to his limo and got in.

Sean watched until the vehicle was out of the driveway, then headed back inside. He plopped down on the sofa and took a handful of popcorn.

"Who was it?" Elizabeth asked.

"Neighbor." He wrapped an arm around her.

She pulled back, and he ground his teeth. "At this time of night?"

"Their dog got out, wanted to know if we'd seen him."

She frowned and leaned back against the sofa. "Oh no. I hope they find him."

He pulled her close and tried not to huff as she stiffened against him for a moment before she *made* herself relax.

Every time.

WRIGHT STOOD inside the capitol with a hot beverage cup in each hand. Patrick approached the building in the dark predawn light and hoped it was hot chocolate, but had the sneaking suspicion that both were coffee. The man was worthless in every other aspect of his life. It didn't surprise Patrick that he'd choose the lesser drink.

"Alex, thank you for meeting me here." He handed one of the cups to Patrick. "I hope you like your coffee black."

"Thank you." The pungent aroma of black coffee wafted up to his nose. He took a sip, careful not to show his disgust. "I assume I'm here because you want me working on the Benson case?"

Now that the media was all over the Benson case again, it'd be easy to scare Wright into thinking that they would dig deeper into his life than he'd like. Wright would hire him out of desperation to close the case quickly. Everything was working exactly as planned.

Wright turned and headed into the building. "Yes. I called around Miami and learned only good things about you. Each officer you worked with said you'd helped them close every case you were called in on."

"Yes, sir." Patrick took another drink of his coffee, making sure this time not to breathe through his nose.

Wright laughed. "No false modesty. I like that."

"I'll need the case files and the assurance that the officers in charge will work with me."

"Of course," Wright said. "You can pick up a copy at my office from my secretary as soon as you're done here."

"Who's in charge?"

Turning down the hall to the conference room, Patrick spotted a bald man pacing in front of the door. The man turned and rested his hands on his hips. It was Brown.

Wright signaled to him. "Sergeant Brown is over the case."

They stopped when they reached him. The last decade hadn't done his hairline any favors. Patrick was glad, but he had to admit the man did bald well, which was annoying.

Brown eyed Patrick nervously. "Who's this?"

"I'm the man who's going to do what you have been unable to," Patrick said.

"Oh yeah?" Brown's voice was gruff. "What's that?"

"Find out who killed Sergeant Benson." It was mean, and Patrick didn't care. It didn't matter that the man hadn't had anything to do with his ruin; harassing Brown would be a nice bonus. Without taking his gaze from Brown, he took another drink of his coffee.

Brown narrowed his eyes. "Excuse me?"

Wright lifted his hands. "He's a private investigator."

"Chief, you can't be serious." Brown faced Wright and intentionally blocked Patrick from the conversation.

"I am," Wright said. "We need a fresh set of eyes on this, and he comes highly recommended."

"Boss," Brown tried again.

"I'm not arguing this. You'll work with him and get him whatever he needs." Wright pointed to the conference room. "Now, if you'll excuse me, I have a statement to make regarding this case. Get it solved, gentlemen. And fast."

Brown scowled at him before going into the conference room. Patrick rolled back on his heels, then turned and headed for the drinking fountain at the end of the hall. He took a sip as a man and a woman rounded the corner and went into the press room. Patrick went down the hall across from him, catching sight of a petite, dark-haired woman in his peripheral vision for just a second before she ducked into the conference room. He stopped in his tracks. He glanced down the hall. For a second he thought he'd seen Elizabeth. He shook his head. It was a trick of his mind, but he would not be stopped.

"WE'RE LATE." Shea and Lee darted through the empty halls of the capitol building.

"We'll make it," Lee said.

Coming around the corner to the press room, they slowed to a walk. At the end of the hall, a man was getting a drink from the drinking fountain. Lee went into the press room first, and Shea followed, noticing the man at the fountain stand tall as she stepped in. She froze, and a shock of heat shot through her. She stepped back and peered down the hall just as the man turned the corner.

Lee stepped out. "Everything all right?"

She frowned. He'd seemed so familiar. He kind of looked like... Patrick.

No. He didn't. He hadn't looked anything like Patrick, now that she thought of it. Wrong hair color and build, wrong posture. Wrong everything. It was bad enough that he was starting to haunt her in her dreams at night, but now she was seeing him in random strangers.

"Shea?" Lee lowered his voice.

She turned to him. "Yeah?"

"You all right?"

She blinked. "Yeah, I'm just tired."

Brown stepped into the hall. "Where have you been?"

"There was an accident," Lee said.

Brown's jaw clenched. "It's over. Wright already gave a statement." He waved them down the hall away from the press room and prying ears. "He's hired a private investigator to work Benson's case with us."

"What?" Shea froze. Why would he do that? Private Investigators were rarely helpful. She thought of the one from Bristle Park—he'd been a pest, constantly sticking his nose where it didn't belong. Though, she couldn't really remember why. She'd kind of blocked him out. Come to think of it, she couldn't even remember what he'd looked like.

Brown nodded. "I'm not happy about it either, but we have no choice. He's going to come into the station this afternoon at four-thirty to meet with us and look at the case file."

Lee folded his arms. "Who is this guy?"

"Alex Westkeys," Brown said. "And from what I can tell, he's a pain in the neck."

CHAPTER TWENTY-EIGHT

In front of the door to Patrick's office sat a package about half the size of a shoe box. Patrick smiled when he came off the elevator. He stuck the case files he'd picked up from Wright's office under his arm and scooped up the box. It had arrived right on time. He pulled out his phone and dialed Zakhar.

"Patrick," came Zakhar's pleased tone. "Did my package arrive?"

"It did." Patrick stepped into his office and closed the door behind him with his foot. "Did you get it ready?"

"You know, before last week I'd never even heard of a telephone transmitter like this, but somehow you, a man who spent a decade in a work camp, does? And I'm a smuggler. What were you doing in that camp anyway?"

Patrick crossed the nicely decorated reception area and went into his office, tearing the box open as he went. "Is it ready?"

"It wasn't exactly easy to come by either—"

Patrick sat in his black-leather, swivel chair, and placed the file on his rosewood desk. He pulled out the transmitter. It looked like a walkie-talkie, but instead of dials, it had buttons like on a cellular phone for dialing, accepting, and ending calls.

"I had to use every contact I had to locate that for you."

Patrick breathed out and looked heavenward with a slight roll of his eyes. "You're amazing, Zakhar, wonderful. The best smuggler I ever met. I don't know what I'd do without you."

Zakhar laughed. "Of course it's ready! Jones's number is already keyed in. Any number, ingoing or outgoing, will appear on the screen and you'll be able to hear their conversations. And just like you requested, there's no range distance on that. You can listen to his calls from anywhere."

"How many numbers can I key up for monitoring?"

"Twenty," Zakhar said. "But if you have to listen to that many people, you're in way over your head."

"Noted."

"Have you seen your girl yet?"

"Bye, Zakhar." He disconnected and turned on the transmitter. If Sean was anything like what he used to be, then he had every reason to expect Sean would be calling Vadim at some point today. After he woke up. It was still early. And Sean liked to sleep in. At least, he used to. Patrick had learned before coming back that Sean was an attorney now, so maybe his days of being lazy were over.

Patrick sat the transmitter aside and opened the file. He flipped through the stack of pages until a name caught his eye, making him freeze.

Detective Shea was one of the first officers on the scene where Benson was murdered.

"Elizabeth." His heart thudded a rapid percussion against his chest. She was on this case? Would she recognize him? What if she didn't? And if she did, how long would it take her to arrest him? He had to know the answers to these questions before he showed up at her precinct.

Looked like Zakhar was getting his wish after all. Pulling out his cell phone, he dialed Shea's precinct. Now, he just needed to remember what time high school got out on Friday.

"LOOK AT THIS." Shea came around her and Lee's desks and set the papers she'd just printed down in front of Lee. "I found Alexander Daley."

Lee turned from his computer.

"He changed his name to William Castile and started a psychic business in Reno, Nevada."

Lee lifted one of the pages. "Is that his house?"

Shea nodded. "And he has another, nicer one in Lake Tahoe."

Lee let out a low whistle. "I thought he was a gambler. How could he manage this?"

"The Reno house is in foreclosure. Apparently he hasn't paid his mortgage in six months— the Tahoe house was paid for in cash eight years ago."

"Let me guess..." Lee leaned back in his chair. "Not long after Miller visited him?"

"He was paid off to stop making a fuss." She stood tall, placing her hands on her hips, and nodded. "Looks like it, anyway."

"I doubt he'd be a fount of information," Lee said. "We already know who paid him off, and Miller wouldn't have been forthcoming, considering how he guarded his client list. Plus it's been years."

"Agreed." Shea pinched her nose up by her brows, the slightest pressure of a forming headache making itself known by a pulse. "What do we do, Lee?"

The desk on her phone rang, and she went around to answer it. "Hello?"

"Detective Shea?" spoke a tired voice.

"Yes." She pushed her bangs off her forehead. "Who's speaking?"

"William Rafferty."

Shea locked gazes with Lee. "Rafferty?"

Lee stood.

"I heard you've been looking for me," Rafferty said.

"I have. You heard about Sergeant Benson?"

"Yes."

"We've found evidence linking him to a murder from eight years ago, and to Patrick Daley's missing person case," Shea said.

Rafferty breathed out. "Finally."

Shea held her breath. "Can we meet?"

"Today. Meet me at the Oakland Zoo at two near the lion exhibit. Tell no one." He hung up.

Shea lowered the phone and looked at her watch. "Twelve-thirty." She'd have to leave now.

"What's going on?" Lee rested his hands on his desk.

"I have to go."

"We're supposed to meet that PI here today at four."

She hung up. "I'm going to talk to Rafferty. You stay and deal with Brown and Westkeys."

She grabbed her jacket and turned, then remembered that she was supposed to pick Luke up from school today. She always picked him up on Friday on her lunch break because he got out early. She faced Lee again.

"Luke?" he asked.

She nodded.

"I got him."

"Thanks." She put on her gray leather jacket and crossed the bullpen.

~

PATRICK LAY on the mat carpet on his office floor with his blazer bunched under his head and his legs crossed. He rocked his feet back and forth as he waited. The transmitter sat next to him, letting off a white noise that Patrick found soothing.

He was so tired, but even now, with nearly six months out of the work camp, he still couldn't sleep. He'd almost slept better while in the camp. Now that he was free, he had nightmares nearly every night.

It didn't help that his bed was way too soft, either. While in camp, he remembered the mattress in his trailer as a luxury but now only the floor brought comfort. Clearly not enough, though, because he was still wide awake even after three days of no sleep.

The transmitter started to ring, and he stopped his feet fidgeting, but kept his eyes closed.

After two rings, a voice came over the line. "I told you never to call me on this line." It was Vadim.

Patrick sat up and moved into his chair. He placed the transmitter next to a recorder and hit record.

"If you didn't want me to call you on it, you wouldn't have given it to me," Sean said.

Seeing Sean, talking to Sean, facing Sean had been a part of Patrick's plan for a long time. A long, long time, but planning out how this would go hadn't prepared him for the reality of it. His muscles tightened so much he started to shake, and he saw red. He realized how close he was to his once friend and now mortal enemy. A twenty minute drive and this could be all over.

Patrick took a deep breath, remembering all his carefully laid plans. Sean had to suffer. Had to know what it was like to lose everything. Patrick leaned forward on his desk and gave all his attention to the conversation.

"What do you want?"

"Your assurance that Patrick Daley is, indeed, dead."

The line went silent.

"Vadim," Sean snapped.

"That kid I took ten years ago?" Vadim's Russian accent got thicker. "Why you ask me about him now?"

"Because Wright asked *me* if he was still alive, and I *assured* him that Patrick was dead. Was that a good assurance to make, or not?"

"He is dead," Vadim said.

"You killed him yourself?"

Vadim took a deep breath. "He is dead. You have nothing to worry about."

"I certainly hope not, Vadim, or you'll find yourself back in a jail cell."

"What is that supposed to mean?"

"Your number isn't the only information I have on you," Sean said. "Does the Oakland Port or the *Siyan* sound at all familiar?"

Vadim cursed.

Patrick chuckled.

Sean waited Vadim out. "If there is any chance that Patrick could be alive, you find him and kill him. Do you understand?"

"He's dead!"

"So you've said."

"If I go down, you go down, too."

"Please, Vadim, I've been threatened by men far more powerful than you today."

The line disconnected.

Patrick turned off his recorder and smiled. "Gotcha." He grabbed his cell and dialed Zakhar.

"Has he called already?" Zakhar asked in way of greeting.

"Where are you?"

"Two days out of Oakland."

Patrick stood. "How fast can you get there? I have a feeling Vadim will be pulling out sooner than we'd anticipated."

Zakhar breathed out. "Yes, we can. We'll try."

"Do it. Get there. It's the Oakland Port, and you're looking for a ship called *Siyan*."

"We're on our way."

CHAPTER TWENTY-NINE

Moving through the crowd, Shea kept her eyes open for Rafferty as she approached the lion exhibit. She passed a class of second graders looking at the camels and slowed when the lion exhibit came into view. Several people had gathered around, but as she got closer, one man caught her eye. He stood in the shade of a tree by the fence, wore a blue ball cap and sports coat, and from her vantage point seemed about the right age to be Rafferty.

When she was within a few yards of him, he glanced over at her, then back to the lions. It was him, all right. She stopped within a couple feet of him and faced the lions. One big male lay out on a rock with several females around him. His head was tilted to the sun, his mane blowing in the gentle breeze.

"Magnificent creatures, aren't they?" Rafferty held a manila envelope in his hands and was playing with the fastener. He hadn't aged well. His face was drawn, and his blue eyes were dull. He looked tired—like he didn't sleep often.

"Rafferty?"

"How did Benson die?"

She turned her head to look at him. "I'm sorry, but I can't disclose details of an ongoing investigation."

He nodded. "Of course not." He faced her. "Did he have a coin in his hand?"

Shea's stomach flip-flopped, but she kept a straight face. "How did you know that?"

"Benson worked Miller's cold case for years—with me. Secretly. Not that we were ever able to find anything. Well, except that he'd bribed Alexander Daley into leaving."

"What?" Shea's breathing came fast and then stalled. "Why didn't you come forward with this information when he was first killed?"

His hands tightened on his folder. "There were no prints on the coin, correct? No way to identify the killer whatsoever?"

She breathed out her nose and looked down.

"Same as Miller's murder. I didn't come forward because Benson was working with me. I waited. He was a good man who was helping to find out what happened to Patrick, and the last thing his reputation needed was to be smeared by association as mine had."

"He deserves justice."

"That's why I called you. And not just him but Patrick. Benson was my friend, and I mourn him, but he was a grown man and a cop. He knew the dangers involved with his career. Patrick was a good boy with no clue what he was getting into. He deserved better."

Shea's eyes stung—she clenched a fist and took a deep breath. It equally brought relief and stung to hear someone speak so kindly of her friend.

Rafferty tapped the folder against his opposite hand. "Let's find somewhere to sit."

Passing the meerkats, they came to a concession and gift shop area and took a seat at the nearest empty table.

Rafferty slid the file to her. "Benson was murdered because we were getting close to finding something that the killer didn't want us to—something about Patrick."

Pushing up the tabs, Shea lifted the seal on the envelope and dumped out mug shots of a man with a pock-marked face and greasy hair pulled back in a ponytail. He was sneering. "Who's this?"

"That's the man I lost my job over."

She lifted the picture. "Vadim Mikhail?"

"Patrick's the reason he was put in jail in the first place—him and his friend, Sean Jones."

She did a double take between the pictures and Rafferty. "Wait, what?" Sean was involved? How could that be? He'd never told her a thing about it?

"It's a long story, and all you need to know is that Vadim hated Patrick. It's taken me years to figure out the things I have, and I'm still no closer to finding the boy." He dropped his head and stared at his hands interlaced in his lap.

She swallowed the lump that filled her throat. "What do you know?"

"This case goes so much deeper than you could ever imagine. I'll tell you everything I know, but you need to be sure you want to hear it. If anyone finds out you're digging into more than Benson's case, that you made the connection between him and Miller—and by them, Patrick Daley—not only your career but your life could be at stake."

She lifted a hand. "I know about the dirty cop."

"It's not just a dirty cop." He raised his voice. "It goes a lot higher up than that. So you'd better be a hundred percent positive that you want to pursue this because half-baked won't cut it. You're either all in or all out."

She furrowed her brow. Higher up? "Tell me," she demanded.

He stared her down.

She refused to blink and straightened her spine.

He nodded. "After Mikhail's arrest, I went to Wright, who was my boss at the time, and asked for permission to look into Samantha Daley's missing person case. He'd closed it, you see. When I mentioned it, he gave me permission but didn't remember the case well until the end of the conversation. He told me that if he recalled correctly, the dad had seemed the most likely suspect, they just couldn't prove it. He told me to not get Patrick's hopes up."

"Husbands are responsible for the deaths of their wives more often than not," Shea said. "Seems like sound reasoning." She still didn't like it. She hadn't known Mr. Daley all that well, but the idea that he'd killed Mrs. Daley made Shea's stomach churn.

"I thought so, too until I started digging. Alexander Daley had an air-tight alibi the night Samantha was last seen, video surveillance of him at a casino on the Nevada/California border. Yet somehow the documentation of that never made it into her case file. That night, while I was out of the office, talking to Daley and his alibis, someone messed with Mikhail's papers to make it look like I'd dropped the ball. Mikhail was released the next day. Next thing I know, he's gone, Patrick is gone, Samantha's case is taken away from me, my reputation is in shambles, and I'm out of a job."

"Okay, so the dirty cop was keeping himself busy."

Rafferty leaned back. "I can't blame you for not seeing it. It took me several years to piece it together."

"You know who it was?" Shea leaned forward.

"Wright."

She pulled her chin back. "The Chief of Police? The man currently running for the office of mayor? You're kidding, right?"

"His signature was all over Samantha's case from the beginning, from the very first day she disappeared. He even went over her case with Brown and Benson two days after they started investigating. He wanted updates," Rafferty said.

She shook her head. "His name is nowhere in her case file."

He leaned forward again. "Just like Daley's alibi wasn't. Benson told me Wright had been involved much later on, after the case was closed and I was no longer in Sacramento. Of course, at the time, neither Brown nor Benson had any idea what the implication of Wright's request was."

"Which was?" Shea asked.

He lifted the bill on his hat a little. "He lied about not remembering Samantha's case. For someone receiving frequent updates, he should've immediately known who she was. He played dumb. After Mikhail's release, he personally accused me of misconduct on handling the kidnapper and led the character assassination that forced me to retire. And he's the one who closed her case. Closed a cold case. The implication is that he knows more than what he's said about Samantha Daley, that he had Mikhail released after I started looking into her case, and that, in exchange for his release—" He pointed to Mikhail's picture. "—Mikhail got rid of Patrick, the one person determined to find out what happened to Samantha. The person who got me, Wright's biggest competition, to look into her case."

Shea stood and turned from him. "No. No. No. No. No." She sucked in a breath.

This couldn't be. Patrick was just a kid. Only eighteen. And Wright was, well, Wright. The man who'd spent close to thirty years of his life in the police force—the last five as the Chief of Police. The man who was leading in the polls to win the mayoral election.

She dropped her hands to her knees and took several long, deep breaths.

Could he really have traded Patrick to slave traders? Have had something to do with Samantha Daley's disappearance and the deaths of Benson and Miller? She thought of the man she'd only officially met half a dozen times, that was constantly on TV and looking for accolades. Yes, it could've been him. And if it was, they were all in big trouble.

Rafferty moved in front of her. "I must say you're handling this better than I did when I realized the truth."

She sucked in another breath and stood tall again. "Please tell me you have proof?"

He dropped his gaze again. "I don't. If I did, I'd have brought him down years ago."

"Could you go to the news?"

He shook his head. "I'm a disgraced ex-cop. He's the soon-to-be mayor of Sacramento. It'd look like I was trying to get revenge. No one would give me the time of day. Our only hope is finding who killed Benson and Miller and making them talk. That, or finding the Daleys alive."

She swallowed. What had happened to him? Had they killed him? Sold him into slavery? Something worse? Not knowing what had happened to him had been a nightmare, but with these options, she kind of wished she could go back to not having a clue.

"I feel sick," she said.

"You look it." Rafferty rested a hand on her shoulder. "I've been where you are. I've spent days and nights panicking for him, wondering what they'd done to him. I don't know if you'll find any consolation in this, but I doubt they sold him into slavery."

She took another deep breath, willing herself not to cry. "Why?"

"Patrick was a physically strong, young man. Not ideal for his market."

She wiped an errant tear away. For a second, that did make her feel better—that was until she started thinking about what Mikhail's market was. "Bastard, slave traders!"

He dropped his hand from her shoulder. "I have one piece of evidence that might help you—a witness."

"A witness?" She stood tall. A witness sounded like a miracle, especially compared to the nothing she'd been expecting.

"The night Mikhail was in holding, the cameras glitched on and off for five minutes."

"You think that's when Wright traded Mikhail's freedom for Patrick?"

He nodded. "There was a young man in the cell down from Mikhail's that night—he'd never talk to me, but he knew something. I could see it in his eyes. It was Patrick's friend, Sean Jones."

~

AT ONE-TWENTY-FIVE, Patrick parked his car across the street from Luke's high school. A crossing guard stood ready two houses down from where he waited. There was hardly any traffic now, but as soon as the bell rang that'd be a different story. He got out of his car and waited for the bell to ring. It was a nice day today—sunny and warm with a comfortable breeze. He glanced around, looking for any sign of Elizabeth.

The bell rang, and kids slowly started to trickle out of the building. A few more minutes passed before a black SUV parked four cars down from him that looked police-issued. That had to be her.

He'd been nervous before, but not now. Now he felt eerily calm. He felt right. Why had he spent all week avoiding this moment? All he felt now was excitement and longing. He took a deep breath and reminded himself that if she didn't remember him, he had to play the part of Alexander Westkeys. Would have to keep playing that part until this was all over. Would she forgive him for lying to her?

The door opened, and he took a step forward. A man stepped out of the SUV, and Patrick froze. He had tan skin and shiny, black hair. He wore a button-up shirt with short sleeves and a tie, dress slacks, and he had a badge on his belt.

Remembering the name of Elizabeth's partner from Benson's case file, he moved toward him. "He must be Lee."

The man was on the phone and staring across the street. He waved over his head, and a hand shot up above the crowd of students. Lee looked right and left, then crossed the street.

A car pulled away from the curb and picked up speed. It raced toward Lee, who hadn't noticed it yet.

Patrick moved, racing toward the cop. "Move!"

Lee glanced at him, just as Patrick pushed him out of the way. The two men went flying toward the curb as the car rushed by.

A young man ran past them as they hit the ground, his backpack bouncing as he went.

"Luke, get out of the street!" Lee yelled, pushing up on one arm.

The boy took another step forward, staring at the car for a moment longer, then turned back to the men. He rushed over to Lee and grabbed his arm. "Are you okay?"

Patrick sat up.

From the boy's raven hair to his sharp features, there was no mistaking he was a Shea, but it was his honey-hued eyes that caught Patrick off guard. The eyes so like his big sister's. That's how he recognized him. Luke was all grown up. The little boy he'd played coin tricks with, the boy he'd let play with Maggie, the boy who had always given him tight bear hugs, was gone, replaced by a tall, strong, almost *man*. What did Kyle and Jake look like? Where were they? Were they happy? Ten years really had passed, and he'd missed it. He'd missed it.

"Yeah, I'm fine. Thanks to him." Lee pointed at Patrick as Luke helped him to his feet. His elbow was bleeding, and he was holding his side.

Patrick got to his feet and brushed the dirt from his pants. "You all right?"

Lee nodded. "Yeah."

Patrick stared off down the road, the car now long gone. He couldn't say he disagreed. He'd started to stir the pot, and now, out of desperation, Wright was acting carelessly. That was good for Patrick, a careless criminal always got caught, but not good for those working the case.

Patrick extended a hand to shake Lee's. "I'm Alex Westkeys. I'm working the Benson case with you."

Lee took his hand, and his eyes went wide. "Why are you here?"

"I wanted to talk to the first officers on the scene of the Benson case before I went to the station today. You're Detective Lee, correct?"

"Yes."

"Where's Detective Shea?"

Lee's jaw pulsed. "She had something come up."

"Will she be at the precinct later?" Patrick had to keep himself from staring at Luke.

Lee shook his head. "No, she's out for the evening."

Luke offered his hand. "I'm Luke, Detective Shea's brother."

Patrick shook his hand and smiled. Luke was as outgoing as he remembered. "Nice to meet you."

"Are you a cop?" Luke asked.

Patrick shook his head. "A private investigator."

"Cool!" Luke grabbed the straps of his backpack.

Patrick chuckled and faced Lee. "Do you think that near hit had anything to do with the Benson case?"

Lee breathed out, his hand still clasped to his side. "Yes."

"It was a blue Toyota Camry, driven by a man with straight brown hair, a medium build, with bulging arm muscles, and he's a smoker, so that's something to go by, but unfortunately I didn't catch the plate number. Did you, by chance?" Everything had happened so quickly; he'd missed it and wanted to deck himself for it.

Lee blinked. "How do you know he smokes?"

"The inside of the car was smoky."

Lee furrowed his brow.

"No plate, then?" Patrick repeated.

"No."

"I got it," Luke said.

Patrick and Lee both faced him.

Luke gave them the license. Lee pulled a pad of paper from his back pocket and jotted it down.

Patrick smiled. "That was quick thinking. Well done!"

Luke fought back a smile, just as Elizabeth would've at his age. He shrugged. "My sister's a cop."

"Looks like you could be one too, one day," Patrick said.

"Nah." He waved the suggestion away, even though he was smiling wide now. "I want to be an artist."

Lee turned his elbow up to look at it and groaned from the movement.

Patrick faced him. "You okay?"

"I'm good," Lee said.

"We can reschedule our meeting with Detective Shea for tomorrow," Patrick offered.

Luke stepped forward. "No, not tomorrow. Tomorrow's my sister's engagement party."

If an elephant-sized fist had landed a blow to Patrick's gut, it wouldn't have been any less painful than what he was currently feeling. It took everything in him to keep his poker face and respond with a smile. "She's engaged?"

Luke nodded. Then a big grin covered his innocent face. "Why don't you come? My sister and Lee and their boss, and their boss's boss are all going to be there. I could introduce you."

Patrick cleared his throat. "I wouldn't want to intrude."

"El won't mind, and neither will Sean," Luke said. The rest of his sentence began to fade into the background like white noise. "There are going to be about a million people there anyway. Another one won't matter."

"Sean Jones?" Patrick asked, and even his voice sounded disembodied.

"Yeah. You know him?" Luke asked.

She was marrying Sean? The betrayer? The seducer? The life ruiner? How could she do it? How could Elizabeth marry *him*? He'd warned her. Told her to stay away from him. And she hadn't. He shook his head.

"Heard of him." Patrick plastered a smile on his face. "I'll see you both tomorrow then."

He shook both their hands and dashed back across the street to his car. He had to get out of there.

CHAPTER THIRTY

S hea parked her car in Sean's driveway and took a deep breath. His Corvette was there, gleaming like it'd been freshly washed. He was home.

On the way here, part of her had hoped he wouldn't be, and she was ashamed of herself for it.

She needed to play cool here, needed to be completely nonchalant. She nodded once. She could do this. It'd be like an interrogation where she played dumb and let the suspect do the talking. She'd done it a thousand times. The fact that Sean was her fiancé and that he'd been lying to her was irrelevant. She could do this.

Letting herself in, she strode past the living room where Sean sat and went into the kitchen.

Sean turned as she passed. "Hey, babe. I wasn't expecting you."

Babe. She'd never been particularly fond of or accustomed to terms of endearment, but if she had to pick, "babe" wouldn't be it. She went straight to the cupboard and grabbed a glass, then to the fridge to fill it with water.

Sean came in and leaned against the counter.

"I'm not staying." Shea faced him and took a swig of her water. "I just wanted to see if there was anything else I needed to do or know for tomorrow night?"

"All you need to do is show up. Everything else is handled. I can't wait for you to see the ballroom when it's finished."

She gave a curt nod and set her glass down hard enough to make the water slosh over the side.

"Whoa, you all right?" He skirted the counter to stand next to her.

"Yeah, long day." She grabbed a paper towel from the holder by the sink and wiped up her spill.

He folded his arms. "The Benson case?"

"It's just one dead end after another." She wadded the paper towel in her hand and rested her fist on the cool granite counter top.

"Want to talk about it?"

"We've resorted to opening cold cases." She reached for her glass, but Sean caught her hand before she could. She almost flinched.

He made eye contact and rubbed his thumb over the back of her hand. "What cold cases?"

She forced a little chuckle. "You know I can't tell you."

He squeezed her hand.

"If you don't need help, I should go." She leaned over and pecked him on the lips. "See you tomorrow."

"I'll be here." He grinned.

She slipped her hand from his grasp as she went around the island and toward the hall. Then she stopped and faced him. "Oh, hey—"

"What?"

"When you were nineteen, you spent the night in jail?" She rested her hand on the arch to the entrance of the kitchen

"Are you asking me or telling me?"

"Drinking and driving, and I think there was something in there about evading a police officer."

He nodded. "You're checking up on me now? Is this some kind of pre-wedding initiation?"

She shrugged. "We've been digging into *everything,* and Lee happened to see your name in the holding cell on one of the nights we were looking into."

"What does that have to do with Benson's case?"

"You in holding? Nothing. Though, I admit I'm curious. You were locked up with a man by the name of Vadim Mikhail."

"Who is he?"

There was no way he'd have forgotten who Mikhail was. No. Way. "He's a human trafficker."

Sean scratched his chin. "Hmmm. I don't recall. I was pretty out of it that night."

"Might have been interesting if he'd talked to you, don't you think?"

He folded his arms. "Maybe. Or creepy. I can't imagine that a human trafficker would be very interested in talking to a drunk teenager."

Except for five minutes? When the cameras were on the fritz? Then maybe.

◦◦◦

KNEELING IN TALL, patchy grass, Patrick ran a hand over their green tips and stared at the open space that had once held Maggie's pen and training area. When she'd occupied it, even for only five months out of the year, the space had been mostly dirt with a few sprigs of grass here and there. It'd looked nothing like the green field before him.

He'd known the circus had disbanded, but he'd idly hoped that Tilde and Jay had been able to keep Maggie on the property. Even more than that, he'd longed to see her. After the news of Elizabeth and Sean's engagement, he hadn't even stopped to think that after all these years Maggie might have forgotten him. All he'd thought was that he needed to get to her.

None of the trailers in the park looked familiar, but maybe someone could tell him where Tilde and Jay were. He needed friendly faces. And then they could tell him where to find Maggie.

"Can I help you?" came a deep voice from behind him at the trailer park.

Turning, he found Jay standing a few yards off with a bucket of water in one hand and a sponge in the other. Suds streamed down the side of his trailer.

Jay was here. Patrick's pulse spiked, and he smiled. Was Tilde here too?

He moved a few feet closer. "Jay?"

The big man scrunched his brow. "Do I know you?"

Patrick looked different, what with his hair being brown and a little longer than he'd previously worn it and facial hair. He could only imagine what irrevocable changes the camp had made to him, but to someone who'd been with him since he was a toddler, who'd helped raise him. He took a couple steps closer and brushed his hair back from his face, willing recognition to seep into his friend's hazel eyes.

Jay raised his brows. "What do you want?" He sounded testy, like how he sounded when he caught towners walking around the back-yard while the circus was going. He sounded like a man talking to an outsider, an unknown element, a sap. Jay didn't recognize him at all.

Patrick blinked and forced himself out of his stupor. "I saw your show. Your strongman routine was incredible."

Jay smiled and straightened his spine. "Had to have been a while ago. The circus has been closed for seven years now."

Seven years? "What happened?"

Jay turned to his trailer and started scrubbing it again. "After our elephant died, the circus lost a lot of its appeal. People weren't as interested in coming anymore, and we couldn't afford another elephant."

When Patrick had played Peter Pan in the trapeze act, getting out over the net was relatively easy, and so was getting back, but when he tried handing off to a partner, he'd missed their hands by inches and had fallen forty feet to the net below. He remembered vividly the sinking feeling in his stomach as time slowed down and he'd dropped. That's how he felt now.

He was dropping in slow motion to a rickety net below.

Maggie was dead? His sweet, loving Maggie.

"You all right?" Jay asked.

Patrick tried to speak, but no words came. He cleared his throat. "Your elephant died?"

"About nine years ago." He nodded. He squeegeed out his sponge and turned his gaze on Patrick. "Are you sure you're okay, mister? You look gray."

"I'm fine."

"Tilde," he called out. "Get out here!"

Patrick spun around and marched off.

"Wait there, fella, you don't look well," Jay called.

"What's all the racket out here?" Tilde's voice found his ears.

He picked up his pace until he was in a full-on sprint.

Elizabeth was going to marry his mortal enemy, Jay didn't recognize him, and Maggie was dead. He couldn't stand the thought of seeing Tilde's blank expression, as well.

Wright and Sean wanted to know if Patrick Daley was dead. Earlier today that had been amusing. Earlier today he'd still had hope that he could come back and reclaim his old life. Now he knew that would never be—could never be. Vadim may not have ended Patrick Daley's life, but Patrick could see now that he'd died all those years ago anyway.

All that was left was Alex Westkeys, the bishop's account, and revenge.

CHAPTER THIRTY-ONE

Stepping out of his Mustang, Patrick tossed his keys to the nearest valet and made his way to Sean's front door. He swallowed hard against the bow tie throttling him and stopped himself from tugging on it. He had to convey confidence, couldn't show signs of anything less.

Unfortunately, tuxes didn't go all that well without ties. Once in the door, he immediately grabbed a champagne flute from a passing waiter and made his way through the crowd, past the kitchen, living room, and stairs, and to the ballroom.

A few tables were set up around the room, and people sat eating, while others were making use of the open space and full band to dance. He took a deep breath through his nose and immediately wished he hadn't when the overwhelming scent of the flowers bombarded him. Roses, tulips, orchids, baby's breath, peonies, and more. Large vases sat on every table, and even larger vases stood about the room. Petals were strewn across the floor.

Elizabeth really was different than she had been. The girl he knew would never have wanted an engagement party like this. Glancing at a woman passing in a ball gown, he shook his head. Nor would she have wanted to dress up. The girl he knew would've wanted something intimate. In a small way, the thought gave him comfort. The girl he'd known had died with Patrick Daley, too, it seemed.

He twisted her ring around his finger, feeling for the dent.

He glanced around the crowd until he spotted Lee, standing in the corner with Brown. The two men gave definition to the term *out of place*. While they looked decent in their suits, neither smiled, but Patrick had the impression that Lee didn't make a habit of smiling. Still, his arms were folded across his chest, and while more than one woman smiled at Lee in passing, he ignored them.

Brown wasn't pleased either, but he at least was making an effort to be polite with those around him. Both men's gazes were fixed on the dance floor and one of the many couples there swaying to a slow melody.

Patrick smirked and followed their gazes, curious as to what would be causing such tension in the men. The man was about Patrick's height and a bit bulkier, but he hadn't gotten his weight up to what it had once been. He still had a pretty tenuous relationship with food—loving and hating it with equal measure.

The woman was petite and wore a cranberry-colored dress, and her dark hair was styled off her shoulders. Her posture was tense. He couldn't see her face very well—not that it mattered.

Whatever was making these men uncomfortable wasn't his problem. He was here for a reason. He started toward Lee and Brown when the man spun the woman around, letting him get a good look at her face—at her flushed cheeks, rosebud lips, and honey-hued eyes.

Elizabeth. He stopped in place and faced her. His heart skidded in his chest. She was as he remembered her, only older, and she had aged well.

He swallowed the thick lump in his throat. Inside, his emotions struggled a game of tug-of-war. Half of him wanted to rush to her and sweep her into his arms, wanted to tell her how much he'd missed her, and how thinking of her had been a big part of the reason he'd survived.

The other half of him wanted to turn from her, curse her, and flee this place and his plans for revenge to get as many miles between them as possible. His memory of her had all been a lie. He'd put her on a pedestal where she'd never had a right to be.

He looked at his feet, studying his shoes, and took a deep breath. Of course, he'd take neither action. He was here for a reason, and he would do what needed to be done. He glanced up at her once more, felt the tug-of-war rope snap in two, and turned his gaze to her partner.

Sean.

Just as he had been, so was he now. *Smug.* He held Elizabeth in his superior gaze. His victory over Patrick still and forever in play. At least that's what Sean thought. Wouldn't he be surprised when he learned the truth about the man whose life he'd ruined?

Patrick tore his gaze away and marched over to Brown and Lee. He plastered his normal smile on his face and straightened his spine.

Lee and Brown saw him coming at the same time. Lee's tight-lipped stare softened; Brown's hardened. Lee was still favoring the side he'd landed on when Patrick pushed him out of the way, but Patrick doubted if anyone else would notice.

"Evening, gentlemen." He lifted his champagne flute to them and looked at Lee. "Any less sore today?"

Lee nodded. "I'm good."

"What are you doing here?" Brown snarled.

Patrick chuckled and took a sip of his champagne. It was nasty sweet stuff that he hated, not that he let his dislike show. He must appear in control at all times. "Good to see you, too."

Brown took a step forward.

"Luke invited him," Lee said, stripping the thunder from Brown's aggressive move.

"You were invited?"

"Isn't it weird how I just keep appearing? First at the capitol, in your office, here... if I showed up at your home, it'd almost be like I was taking over your life," Patrick said. "Wouldn't that be fun?"

Brown frowned. "A riot."

"Alex!" Luke rushed through the crowd, coming from the direction of the band as they finished their song. "You made it."

Luke and Patrick shook hands. Brown's gaze darted between them.

"It's good to see you," Patrick said. It was a slight balm to the ache he was desperately trying to ignore to realize he'd meant it. He'd always had a soft spot for the Sheas and knew now that that would never go away, even though he'd lost Elizabeth.

Lee faced Luke. "Would you grab your sister? Might as well get the introductions out of the way."

Luke smiled and nodded. He turned and rushed toward Elizabeth.

"You know him?" Brown turned to Lee.

Lee nodded. "Yeah, he's the investigator Wright hired to work on Benson's case with us."

"I know who he is," Brown said.

From his peripheral vision, Patrick saw Elizabeth and Sean getting closer and closer, but he didn't turn to them, not even when Luke stopped beside them. Instead, he kept his attention on Lee and Brown.

"Mr. Westkeys," Luke said. "This is my sister, Elizabeth Shea, and her fiancé, Sean."

Pushing his suit coat back with his left hand, Patrick rested it on his hip and faced the couple. Unwittingly, he faced Elizabeth first. They locked gazes, and she sucked in a breath. Her hand immediately went to the crucifix she still wore around her neck.

And yet God had failed him once again. Patrick clenched his jaw.

He reached for her hand and kissed it, never removing his stare from her unblinking one. "Detective Shea."

A hand extended to him. "Luke tells us you're a private investigator?" Sean asked.

Patrick ripped his gaze from Elizabeth's and took Sean's hand. "That's right." He looked for any recognition in Sean's gaze but there was none.

"What exactly does that entail?" Sean seemed more bored than interested.

Patrick flicked his gaze to Elizabeth. "Mostly it involves finding and photographing cheating spouses." He then held Sean's gaze. "But I also find missing persons, take legal cases for individuals and businesses, and occasionally the police deign to request my services."

"Interesting," Sean said. "Perhaps my law firm could use your services. Occasionally we have need of private investigators."

"Perhaps," Patrick said.

"And you're working with the police now?" Sean picked at something invisible on his tux.

Patrick almost rolled back on his heels, but stopped himself. If Sean had recognized him, that would be one thing, but it wouldn't be because Patrick made it easy for him. He glanced over at Lee, who was scrutinizing him as though he'd just figured something out.

It made Patrick nervous.

"He can't discuss cases he's working on with us." Lee fisted a hand.

"Right, of course." Sean glanced at Elizabeth over his shoulder. "Must be the Benson case?"

Elizabeth pursed her lips.

Brown stared at her.

Sean's gaze trailed off behind Patrick, and Patrick turned to see what he was staring at. Wright walked into the ballroom with his wife on his arm. Mrs. Wright saw Patrick and waved. Patrick was grateful they hadn't brought Haydee. She should be as far from this mess as possible.

Sean's eyes narrowed as Wright approached.

"Alex," Mrs. Wright said. "It's so good to see you. I only wish we'd brought Haydee along. She would have been so glad to see you again."

Patrick took her hand and kissed it. "I'm very glad to see you again as well."

Sean stood tall, intentionally trying to dwarf Wright's shorter height. "I wasn't expecting you this evening."

Wright took a deep breath. "Yes, well—"

"I invited him," Patrick said.

"And who invited you?" Sean tried to keep his tone friendly, but the undercurrent of irritation was clear.

Luke lifted his hand. "I did."

Sean turned to him, blank-faced. Elizabeth tightened her grip on Luke's arm in a reassuring gesture. The tension building was not unlike the moment in the circus right before they shot the man out of the cannon.

Patrick cleared his throat. "I hope I didn't ruin your engagement party by inviting Wright, but I thought, considering the delicate nature of the Benson case, that it'd be prudent to have a quick meet with the officers on the case."

"Certainly." Wright lifted his glass he carried, sloshing it a little over the side. "Give me a few minutes. Senator Morrel is here, and I must have a quick word."

Wright escorted his wife away.

Another song came on, and Patrick turned his gaze to Elizabeth once more.

"Would you mind terribly, Mr. Jones, if I steal your lovely fiancée?"

Elizabeth pulled her chin back and flushed.

Sean's eyes narrowed.

Patrick smiled. "For this dance?"

Elizabeth lowered her head and took a deep breath.

"You'll have to ask her." Sean signaled to Elizabeth with his right hand.

Patrick held out a hand to her.

"Thank you." She took his hand and lifted her chin, refusing to look at Sean. "I'd be delighted."

Patrick felt a small pang where his heart used to be when he realized she'd only said yes to irritate Sean. Still, he was glad to see it worked.

He led her to the dance floor, spun her wide, and then pulled her close.

~

SEAN GLARED at the PI as he led his fiancée to the dance floor. Whoever he was, he didn't like him. There was something off about the guy. How was it possible that Wright, Wright's wife, and their daughter, Haydee, all knew of him? That Wright felt comfortable enough to have him on Benson's case? And after all of that, how had Sean never heard of the man?

Wright and his wife approached Senator Morrel.

Luke spoke. "What did you think of Alex? He's pretty cool, right?"

"Excuse me." Sean crossed to Wright and grabbed his arm. "Sorry to interrupt, Senator Morrel. Are you enjoying the party?"

"Yes, thank you," Morrel said.

"Can I borrow Wright for a moment?" Sean led Wright away at the slightest nod from Morrel. They went to the second floor and stared over the banister.

Sean released him. "Please explain to me why you thought it would be appropriate to come to my engagement party?"

Wright puffed out his broad chest. "Saying no, especially while I'm running for office, would have looked suspicious. In fact, considering your position in society and mine, it was strange that you didn't invite me in the first place."

"You know why I didn't." Sean placed a hand on the landing. "We can't be seen together."

Wright spoke under his breath. "If that boy is still alive, then certainly not, but if he's as you've assured me, then there's nothing to worry about. Correct?"

Sean ground his teeth and counted down from ten. "Who is this PI?"

Wright rested his hands on the landing as well. "His name is Alex Westkeys. He recently moved here from Florida."

Sean breathed out. "What do you know about him personally?"

"Not much. Just what I've told you, and he's very wealthy and only recently came into his fortune."

"Wealthy?" After his parents died, Sean had barely enough to get through college. Everything he had now was of his own making, and his law firm was struggling, and this man just came into money?

"Did he ask for the Benson case, or did you give it to him?"

Wright furrowed his brow. "I gave it to him."

"You're sure?"

"Yes, of course. Why are you asking me this?"

Sean leaned his head back and looked at the chandelier. "Is he any good at what he does?"

"He came highly recommended by Miami PD."

Fantastic. "Look into him. I want to know everything. Where he's from, who his parents are, who his favorite Stooge is. Leave no stone unturned."

"Why would I do that?"

Sean twisted his hands on the banister in a throttling motion. "I have a strange feeling about him. You send me the information on him I requested, and I'll determine what to do next."

Wright faced him. "How exactly am I supposed to find this information?"

Sean made eye contact. "You used to be a detective—detect. Unless, of course, that's too hard for you from your gilded throne of authority. If that be the case, then perhaps you could hire a private investigator to do your work for you?"

Wright turned from him and marched down the stairs.

Sean walked down the hall and into the library. He went straight for the decanter of whiskey sitting on a table in the middle of the room and poured himself a lowball of gleaming copper liquid. It burned its way down his throat.

First Elizabeth started acting weird around him, and now this detective was digging into things he had no business digging into. Westkeys was a loose cannon on a stormy vessel with no way to predict his movements. A problem that had to be taken care of.

Sean went to a bookshelf on the wall to his right and pulled out a stack of about ten large encyclopedias. Behind them was a safe. He put in the code and yanked the door open. Now, all he needed to know was if this man was a knight, a bishop, or a rook. A nickel, dime, or quarter.

CHAPTER THIRTY-TWO

S hea couldn't help but stare into the eyes of the man who held her in his arms. When she'd first seen him, for a split second, she thought it was Patrick. Then she'd looked at him, really looked at him, and the thought vanished.

The differences were too great. His hair color, his scraggly beard, his skin tone, and his posture. Patrick had been fair and soft in a lot of ways, unlike this man, whose countenance, every edge, and pretense were hard. Except for his eyes. His sea-green eyes.

They reminded her so much of Patrick's, only tired.

"Is everything all right?" Westkeys spun her out and back.

She used the moment free of his grasp to clear her mind. Facing him again, she said, "Yes. I was staring. I'm sorry."

"Not at all. It's every man's dream to be stared at wistfully by a beautiful woman." His lip quirked up ever so slightly at the corner.

She glanced to her side at the other dancers on the floor, colorful fabric swirling around as if caught up in the wind. "I don't know about that."

Under this man's scrutinizing gaze, she suddenly felt like how she imagined Eliza Doolittle had when she'd danced with the prince in

My Fair Lady—nervous, a little giddy, and above all like she had something to prove.

"What was it?" he asked.

She glanced to the other side. "What was what?"

He tightened his grip on her hand as they spun around, the cool metal of a ring pressed against her hand. "What was it that so arrested your attention?"

"Noth—" She stopped talking. She'd spent so many years censoring herself on Sean's behalf, but this man wouldn't care. Wouldn't be hurt or saddened. She made eye contact, forcing herself not to shirk back from the familiarity there.

Westkeys stared, brows raised, as he waited for her response.

"You remind me of someone. A dear friend." The last time her heart had beaten so sporadically and fiercely had been last year when she'd been on her first murder case.

"What happened to him?"

"He..." She cleared her throat. "My brother tells me you pushed my partner out of the way of a speeding car yesterday."

He nodded. "Right place, right time."

Now they were on the topic she wanted to discuss. "Why were you at my brother's school yesterday?"

He smiled at her.

She sucked in a breath. Even through the beard, that smile, the one he'd kept to himself the entire time he'd been here, it was so familiar. It was...

"I came to meet you," he said.

The music ended, and he stepped away from her.

She felt strangely bereft as she stared at him once more.

He rubbed his thumb over the side of his index finger.

She stopped breathing.

"Thank you for the dance." He nodded toward Brown, Lee, and Wright, who all stood waiting for them at the edge of the dance floor. "They're ready for us."

~

PATRICK TOOK ALL of two minutes with the team before wrapping it up. He'd really only invited Wright as an excuse to rile Sean, and if Sean's disappearance was anything to go by, it'd worked.

Taking his leave of the group, he headed upstairs and past the library, where a stream of light flooded through the crack in the door. He walked down to what had once been Mr. and Mrs. Joneses' room and pushed in.

He left the lights off and sauntered toward the bed.

Sean had redecorated the suite that had once been painted and draped in light tones. Now red was the dominating theme, from the bedspread to the modern paintings hung on the walls. Reaching into the inside pocket of his tux coat, Patrick retrieved the silver coin Sean had given him.

He went straight to the bedside table and set the coin under the lamp, which he turned on to illuminate the coin. When Sean saw this, he'd know. And he'd be afraid.

"Hello, Peter." Elizabeth's voice came from behind him.

He started to turn, then froze, and cursed himself for doing it. He'd reacted to the nickname. If he'd only turned, he could've played it off as wondering who was in the room with him but freezing too? He doubted he could be that lucky. This was Elizabeth, after all.

Setting his jaw, he faced her.

She was blocking his escape.

"Detective?" He extended a hand out to the room. "I apologize for snooping, but this is such a marvelous house, I couldn't help but look around. I've just purchased something similar."

She said nothing, only stared at him, unblinking. The golden depths of her eyes and her unrelenting stare unnerved him. Leaving the door open behind her, she slowly crossed the room until she stood directly in front of him. Until the toes of their shoes nearly touched.

Patrick should speak. He should say something and break this strange trance they were in, but curiosity got the best of him. He didn't just want to know what she was doing; he had to know.

She brought her hand up to his face and touched his cheek. He flinched back, but she grabbed his hand with her free one and held him there. She slid her hand over his beard to his jaw and cupped it as she stared into his eyes.

She gasped. "Patrick." Her hands went to his shoulders, and just as when they were kids, she went up on her toes and leaned in to kiss him.

Never in his life had he wanted a kiss more but this couldn't happen. He leaned away from her, placed his hands on her shoulder, and pushed her gently away. She'd betrayed him. "Detective, I don't—"

There was hurt in her eyes, hurt from his rejection and so much more. But he couldn't care. Couldn't. Regardless of the need he felt for her growing inside him like some uncontrollable... thing.

"Where have you been?" Her voice hitched, and she clung to his shirt. "I thought... I thought you were dead. What happened? What happened to you?"

He clenched his teeth. He had to get this situation under control, and now. "Detective Shea, please. Stop."

"Patrick."

"My name is Alex Westkeys."

She shook her head, and another tear threatened to fall. "No, I know you. Please. Just tell me what happened to you? All these years..."

He grabbed her hands that held tight to his shirt and removed it from her grasp, then stepped back again. There was no use. He'd always easily lied to everyone, everyone but her. And despite her betrayal, he found he had no wish to keep up the pretenses. She knew.

He stared her down, and could practically see her shrink back from his icy stare.

"Patrick Daley is dead."

She flexed her hands, as though desperate to reach for him again. "What happened to him?"

"Why don't you ask your fiancé?" He barely saw the look of confusion that crossed her face before he went around her, and fled the room.

AS PATRICK WAITED for the valet to bring his car, he shoved his hands in his pockets and looked at his shiny black shoes. What had he been thinking? She couldn't have really known, could she? If he denied it tooth and nail, she would have doubted. He should have denied it.

The valet stopped his car, and he hopped in.

Before he could drive off, his passenger door opened and in stepped Detective Lee. "Can I have a word?"

Patrick breathed out an annoyed sigh, not bothering for a moment to disguise it as otherwise. "No, get out."

Lee didn't flinch. "Fine, I won't talk, but I'm not leaving."

Patrick rubbed his eyes with his thumb and index fingers. "What do you want?"

"I have a contact down in the crime lab who owes me a favor—a big one."

Patrick couldn't help but grin as he furrowed his brow. This had to be good. "Okay."

The stoic detective continued. "Normally to get fingerprints back we could be waiting months, but I called in my favor and jumped the line."

"Does this have to do with the case? Because if it does, you should have brought it up while we were with everyone," Patrick said.

Lee removed Patrick's cell phone from his tux coat pocket and handed it back.

"I was wondering where that went." Sort of. He'd noticed it was gone earlier in the day, but hadn't cared enough to worry about it.

Patrick took the phone. He'd missed five calls from Zakhar. He hoped he hadn't worried him. "Thank you."

Patrick opened his text messages. Zakhar had texted him half an hour ago. The message read, "We have him. If you want to talk to him, you need to get here now."

He had to get out of here. "I'm sorry, detective, but I'm in a bit of a hurry."

Lee continued, unconcerned. "He pulled your prints off that phone."

Patrick could feel his ire building. Of all the things Lee could have done, he'd been just shrewd enough to do the very thing he'd have done himself. "Oh yeah?"

"How is it that you and a boy who's been missing for ten years have the same fingerprints?" Lee folded his arms.

"Obviously there was a mix-up in the lab." He shrugged.

"Apparently, Wright had a napkin checked for prints as well. Any guesses whose fingerprints came up that time?"

Well, this was swell.

Lee faced him. "I don't care where you've been, Mr. Daley, but if you're back to mess with my partner, I need to know."

Patrick had to play this cool. Lee was obviously not a guy to be messed with, and his time was running down. "Your partner?"

"You were friends. She's spent the better part of a decade worried about you, and the last year digging into your missing person case. Don't play dumb with me. I know all about you. So, do yourself a favor and be straight with me."

Patrick gripped the wheel.

"I could just drag you downtown right now." Lee produced a pair of handcuffs from his suit coat pocket. "I bet Wright would be interested to know who you really are."

Patrick's mouth fell open. "You brought handcuffs to a ball?"

Lee flipped one of the metal bracelets open.

"I'm not after her." Patrick sighed.

"What are you after?"

Patrick shot a side-glare at the cop. "I saved your life."

"Which is why I haven't arrested you... yet," Lee said. "Look, it's not a coincidence that you've miraculously reappeared now, after all these years, when one of the officers who was on your case and your mother's was murdered, and it's not a coincidence you being on this case. You got yourself assigned."

"What makes you think Wright didn't seek me out?" Patrick asked.

"He probably thinks he did. The man's not exactly a mental giant. That said, he's never once considered bringing in an outsider, much less on the case of a murdered cop."

Man, Lee was shrewd. "I'm impressed."

Lee stared him down. "Either you're behind Benson's murder, or you're seeking revenge. Which is it?"

"I liked Benson," Patrick said.

"Revenge it is, then." He flipped the cuffs closed again and shoved them back in his pocket. "Against who? And is it just for Benson's murder, or is there more?"

Patrick turned in his seat and faced Lee. He needed to see his face while he told him. "Wright killed my mom. He released Vadim Mikhail—"

Lee's eyes widened. "The human trafficker?"

"—who kidnapped me as a thank-you."

Lee glanced out the front window. "He ruined Rafferty's career?"

Patrick nodded.

"Did he kill Benson?"

"No. That was someone else."

Lee faced him. "Who?"

Patrick clenched his jaw. He didn't have time for this.

CHAPTER THIRTY-THREE

Shea stood silently after Patrick left. Part of her wanted to chase after him, but his voice had been so cold, so seething with hatred —for her. What had happened to him? After she'd composed herself, she'd headed back downstairs to look for him, but he was long gone.

She'd wanted to leave right then, to find him, but she didn't know where he was or how to track him down. Not that it'd mattered. Soon she was surrounded by well-wishers and before she knew it an hour had passed. Her only comfort in this mess was Lee standing with her brother all night, keeping him entertained while she made the rounds. Without Sean.

He'd apparently vanished as well, but now she needed to find him, not just to make him come out and talk to their guests—ninety-five percent of whom he'd invited. Now he was her only hope of finding out what happened to Patrick. She was certain Sean knew what happened in the holding cell the night the cameras went out.

She excused herself to the ladies room and ran cold water into her hands, then gently patted the back of her neck.

She'd never wanted her engagement party to be like this. She hadn't wanted a fuss, but when she'd suggested they do something small and intimate with friends and family, she'd been quickly rebuffed. And now, she'd just faced the one man she'd truly had feelings for, for the first time in a decade, and she barely recognized her own reflection.

She dried her hands and clenched the satiny fabric of her dress. She had to find Sean. She couldn't do this anymore—pretend. Sean had been a shoulder to cry on for years, and then he'd been safe. But he never really wanted her. He'd wanted her to be something she'd never be. This dress he'd picked for her was proof positive of that.

It finally occurred to her why she'd really said yes to Sean, and she was ashamed of herself for it. He could never break her heart because it'd never belonged to him. He'd been safe but safe was now long gone.

She released the folds of her cranberry dress and spun on her heel. In a fast walk, she exited the bathroom and passed several people calling out to her as she made a dash for the stairs.

Passing the stairs that went to the third floor, she pushed into the library and came to a stop. Sean sat in a leather recliner across from the fireplace with his head back against the headrest and his eyes closed.

Behind him and to her right on the bookshelves, she saw something she'd never known existed. An open safe with a pile of books sitting next to it. It had several items in it.

"Sean," she said, making her way to the safe.

"What?" he grumbled.

Had he always been so careless? Yes, he had, and she'd just ignored it. Until tonight, when he'd implied in front of her boss that she'd been sharing key details of Benson's case with him. That'd pissed her off. "You can't just leave these things open when you have a house full of strangers."

She stopped at the safe, reaching up to close it when something caught her eye.

"Wait, Elizabeth, don't—" He must have seen her then because he cursed.

She barely heard it, her gaze fixed on a ten-year-old library card with Patrick Daley's signature on it. The very card he'd gotten the day she'd ditched school to hang out with him, the day before he disappeared. It sat behind a black velvet bag filled with coins, one of which sat next to the bag at the very front of the safe, and to the side of a stack of papers.

She picked up the card, her gaze dropping to the coin at the front of the safe. It was a wheat penny, and even without her coin collector, she could tell this one was in good condition. She glanced into the open velvet bag to see a whole slew of old coins all in perfect condition—like the ones found on Miller's and Benson's bodies.

A flash of the first time her father had gotten rip-roaring drunk, three years after the death of her mom, crossed her mind's eye. In a confused stupor, he'd shoved Jake, who'd been eleven at the time, and had knocked him into a wall, winding him. Kyle, who'd been fourteen, had rushed forward to help Jake, but her father had taken it as a threat and had hit him. She felt the same shock now as she had then. The same betrayal.

She closed the safe and turned, Sean's ring suddenly weighing down her hand. He'd done it. He was responsible for all of it.

Sean stood a few feet from her. His short brown hair was mussed over his forehead, his deep blue eyes blood-shot, and he had a translucent amber, wet spot on his tux shirt. If the smell of liquor was anything to go by, she could guess the cause of his current condition. He was drunk.

She thought of her father once more, remembering how he'd been the last year of his life, and shivered. She hadn't seen Sean drunk since they were kids and even then it'd been brief. But if alcohol could turn her father, who she'd always thought to be sweet, into Mr. Hyde, she didn't want to know what Sean would be like. The type A personality with extensive fight training. Especially while she was dressed in this getup and unarmed.

He narrowed his eyes at her.

She hid the card in her hand. "Why didn't you ever tell me about that safe?"

He blinked. "It was my father's."

"Ah."

"Did you see what was in there?"

She furrowed her brow. "Yeah, papers, and a bag of coins. Did your dad collect?"

He breathed out slowly, and the tension in his jaw loosened. "Yeah."

"I came to bring you back to the party." She signaled to his tux. "You're a mess. What have you been doing?"

He moved closer. "Just thinking." His arms went around her waist, and he leaned down to kiss her.

She turned her head. "You smell like booze."

He tried to kiss her again, and she took a step back and out of his grasp.

"Get cleaned up and come back down. There are a lot of people here to see you." She headed to the door, stopping in the frame, then turned her gaze back to him. "Was Patrick here the day he went missing?"

Sean's eyes flared. "What? Why would you ask me that?"

"Curious is all."

"Not that I know of." He rubbed the back of his neck.

She nodded and pulled the door closed. She'd found out all she needed to. All this time when she'd brought up Patrick, she'd thought Sean's response was sadness and anger for his missing friend. She'd been reading it wrong for years. It'd actually been contempt. She needed to find her brother, Lee, and Brown and get out of here.

She lifted her left hand and stared at Sean's engagement ring. But first, she had something she needed to do.

AFTER ELIZABETH HAD CLOSED the door behind her, Sean

went back to the safe and opened it. She'd been acting weird. She'd seen something that had made her pull away from him. He reached over his coins and dug through the papers. It took him only a moment to discover that the library card was missing.

He cursed.

She'd be long gone before he could get changed and down to where she was. But he could head her off if he hurried. There was no way she'd want to go anywhere in that dress, which meant she'd go to her apartment to change first.

He went to his room and to his closet where he grabbed a pair of jeans and a T-shirt. He set them on his bed and started to disrobe. He shucked his shirt aside, and it hit the bedside table. Something on the table made a metallic clink against the wood.

He stooped to pick up his shirt, and under it found a silver dollar. Aside from being filthy dirty, it was still in excellent condition and regardless, silver was silver. He flipped it over to the face side to see the date, and a rush of ice shot its way from head to toe and back again.

Slowly, he pushed himself to his feet. This was the coin he'd given Patrick before Vadim took him. He'd been here, been at the party. He had to have been.

"The PI," he ground out. It was so clear now.

Sean was going to kill Vadim. He pulled his cell from his pant pocket and dialed. It rang three times before he answered.

Sean spoke before Vadim could. "He's alive, you idiot!"

"Yes. I am, Sean," came the PI's voice. Patrick's voice.

Sean sucked in a breath, and his hand tightened on his cell. "Where's Vadim?"

"He's hanging around." His voice was cool and calculating—unlike anything he'd ever heard from Patrick in their youth.

"Did you kill him?" Sean asked.

"You'd like that, wouldn't you?"

Sean breathed heavily.

"You're next. And I promise—you'll never see me coming."
Patrick disconnected.

Pulling the phone back, Sean glanced blankly at Vadim's
number. Heat passed through his body, finding all the places that ice
had filled moments before, as fear and anger suffused him. He threw
the phone, shattering it against the wall and the side of a painting that
hung there.

If Patrick thought he could outwit him now, he was sorely
mistaken. He may think he had stacked his deck, but Sean knew the
game better than anyone. This would end *his* way. He slammed the
coin down. Something sparkled up at him from the floor. He bent
down and picked up Elizabeth's engagement ring.

WALKING up the rusty ramp of Vadim's even rustier ship, Patrick's
mood grew darker and bitterer. He untied his noose of a neck tie and
let it hang.

The ship seemed smaller to him now than it had when he'd first
been brought aboard. Of course, while it had been the middle of the
night when he was brought on board, like now, he had also been
blindfolded and drugged.

He wondered how many "passengers" were currently on the
boat, and had the sudden urge to kill every trafficker on board. The
soft, cradle-like rocking of the vessel made him queasy.

Zakhar stood at the top of the ramp and greeted him as he
boarded. "We've called Oakland PD. You have minutes."

Patrick nodded and continued around to the hull of the ship,
where more of Zakhar's men waited. They stood around two men
who'd been tied to two metal chairs at the back of the ship, which had
no rails, nearly teetering on the edge.

Both men were whining loudly through the gags that had been tied
over their mouths. Their gazes kept sweeping from Zakhar's men, who

were egging them on in Russian, to the open water behind them. Of course, at the dock, the water here couldn't be more than twelve feet deep. Not that that would do them any good tied to the chairs as they were.

"Where are the rest of his men?" Patrick was sure from the size of the ship and from the cargo that there had to be at least fifteen men on board.

"We found them about an hour off shore, heading north," Zakhar said. "When we took the ship, it was the weirdest thing—all their men jumped overboard."

Patrick's lip curled up at the corner. "Is that right?"

Zakhar repeated himself in Russian, and the men nodded and said, "Da, da!" with enthusiasm.

"See? Strange, yes? Like a mass exodus."

Patrick eyed the automatic weapons that each of Zakhar's men held. "I don't suppose they were given an incentive?"

Zakhar stuck his thumbs in his belt loops and puffed out his chest. "I can't believe you would suggest such a thing."

Vadim and Bogdan struggled against their restraints, and Vadim hollered through the cloth jammed in his mouth.

Zakhar hit him over the head. "Is that how you were taught to treat your betters?"

"Pull the gag out," Patrick said.

Vadim gasped in air when his gag was removed, and he spoke through a ragged breath and a Russian accent. "You blind-fold my men and force to jump."

Zakhar shrugged. "I'm sure the coast guard will happen by."

"I would like to make a deal with you, Vadim," Patrick said.

Vadim's hateful glare turned on him. "I'm listening."

From his inside tux pocket, he removed the jack of hearts, and held it out to Vadim and then to Bogdan.

Vadim's and Bogdan's eyes nearly burst from their heads, as their gazes whipped up to Patrick's face from the card.

"You were dead," Vadim said. "They tell us you die years ago in work camp."

Patrick flipped the card at Vadim, striking him in the nose. "Surprise."

"What do you want?" Bogdan asked.

Patrick dropped to one knee in front of Vadim and made eye contact. "I want Vadim to roll over on Sean Jones and Robert Wright."

Vadim spat in Patrick's face. "I'm no rat."

"That is a matter of opinion," Zakhar said, making several of his men chuckle.

Patrick stood and wiped his face, then pointed to Bogdan. "Remove his gag."

Bogdan let loose a slur of Russian that Patrick recognized as the foulest of curse words.

"Does that mean that you're not willing to negotiate either?" Patrick rested a hand on his hip.

"Never," Bogdan said in his thicker-than-spit accent.

Vadim lifted his chin in silent protest.

Patrick smiled. He took two steps toward Bogdan and stopped in front of him, then looked at Vadim. "I hoped you'd say that." He kicked the chair between Bogdan's spread legs, sending the chair and Bogdan over the back of the boat.

Vadim started screaming. Patrick stopped in front of Vadim again, resting his foot on the seat between his legs.

"No, no!" Vadim continued to scream. "If you kill me, you won't have your witness!"

Patrick shrugged. "True, but you'll be dead." He tilted the chair off its front legs, leaning him off the back of the boat. "It's a tough call."

"Okay, okay, I'll do it, just don't. Don't kill me!" He glanced behind him, trying to crank his head to see the water.

"Excellent," Patrick said, and pushed him off as well.

The screams followed him down ten feet, where they temporarily stopped as the rope tied to his chair caught him in a violent jerk and swung him with a loud metallic thud into the side of the ship, next to where Bogdan also hung. He kept screaming for a moment, then gasped for air when he realized he wasn't about to die.

Patrick stared over the side of the boat. "If you thought this was bad, try going back on your word. Ten years in Lazerev gives a man ample time to come up with ways of killing that would be slow and painful."

Vadim and Bogdan glanced up at him, trembling and pale.

Patrick faced Zakhar.

"Cut them down, and get out of here." He shook his friend's hand. "As soon as the police see what's on this ship, there'll be cops all over the place."

"Where are you going?" Vadim asked.

"Home. I'm tired." So far his revenge was coming along exactly as planned, but wasn't nearly as fun as he'd thought it'd be.

He turned to leave, but Zakhar held his hand tight. "And what about your girl?"

Patrick looked down. "She's not my girl anymore."

A phone vibrated from Zakhar's pocket, and he pulled it out. "Right, I almost forgot. This was on Vadim."

Patrick took it and answered as he headed down the ramp to the deserted dock.

"He's alive, you idiot," Sean barked.

Sean had found the coin.

CHAPTER THIRTY-FOUR

Shea drove up the long driveway leading to the address Lee had given her when she'd fled Sean's place with Luke. Pulling around the fountain that sat in the middle of the driveway, she parked in front of a large staircase that led to the front doors. The house was about the same size as Sean's provincial-inspired mansion but homier with a very Colonial look to it. Large gardens fanned out around the mansion, and all the many windows stood dark and empty.

She pulled her trembling fingers from the wheel and clenched them into fists. She'd faced two huge shocks tonight. Patrick was alive, and there was a good chance Sean was a murderer. She wasn't sure which had most thrown her for a loop.

"Is this where Patrick lives?" Luke stared up at the house, mouth agape. "I never would have pegged him for mansion living."

She removed her seat belt. She wouldn't have either. He'd always seemed like he'd end up in a ranch-style home or a bungalow. He had been gone ten years. A person could change a lot in that amount of time. She'd changed, and the man she'd met earlier tonight certainly had. He didn't seem to have any of the good humor or lightness that he'd had when he was a kid.

"Wait here. I'll be back in a minute." She opened the door.

Luke yanked off his seat belt. "No way. I'm going in too." His eyes were wide with alarm, and he suddenly seemed so young, not even old enough for his tux. "He's my friend too. And after all this stuff with Sean. I don't want to stay out here."

She nodded. "Fine, but you're to do exactly what I say once we get inside, understand?"

He nodded and hopped out.

After she'd found Patrick's library card in Sean's safe, she went in search of Lee and Brown. Brown had already left, but Lee was still with Luke. They'd left, and she'd told him about Patrick and about what she'd found in the safe. Lee then confessed that he knew Alex Westkeys was really Patrick and had told her about the fingerprints. He'd also given her Patrick's address. Luke had heard it all.

Lifting her dress skirts, she hurried up the stairs to the front door with Luke at her side. While she tried to locate a doorbell, Luke went and peered in a window.

"There's a ton of boxes in there, El. He must have just moved in," Luke said.

She gave up on the doorbell after a moment's search. Either there wasn't a bell, or the front porch was just too dark to find it in its secret hiding place. She knocked.

No lights came on. There didn't appear to be any movement whatsoever. She knocked again.

"What if he's not home?" Luke came to stand by her.

"Then we'll wait." She stared through the glass window in the door but saw nothing. It was late, and he was either asleep or had run off again somewhere.

She reached her hand toward the door, stopped, then grasped the handle and pushed in. A light burst of air whooshed out. They stood silent for a moment.

Luke leaned forward and peered through the door. "That was creepy."

No kidding.

From the foyer and to their right looked like what would be a library, and to the left was a dining room. Stairs stood directly in front of them, and a hall to the left of those led to the back of the house.

They stood in the darkened foyer for several minutes until their eyes adjusted. Up the stairs, a faint warm light came from the hall.

She faced Luke. "Wait here."

"But El—"

"He's not the same man we knew. As far as we know, he could be dangerous."

"Not to us." Luke lifted his chin.

She placed her hands on her hips. "This was the deal, Luke. You could come inside if you do what I say once we got in here. We're not here to visit an old friend. I'm working."

"Fine." He backed into the corner by the door and leaned into it.

She shook her head at him, then went up the stairs. She froze midway up when a step creaked, and her other foot hung just above the next step up. She set it down gently and made her way up the rest the stairs and down the hall toward the warm light. At the end of the hall was a large door opened to the master bedroom.

The room was lit by a fireplace that sat across from a large California king bed that was neatly made and empty. She took a step in, her gaze landing on a painting of a girl in front of a tree above the fireplace in an ornate frame. The room was simply and elegantly decorated in light, clean hues. There was also a small sitting area with a plush couch and bookshelves built into the walls that were already filled with books. A white tea cup with gold filigree sat on his bed side table with a creamy brown liquid that Shea would be willing to bet was hot chocolate.

Everything about the room's style spoke of the boy she'd once known. The man who was nowhere to be found.

"Patrick, are you here?" For some reason, she kept her voice down.

No one answered, and she felt a lump start to form in her throat. Now what was she supposed to do?

She turned to leave when a heap of white cloth sticking out around the edge of the cottage-style bed on the far side caught her eye. She inched closer and peered around the end. In a mound of cream blankets and white sheets, Patrick lay on his stomach, nearly buried in the material.

She pulled her chin back. "Patrick?" Why was he on the floor?

He moaned, and a moment later he was pushing himself up on his arms. The sheets and blankets slid down his back, exposing several deep scars.

She gasped.

He turned into a sitting position. "Elizabeth?" He sounded groggy like he thought he might still be dreaming.

"What happened to your back?" She blinked several times, not sure that what she'd seen had been real.

Scooting toward his bed, he grabbed his discarded tux shirt from the floor and quickly slid it on as he stood. He was still wearing his tux pants and socks. "What are you doing here?" he snapped.

"I..." She was at a loss. She'd come here for a reason, but right now it was evading her.

"If you're here to go over the conversation we had earlier, then you can go ahead and let yourself out. You're not welcome." He pointed toward the door.

She frowned. "I'm not here to argue over whether or not you are who you are."

He picked up one of the blankets from the floor and folded it. "Then why are you here?"

Something in her snapped. "Oh, for crying out loud. If you want to be mad at me fine. I wouldn't ask you to stop, though I think it's incredibly selfish of you to judge me when you have no idea what my life's been like."

He stared her down. "Yeah, I'm sure it's been real tough. That boulder on your finger has got to be a real trial, along with all the benefits that come with being with Sean and his trust fund."

She wanted to slap him. Instead, she lifted her left hand. "What boulder?"

He stared blankly for a second, then sneered. "What, you lost it already? What a shame."

Ugh! "I gave it back."

"Is that why you're here?" He finished folding the first sheet and set it on the bed, then grabbed the second one. "To trade one rich man for another? I'll admit that outfit is stunning on you, but I'm not interested in Sean's sloppy seconds."

She swallowed the lump in her throat. "I knew you could be cruel, even when we were kids, but this... What happened to you?"

He dropped the sheet he was folding on the bed, looked down, and took a deep breath. "Why are you here?"

He clearly had no intention of making this easy. And that was fine by her. She knew how to handle hostile witnesses; she'd done it more than a few times. If that's what he wanted, then she'd give it to him. She squared her shoulders. "Patrick Daley—or Alex Westkeys, if that really is your name now—you're under arrest."

PATRICK STARED at the infuriating woman in front of him. He'd known this might come, but it still shocked him. She lifted her chin.

"I'm sorry," he said. "What?"

"You heard me." She gritted her teeth.

"Did I? Because I'm pretty sure you just said I was under arrest."

She glared at him. "We can do this the easy way or the hard way, but either *way* you're coming with me."

He clenched his fists, then straightened his fingers. "Under what charges?"

"How about fraud, *Alex Westkeys*, or faking your own death?"

"I didn't fake my death. If I had, I wouldn't be stupid enough to come back, now, would I?"

"Getting yourself assigned to the murder case of an officer who was responsible for your missing person case? That's enough to make you our number one suspect."

He placed his hands on his hips and narrowed his eyes. "I didn't kill Benson; you know that."

"How could I possibly? You've been gone for a decade. I don't know Alex Westkeys." Her gaze trailed to his bare chest and then dropped.

"Like what you see?"

She rolled her eyes. "I don't want to arrest you, whoever you are, but I have to take you in. You're a key witness—"

He laughed out loud, effectively cutting her off, and turned his back on her. "A key witness to what?"

She was silent for a moment, and then something the same size and shape of a credit card, but not one, landed on the bed next to him. An ID card. He picked it up. His library ID from when he was eighteen.

He furrowed his brow and faced her. "What's this?"

"The man who killed Benson killed another man by the name of Miller a few years after you vanished. I later found out that Miller was hired to buy your father off. To get him to leave town and start over. Whoever killed Benson and Miller left a calling card at both deaths. Old collectors' coins. You left an old coin by Sean's bed tonight. And in his safe are more old coins similar to it. There was also that." She pointed to the library card on the bed.

Patrick swallowed. He had to deflect. He wasn't going through all of this so that Sean could be arrested. He wanted his revenge. "So what if Sean has coins? Lots of people do, and I probably just left the card at his house by accident as a kid."

She shook her head. "No, you didn't. You got that card with me the day before you disappeared. The day that Sean swore he hadn't seen you. You were at his house, and now I'm guessing he had something to do with your disappearance and with Benson's and Miller's deaths."

"You don't know what you're talking about."

She produced a pair of handcuffs from somewhere behind her. "I thought you'd say that."

He threw his arms in the air. "What is it with you and Lee?" Lee and Shea made the perfect partners. Both too serious and way over-prepared. "Where were you keeping those things, anyway?"

"You're coming downtown with me." She took a step forward.

"No, I'm not."

"And that's resisting arrest. Don't make this any harder than it has to be."

He quirked a smile and stuck his hands up defensively. Before he realized what she'd done, she grabbed one of his hands, twisted it behind his back, and shoved him against the wall.

"Ow." Okay, he deserved that. He'd let his guard down, and that was the one thing the bishop had constantly warned him about. Situational awareness.

The cool metal of one bracelet slid over his arm. He gripped her wrist with the hand she held against his back, stuck a foot between her legs, hooked her ankle, and pulled out. She lost her balance and started to go down, dropping the cuffs with a loud thunk. He spun and yanked her back up from where he held her wrist. She fought his hold, so he pulled her back against his chest and wrapped her in a bear hug.

"Let me go!"

"So you can arrest me? I don't think so."

She stomped on his sock-only-covered foot with her heel.

He hollered but didn't let go. He stepped back and turned her to face him, and pinned her arms behind her back.

"Elizabeth, stop."

She continued to struggle. He'd known she was as a fighter, but this was ridiculous. At least her dress was doing her no favors. Still, if she didn't stop struggling, he was going to have to subdue her or knock her out, and he took no pleasure from the thought.

She lifted her foot again, probably to land another well-placed kick, so he backed her up until her knees hit the bed and shoved her down on the mattress. He continued to hold her hands behind her back and let his body weight do the bulk of the restraining.

"Get. Off. Of. Me." She huffed.

Finally, she was tiring down. "Will you stop trying to arrest me?" he asked.

She bumped her hips up, then her back, then thrashed to the left and right. Her face reddened from the exertion, and suddenly, he found the entire situation amusing.

For years he'd dreamt of holding her and kissing her, and now here he was, restraining her on his bed in probably the least romantic situation he could ever imagine. *Careful what you wish for.* He quirked a smile.

"This isn't funny," she snarled, then tried to toss him to the side again without luck. "It's... it's..." She let out a frustrated growl.

He held her hands tight behind her back and was super aware of her lack of engagement ring. Maybe he did have this all wrong. "Why'd you give the ring back?"

Her squirming stopped—her chest rose and fell rapidly. She glanced away. "I'm a cop, and he's the best suspect I have in a murder case."

As far as excuses went, it was a good one, but it wasn't why. She was no less stubborn today than she'd been when they were kids. If that had been the real reason, she would have held eye contact. "Liar."

She'd seen him, nearly kissed him even. She'd been shocked, sad, and excited to see him.

She glowered. "Excuse me?"

He stared into the golden depths of her narrowed eyes and remembered what she'd told him when they were kids. That she didn't want to be like her dad. Heat suffused him, warming every inch of his body.

Her eyes widened as though she'd seen the change he felt overcoming him and she stopped fighting him all together. She'd never wanted Sean. His gaze trailed to her lips, and back up to her eyes. He released her hands from behind her back, his left hand trailed up her arm and cupped her cheek.

She reached up and took his hand, her eyes flitting to the ring he wore, then whipping back to it. She recognized it. Her gaze came back to his.

She whispered. "My father's ring."

He clenched his jaw.

Her hands went to his arms, and her breathing grew heavy again, this time for an entirely different reason. He leaned forward an inch from her lips and watched her pupils dilate in the dim light of his room. She still wanted him.

"El?" Footsteps pounded down the hall and into his room. "Are you okay? I heard loud noises—"

Patrick glanced over Elizabeth and toward the door where Luke skidded to a stop.

"Oh." Luke turned his back to them. "Bleh."

Elizabeth shoved Patrick off and jumped to her feet, facing her brother. "It's not. I was... Ah jeez."

Patrick fisted the sheets under him. So close; he'd been so close. He could practically feel her lips against his. Would his bad luck never end?

Luke raised his hands. "I don't want to know."

"I was arresting him," Elizabeth said.

Luke chuckled. "They do it differently on TV."

"Quiet, you." Elizabeth grabbed a pillow from the floor and chucked it at the back of her brother's head.

"Hey!" Luke cried out when it hit its mark.

Patrick rolled over and placed his arms behind his head. He

smiled up at her when she faced him. "Anytime you want to *arrest* me —I'm at your disposal."

Luke sniggered.

She rested her hands on her hips. "This isn't going away, Patrick. We need to work together." She took a step forward, her up do now hung in loose curls about her shoulders. "You need to turn state's witness."

Patrick stood and buttoned his shirt. "No, I need to do this on my own."

"Do what? Get revenge? First, it was your mother, and now Sean? Ten years and it's the exact argument we had as kids." She moved in front of him and cupped his face. "I don't know where you've been. I don't know what happened to you, but you have a chance to get your life back, and you want to—what? Kill him?"

He grabbed her hand. "It's my right."

She yanked it from his grasp. "It's not. That's what the justice system is for."

"And the justice system always gets it right?"

"More often than not."

He ground his teeth and took a deep breath. "Not in my experience. Wright killed my mother, and when I found out about it, he made a deal with a slave trader and Sean to get rid of me. And now, it seems, the justice system is also allowing Sean to get away with murder. My mother, ten years of my life, and so much more were stolen from me." He made eye contact with her as her jaw fell slack.

"You were sold into slavery?" Tears brimmed in her eyes, and her hand once again lifted to her crucifix.

He stepped forward so that he was right in front of her. "It *is* my right."

The sympathy in her eyes never faltered, but she threw her shoulders back as resolve came over her. "I can't imagine the horrors you faced, and I wish—I wish I could take it away. Even more, I wish you could let it go. I wish you could forgive."

He scoffed.

She lifted a hand to him in a staying motion. "Not for their sake. For yours. For your sanity and your soul. Because if you don't, you'll be no better than they are." She took a deep breath. "If you try to do harm to Sean Jones, I'll stop you. If you succeed in doing harm to him, I'll arrest you."

At that, she turned from him and marched across the room. Luke had turned back around and was staring between the two. He held his hands in front of him, and even though he was a little taller than Patrick now, even though he was almost a man, Patrick could see the fear of a child in his wide, golden eyes.

"Let's go." Shea took her brother's arm and the two headed for the door. "There's nothing more we can do here."

CHAPTER THIRTY-FIVE

"What are we doing?" Lee asked, barely loud enough for Patrick to hear over the bustling sounds of the bar and grill where they were having lunch. Nearly every seat in the joint was taken, and large flat-screen TVs were mounted in three corners. This was the perfect spot. Patrick glanced over his shoulder at the table behind him where Lee sat with his back to the door and to Patrick.

The detective held a menu as he surveyed the restaurant over the top. He wore a bomber jacket and a black baseball cap. A lovely blond sat across from him, glancing intermittently between him and her menu. She'd come in alone, and Lee had flirted his way into a lunch companion and a useful cover.

Patrick grinned. He liked the man. He was clever, easy to work with, and while he never gave any reaction, Patrick enjoyed prodding him, imagining him to be a slow-burning volcano.

"We're waiting and sitting at different tables because you're not supposed to be seen, so stop talking to me." Patrick rubbed his freshly shaved face, not quite used to the sensation. Since escaping Lazerev, he'd kept a trim beard to help hide his identity.

"If he's not here in ten, I'm calling it," Lee said.

Patrick's gaze went to the door, just as the man in question entered. Wright scanned the crowd and Patrick waved to him. He waved back and made his way through the diners, stopping now and again to shake hands and wave across the room. Everyone knew he was here now.

"Sorry about that. My constituents love me." Wright removed his jacket and took a seat. He grabbed his menu. "So, there's been a break in the case? I can't wait to hear all about it."

Patrick could practically see the wheels turning in his mind—see the man's plan to turn Detective Benson's case into a career-making one. Patrick said nothing, only stared him down until the man raised his eyes to him.

"I almost didn't recognize you," Wright said. "Is the new look for the case?"

"Detective Shea solved the case last night."

Wright set his menu down and grinned. "Well, who killed him? What's being done? Why wasn't I informed?"

"Last I heard, she got a search warrant, and she and a team are about to make an arrest."

Wright clasped his hands together. "That's excellent."

"You don't recognize me, do you?" Patrick said.

"Recognize you?" Wright rubbed his hands together.

"It's been ten years—no one knows that better than I—but it's not every day that a man is reunited with the person whose life they destroyed."

Wright furrowed his brow, his attention finally torn from his short-lived victory. "I'm sorry, what?"

Patrick leaned forward. "Take another look."

Wright stared at him blankly, and then his face fell. "Daley? But you're... you're dead."

"Careful, Wright." Patrick signaled around the restaurant. "You wouldn't want to share your secret with your adoring constituents, would you?"

Wright's gaze darted around and then back to Daley. "What do you want?"

Patrick gripped the table. "I want my life back."

"I can pay you."

"For what? Killing my mother or trading me to a slaver?"

Wright's face drained of color. "Your mother?"

"Are you offering to pay me for murdering my mother, or asking a question?"

Wright lowered his voice. "How did you know? Your mother's death was an accident. I didn't mean to..." He swallowed thickly. "It was a drug bust gone wrong. We'd received intel that an old building near the circus grounds was being used as a shipping grounds for heroin and cocaine. Half my team was sick, so I went on my own. There was only one man guarding the building, but he pulled his gun, and I returned fire. Your mother was walking by with her groceries and got caught in the middle. I felt horrible about what happened to her, but I couldn't have that on my record. I had a promotion coming up, and I needed the money. My daughter, Haydee, she had cancer, and our insurance barely paid half. I was desperate—"

A feral fire burned deep in Patrick's gut. "What did you do? What did you do to her?"

Wright paled and glanced around. "I took her body out of the city and buried her."

All this time wondering what had happened to her. Years in a work camp, because Wright had accidently shot her? "And I was what? Collateral damage?"

Wright's gaze dropped to the table-cloth. "I was in too deep, and you just wouldn't let it go. I didn't want to hurt you. You have to believe me."

Patrick closed his eyes and took a deep breath, then looked at Wright. "I do, but that won't stop me from bringing you down."

Wright clenched his jaw—all remorse vanishing under years of making one bad decision after another. "You can't prove anything."

"I don't need to. Have you seen the news today?" He nodded to the bartender. The man changed the channel to the news where footage of Vadim's arrest played.

It took Wright a moment to piece it together. He wrung his hands.

Patrick stood. "I've given Vadim plenty of motive to tell the whole story, Wright. Everyone will know what kind of man you are. Oh, and you're other co-conspirator is responsible for Benson's and Miller's deaths. Even if Vadim stays quiet, we both know Sean never will."

Lee came to stand at his side, arms folded over his chest.

Wright's gaze flitted to him. "What is this?"

"Your arresting officer," Patrick said.

Wright jumped to his feet and made a run for the door, but more officers waited for him.

"Enjoy your perp. walk." Patrick strutted through the rapidly quieting restaurant. The last thing he heard as he exited was Lee's voice reading Wright his rights.

"ARE you sure there were coins here like the ones we found on the bodies?" Brown stood at the foot of the grand staircase in Sean's house as several officers searched the premises for the coins she'd seen in the safe last night.

Shea sat on the stairs, her latex gloved-hands clasped in front of her. "Yes."

Brown took a deep breath and squatted in front of her. He made a cursory glance around, making sure no one was within hearing distance. "I didn't say anything at the station. You're a good cop, but I've got to be sure, Shea. Sean's your fiancé."

She tore her gaze from the stair where her feet rested and looked him in the eye. "That's exactly why you know I'm telling the truth. He did it, boss. He killed Benson."

"Why?"

She stood and grabbed his arm, pulling him back onto the stairs. "It has to do with Patrick Daley. Sean was part of a plan to kidnap and disappear Patrick. He killed Benson because Benson found something he shouldn't have. He killed Miller because Miller was the man who bribed Alex Daley to leave Sacramento at Sean's bequest."

Brown placed his hands on his hips. "And you know all this because you found a library card?"

It all sounded crazy; she knew that. There was only one way to convince him. "I have a witness."

Brown stepped forward. "What?"

"At least, I think I do. I hope I do." She just had to convince him to talk.

"Who?"

She swallowed. "Patrick Daley. He's back." And he was turning her life upside down. Making her feel things she hadn't felt since before he'd disappeared. Making her crazy.

Brown's eyes widened in disbelief. "Back?"

"Alexander Westkeys," she said.

"Found him?"

She shook her head. "No, he *is him*."

Brown stepped back and ran both his hands over his head.

Her phone rang; her caller ID read Rafferty. "I have to take this. Hello? Rafferty?"

Brown's head whipped up. "William Rafferty? As in my old boss?"

She nodded.

"Where are you?" Rafferty asked.

"I'm at Sean's house with a search warrant. All the evidence is gone."

"Vadim's been arrested," Rafferty said.

"Vadim's in custody? How? When?" She reached a hand out to the wall to brace herself.

Brown threw his hands up. "What is going on?"

Rafferty continued. "He was arrested last night. I've already contacted Oakland PD. How fast can you get here? We need to talk to him."

She turned to Brown. "Vadim's in custody."

He stared at her, his dark brown eyes boring holes into her. He shook his head. "Fine, go. I can handle this."

She smiled at him. "I'll be there in an hour," she told Rafferty as she turned and ran from Sean's house.

THE MOMENT SEAN had talked to Patrick last night, he'd emptied the contents of his safe and high-tailed it out of his house. After disposing of the evidence of his past indiscretions, he went to Elizabeth's apartment. He had to know what she was doing.

She wasn't home, so he sat in his car and waited. She didn't return until early that morning with her little brother, both still in the party clothes, and with two uniformed officers. She'd left an hour later by herself, leaving the two uniform cops to watch Luke.

He'd almost followed her, but now he knew the situation was beyond repair. She knew Patrick was alive. She knew what Sean had done. Patrick would have made sure of that. Sean's only option now was to run. Or was it?

He couldn't let Patrick win. Wouldn't. Patrick thought he'd planned for every contingency, and now he was just toying with him, letting Sean wait for the hammer to drop. The only problem with that logic was that Patrick never really knew Sean. Ten years and Patrick still thought he was smarter than him.

Leaning forward, Sean popped open the glove compartment and pulled out his .40 millimeter and a silencer. He stepped out of his car, slamming the door behind him, and crossed the street to Elizabeth's apartment.

First, he needed to collect a little insurance.

~

STEPPING out of his shower where a puddle of brown hair dye slowly swirled down the drain, Patrick wrapped a towel around his waist. He went to the mirror and wiped away the steam from the glass. Even wet, his curls were still golden. He was pleased with the return of his natural color.

Patrick had intended on regaining his identity all along, all the more fun to torment his victims, but it was more than that now.

Until last night when Elizabeth had said he could have his life back, he'd never considered the idea. He had wanted to find her, but he'd never entertained the idea that they'd end up together. That felt too much like a dream—one that he couldn't indulge in at the same time he was seeking revenge. And now with her real life threat and promise to arrest him should he harm Sean looming, he found himself confused.

What if she was right? What if he could be Patrick Daley again? What if he could start anew?

He'd never trusted the cops to do anything except fail, but things were different now. Elizabeth had figured out that Sean was a murderer and kidnapper, and Lee had figured out who he was, and while Rafferty had failed, Patrick had to admit he'd been a good cop.

Maybe he could trust them to do their jobs now. Maybe he could finally let go of his revenge and move on. Maybe he could have a life with Elizabeth.

But not if he stayed this course. Not if he sought revenge. Elizabeth believed in justice, and he'd have to give that to her if he ever had a hope of her being in his life. This was what the bishop had wanted for him all along, but it had taken her to really make it sink in.

Hope filled him as he made his decision. He could be the man Rafferty had tried so hard to steer him toward. He could be the man the bishop had always thought him capable of. He could be the man she wanted.

And he even knew his first step.

From his room, the soft trill of his cell phone sounded. He padded out of the bathroom, grabbed the device from his bedside table, and answered it.

"Hello?"

"Patrick, he killed them, you've got to help me," Luke's panicked voice came through the line and then it went deadly quiet.

Patrick's chest tightened like a hug from the strongman at the circus.

"Patrick," Sean spoke, "you there?"

"If you hurt him, Elizabeth will never forgive you," Patrick said. It was the only card Patrick could play with Sean.

"That's true, but I'm afraid it's too late for us now anyway. You see, somehow, my fiancée found out that I killed Benson, and she's too moral to let that one go."

Patrick sat on the edge of his bed. "What do you want?"

"Your money. All of it. I know you're wealthy, somehow, and I need it. You're going to transfer the money into an offshore account, and once I have it, you can have the boy. Meet me at the end of the day, or he's dead."

"Where are you?"

"In the last place we spoke before Vadim took you, the place where I gave you the coin."

The factory. "I don't know where that is. I was unconscious in and out of there, remember?"

"That should make it all the more interesting. Clock's ticking, old friend. You have until sunset." Sean disconnected.

Patrick went straight to his closet and dressed in a three-piece suit. There was no way Sean would do anything to Luke until he had his money, which was why he'd told him that he didn't know where the factory was, but he actually had a pretty good idea. He remembered hearing a plane take off and knew he'd been in an abandoned building in a smaller airfield. That narrowed the possibilities substantially and would buy him more time.

After he dressed, he called Elizabeth. Lee had given her his number. Her line rang once, then disconnected. It hurt more than he thought it should. He tried Lee next. His line when straight to voicemail.

Patrick scrubbed a hand through his wet locks and frowned. There was only one other person he could call. And he'd almost prefer to jab himself in the eyes with a hot poker than ask the man for help. But wasn't this what the bishop had wanted him to do? To trust someone? And now he had to.

CHAPTER THIRTY-SIX

P atrick rushed through the bullpen and toward the office that used to belong to Rafferty. As soon as he'd found Elizabeth and Lee were gone, he'd made a beeline to Brown. He'd thought about calling the man, but the two of them had never gotten along, not now and not before. Patrick was smart enough to know he had a better chance of getting his help in person than by phone.

Halfway there a uniformed cop saw him. "Sir, where are you going? Sir?"

Patrick ignored him, picking up his speed. The officer chased after him, so he went into a full sprint. Reaching Rafferty's old office door, he grabbed the handle and pushed in without preamble.

"You can't go in there," the young officer called out.

Brown sat at his desk, going over paperwork. The phone on his desk blinked a red light, indicating he had a message. Brown jumped to his feet. "You," he all but snarled.

The young officer grabbed Patrick's arm. "I'm sorry, Sergeant, I tried to stop him."

Patrick yanked his arm away and moved to stand right in front of the desk and Brown. "I need your help."

Brown looked him over. "When Shea told me you were back, I didn't believe her, but here you are, from your blond head to your finely tailored three-piece suit. Where have you been? And why on earth would you think I'd help you?"

Patrick didn't have time for this. "Sean Jones kidnapped Luke. If you don't want to help me, fine, but you care about Elizabeth, and I know you wouldn't let her brother get hurt to spare you your pride."

Brown came around his desk, passing a large dormant box fan, his eyes slightly narrowed as though he were thinking. "And I'm just supposed to take your word for it?"

Patrick faced him, the blasted blinking red light seeming to flash like a strobe in his peripheral vision. Who just left a message sitting like that?

"Are you willing to take the chance that I'm lying?" Patrick honestly wasn't sure. As far as he was concerned, Brown had always been a waste of space. He just hoped coming here wasn't the wrong decision. *Please don't let it be the wrong decision.*

Brown made a fist with one hand and encircled it with his other. "Yeah, I think I am. Because I happen to know for a fact that Luke is with two officers as we speak. We put him under protection this morning."

"Those officers are dead." That's what Luke had meant earlier when he'd said that Sean had shot them.

"You know, Patrick, you've always had a screw loose, but this is pushing it too far," Brown said.

"You don't like me; I get it. I'm not asking you to. I don't like you either, but I'm willing to ignore your many failings in order to save the life of the little brother of a woman we both care about. I came to you because I can trust you to do that. And I'm asking you to trust me when I say that Luke Shea's life is in danger."

Brown's jaw flexed.

"Call the two officers watching Elizabeth's house," Patrick said. "That's all I'm asking. Just for that much trust. And then we'll go from there."

SHEA AND LEE sat at the table across from Vadim in the interrogation room, with Rafferty behind them. Vadim held a pen in his hand, his confession in a ten-page document in front of him waiting to be signed.

Vadim tapped the end of the pen on the table a few times. After finding him on board their ship with ten kidnapped girls between the ages of eight and fifteen, all of whom were willing to testify, they had an open-and-shut case. He was going to jail for a really long time.

But they wanted more. They wanted Wright. So they'd bargained. Vadim claimed he never touched any of the girls he sold into slavery, but they were sure he'd still be considered a child sex offender in jail, which meant he had a lifetime of brutal beatings ahead of him. So, they granted him protective custody in a medium-security facility and took the death penalty off the table. At least that meant there was a chance that they could learn more information about who was involved in his syndicate, and with any luck, they could shut it down.

She wasn't totally pleased with the deal, but he turned state's witness against Wright, so she bit her tongue.

Vadim ground his teeth and signed. "There. It is done."

Shea took the document and glanced over her shoulder. She made eye contact with Rafferty and smiled, and he, in turn, took a deep breath, the weight of the last ten years almost visibly lifted from his shoulders.

Lee stood as Rafferty headed for the door.

"Raff-er-ty." Vadim leaned forward, resting his hands on the table.

Rafferty paused, his hand on the doorknob.

"You are vindicated man now. People will know that you did your job. Must feel good, da? But you and I still know that it was your fault. If you had been better cop, I would not have taken Patrick. And if I hadn't taken Patrick, the monster that he is today would not exist. That is on you."

Rafferty faced him. "Monster?"

Vadim smiled. "How could he not be? After what we put him through. After being exposed to..." He shrugged. "...darker side of life."

"He survived," Rafferty said. "That says a lot about the kind of person he is. He's a fighter. And I believe in him."

"Just as children believe in Baba Yaga," Vadim said.

"Baba Yaga?" Shea looked at Lee.

"The boogeyman," Lee said.

"Yesssss," Vadim practically hissed. "Boogeyman. Believing in him does not make him good; as signing this means nothing to me."

Shea grabbed the confession. "But it means a lot to the State of California."

Vadim chuckled.

She glanced up at him, just as he encircled the pen in his hand and lunged at her. She scooted back just in time. Instead of the pen jamming into her throat, it slid down her neck and chest, scratching through several layers of skin. A loud bang filled the small room, and Vadim fell back into his chair. Blood seeped out over his white T-shirt like a Rorschach test. A smile spread across his face, and he coughed up blood. Then his eyes rolled back into his head.

Shea blinked. Hands were on her shoulders, a voice speaking to her. She blinked again and glanced to her right. Lee held his gun high, aimed at Vadim. Her ears began to ring. The hands on her shoulders squeezed, and someone squatted on the other side of her.

Rafferty shook her.

"Are you all right?" He was speaking loudly, but the ringing in her ears was louder.

She glanced down at herself, at the blood dripping onto her chest and shirt. She couldn't feel it—felt no pain at all.

Several officers crowded into the room, holding their own weapons. Lee said something she didn't quite catch.

She glanced at Rafferty again.

"Are you all right?" he asked.

She shook her head to clear it and got a hold of herself. "Yeah, yes. I'm okay."

She glanced down at his signed confession, now covered in droplets of blood. Vadim was dead. They still had the testimony, but would it stand when the judge saw it smeared in his own blood? When she learned he'd been killed in custody? Would it, alone, be enough to get Wright?

Rafferty's gaze followed hers to the confession as several officers spilled in.

One of them came straight to her with a phone. "It's Sergeant Brown."

"Can't this wait?" Rafferty asked.

"No," the officer said.

She took the phone. "Boss?"

"Sean took Luke."

She heard nothing else as she dropped the phone and ran from the room.

CHAPTER THIRTY-SEVEN

Patrick found the factory near the McClellan airport and parked his car out front. The sun was maybe twenty minutes from setting. If he remembered correctly, the building, being abandoned and out of use, had no electricity. Once the sun went down, it would get dark inside.

He popped a small pill into his mouth, sticking it in his cheek, then lifted his hand to his vest pocket and tapped it. He took a deep breath, the weight of the gun at his back reassuring him, and crossed the cracked cement parking lot to the door of the building.

It hung slightly ajar. A chain draped from the handle to the fence next to the door left enough space for him to squeeze inside.

His steps crunched in the dirt and echoed lightly through the room. The gray light gave the space a near sepia-like feel, but aside from new graffiti on the walls, it looked almost exactly the same as it had on the day he was taken.

Patrick stopped in the middle of the building and looked up through the rusty scaffolding, then turned around. He took a deep breath. Never had he imagined returning to this place, a doorway that led him right back to where it had all started.

When this was all over, he would buy this building and level it.

"It is you." Sean came from a stairwell set back against a far wall, emerging from the shadows like a monster from the deep. His normally perfectly styled brown hair was messy, and he had dark circles under his eyes, accentuating their deep blue color.

Patrick lifted his hands in a here-I-am gesture. "Would you like me to spin?"

"When Vadim dragged you out of here all those years ago, I never imagined I'd see you again." Sean stopped ten feet from him, stance open, and put his hands in his jean pant pockets. "You were always full of surprises."

"Where's Luke?" Patrick's initial scan of the room hadn't yielded any sign of the boy or where Sean might be keeping him. Patrick was fairly certain that Luke was either on the property or very nearby. Sean was a control freak like that.

"It's fitting, isn't it? Being back here?"

Patrick smiled. "Being back in the place where you destroyed my life?" He pulled his gun, aiming it at Sean's head. "Especially since I now get to destroy yours."

Sean stumbled back a step while Patrick advanced. "Wait, wait." He reached behind him.

"Pull that on me, and you'll be dead before you can aim," Patrick said.

Sean paused.

"Bring it out with two fingers and throw it away."

Sean did as he was told and grinned. "You surprise me, Patrick. I didn't see this coming."

Patrick stopped in front of him; his gun poised inches from his forehead. "You think you know me, Sean? I'm not the same kid you disposed of all those years ago. I don't care about that kid. What I care about is seeing you dead. And you led me here."

Sean's eyes widened as Patrick pulled the hammer back.

"Patrick Daley, lower your weapon!" Brown's voice boomed through the concrete space.

Patrick took a quick glance over his shoulder. "What are you doing here?"

"I called the officers. You're right; they were dead. I tracked your cell phone." Brown inched into the room, his own gun aimed at Patrick.

Patrick's grip tightened on his gun, his gaze narrowed at Sean. "You're too late, Brown. I came to you in good will, and you turned me down. Now Sean's mine. He's not leaving alive."

"If you shoot him, I will shoot you." Brown stopped behind him and to the side.

"Do what you have to do." Patrick made eye contact with Sean. "But first, he's going to tell you everything he's done."

"I'm not kidding," Brown warned. "I will shoot you."

Sean pursed his lips and glowered.

Patrick took a quick step forward and pressed the barrel against Sean's scalp. "One." He lowered his finger to the trigger.

Sean breathed heavily, his face reddening. Patrick thought more from fury than fear.

"Two." He started to squeeze.

"Stop." Sean's tone was a low warning.

Patrick peered around the gun. "Make me."

"Patrick!" Brown yelled.

Sean huffed. "I did it."

Patrick twisted the barrel, pushing it harder into Sean's head. "Did what?"

"I ruined your life," Sean said.

Patrick sneered. "How?"

Sean clasped his raised hands into fists. "I helped Vadim Mikhail kidnap you."

"What else?"

"I killed Miller and Benson to cover it up." A vein in Sean's forehead started to bulge.

"How?" Patrick tapped the trigger.

"I executed them both. And I fought Benson. I'd heard for years what an amazing fighter he was, but I was better."

"This is all information I could get from the ten o'clock news. Convince me you did it and I might consider paralyzing you instead of killing you," Patrick said.

Sean growled. "I left coins on their bodies. Old coins."

"Like the one you gave me?"

Sean nodded.

Patrick grinned and looked at Brown, lowering the gun a fraction in the process. He put one hand in his vest pocket, over the small package there. "He just gave you everything you'd ever need, Brown."

Sean grabbed the gun, yanking it from Patrick's grasp. "Idiot."

Situational awareness. Patrick raised his hands and took several steps back. The bishop would be proud.

"How's it feel, Paddy, to come this far only to die now?" Sean pulled the trigger and fired seven shots.

Patrick grabbed his chest, felt the blood seep through his shirt, and dropped. It was colder than he'd imagined it would be, but nowhere near as cold as the concrete floor beneath him. He closed his eyes as blood seeped from the corner of his mouth.

"Drop it!" Brown yelled.

"Don't make me kill you too, Brown," Sean responded. "I've come too far to stop now. Lower your gun, and I'll let you live. I'll tell you where the boy is."

"I can't do that," Brown said.

The rapid clicks of the trigger being pulled, followed by several loud bangs, filled the old building, bouncing off each wall in turn.

"What is this?" Sean yelled. "What happened?"

Patrick sat up and wiped the blood from the corner of his mouth with his sleeve. "Gotcha." He chuckled. *Situational awareness.* The bishop was right.

"Blanks? You gave me a gun filled with blanks?" Sean lowered his voice, making the venom there sound even more menacing than usual.

Brown moved forward. "Mine are real, Mr. Jones, and you are under arrest. Put your hands up. Now!"

Sean raised his hands again.

"You see, Brown, the fake blood makes all the difference. Really sells it." Patrick stared down at his shirt where he'd slammed the package of cackle bladder blood and frowned. It was everywhere, all over his brand-new suit. He stood and removed his jacket, using it to wipe the blood from the pill he'd hidden in his mouth, then dropped it to the floor.

"Cackle bladder blood?" Sean sneered.

Brown removed a set of handcuffs from his belt and tossed them to Patrick. "Cuff him."

"You haven't changed. You're just the same as you always were— using tricks and cons to get your way," Sean said. "You're nothing but a circus freak, just like you've always been."

Patrick moved toward Sean with the cuffs. "A circus clown that just got you to 'kill' me and unload seven rounds at a cop." With everything they had on him, Sean would be lucky if he only got life in prison.

Sean chucked the empty gun at Patrick and lunged. Patrick dodged the weapon, throwing the cuffs at Sean in the same instant. Sean flinched back, and Patrick moved in, slamming a fist into his kidney.

Sean twisted, his face red with pain, but still managed to throw an elbow into Patrick's back. Patrick collapsed to the floor. The pain of Sean's blow shot through his body as though he'd taken a blade to a nerve.

Sean didn't wait to catch his breath, but jumped forward, lifting one foot high. Patrick rolled out of the way, and Sean's foot slammed into the floor where Patrick's stomach had been. Patrick rolled back, grabbing Sean's foot, and held fast as he continued to roll. Sean lost his balance and hit the floor.

Patrick jumped up, placing himself between Sean and Brown's

gun. "I'm not *just* the same, Sean." He was better, and now Sean knew it. Only problem was that Sean was better, too.

Sean sprang up.

Patrick glanced over Sean's shoulder. "Luke?"

Sean bought it and looked over his shoulder.

Patrick rushed him and threw a left hook. Sean managed to keep his balance, but just barely, and dodged a second punch from Patrick as he backed away.

"Still easily fooled," Patrick said.

Sean pulled a switch-blade from his pocket and flipped it open. "Let's see how you handle this." He lunged forward, and Patrick twisted away. Patrick blocked his second lunge at his midsection with his forearm, but Sean twisted the knife as he pulled back, slicing deep into Patrick's arm.

Now filled with confidence, Sean thrust the blade a third time, but Patrick kicked him on his instep at the same time that he hit Sean's wrist with one hand and the back of Sean's hand with his fist. The knife flipped out of Sean's hand, landing at their feet.

Sean threw a punch into Patrick's cheek and scrambled for the knife. Patrick turned his head with the punch, making it lose most of its impact, then lunged after Sean, grabbing his waist and dropping them both to the ground. Sean reached the knife and rolled. He brought the knife down toward Patrick's head, but Patrick grabbed his wrist again.

The two struggled against one another. Sean grabbed the knife with both hands, forcing it up toward Patrick's neck. Patrick grabbed the knife with his other hand, and with the forward momentum of the move brought the knife down hard.

Sean's eyes widened as he dropped his gaze to his mid-section where the knife had plunged in. His hands went to Patrick's neck, where he got a firm hold. Patrick had had enough. He released the knife, lifted his right hand and brought it down hard into Sean's face.

Sean's head dropped to the dirty concrete floor.

Patrick moved off Sean and rolled onto his back.

Brown holstered his gun and came and stood over him. "You okay?"

"Winded." Patrick nodded.

Brown knelt next to Sean and felt for a pulse. "He's still alive?"

"Yes." It'd been a challenge to land the blade in a place that wouldn't kill him but stop him. He'd wanted to kill him. Badly. But there was something he wanted more.

Brown spoke into the radio he wore on his shoulder. "10-33. We have a suspect with a stab wound and need an ambulance now."

Patrick glanced toward the stairs and sat up. "Luke!"

"I'm here! I'm down here," Luke's voice echoed from the basement.

"You, stay." Brown stood and turned to the nearest cop and pointed to Patrick. "Don't let him go anywhere." He rushed off toward the stairs.

Patrick lay back again, exhaustion hitting him hard. Ten years of his life, and in less than ten minutes, it was all over.

CHAPTER THIRTY-EIGHT

"Stop here," Shea told Lee as they pulled into the parking lot of their station. There was a parking spot only a few spaces down, but she had no patience to wait for that and threw her door open.

Lee stopped the car as she jumped out.

"Careful," Rafferty admonished from the backseat as she slammed the door and sprinted up to the building.

She sprinted past the front desk and rushed to the bullpen. Luke sat at her desk, spinning in her swivel chair with his head rested on the back. Next to him in Lee's swivel chair sat Patrick, spinning in the opposite direction. She stopped in place and stared.

Their chairs slowed, and they reached out their hands to one another, then propelled each other in the opposite direction. Her brother let out a happy whoop as he was flung around.

Ten years Patrick had been missing. Ten years she'd thought he was probably dead. But now, looking at him there before her—with her brother, taking care of her brother, making her brother laugh in a way that she was sure only he could manage with a person who'd just been kidnapped—she realized just how much he'd always meant to her.

She'd dated Sean because she thought he was safe. Because she didn't love Sean and couldn't. For ten years, she'd been making decisions about love with the ridiculous idea that she could protect herself from getting hurt. Like that was a possible thing to do. She'd suffered for Patrick. So much so that the mere thought of him was too painful to bear. And now, here Patrick was. Seemingly from the grave, taking care of her family and making them laugh again.

She couldn't control the future, just like she couldn't control the past. All she could do was make the most of the time she had. That was the lesson her father had failed to realize, the one that was so clear to her now. Whether she lost him in sixty years or in one week, having him for a time was better than not having him at all.

She moved slowly toward them until she caught Patrick's eye. He stopped spinning. She got a better look at him; underneath his blazer and vest, his white dress shirt looked to be covered in blood. Patrick grabbed Luke's chair to stop him spinning, and turned Luke's chair to face her.

"El." Luke jumped up and ran to her.

She reached him and threw her arms around his neck. "Are you okay?"

"Yeah. Sean didn't hurt me. He didn't even touch me, except to zip tie me to a pipe in this creepy old building." Luke pulled back. "Patrick and Sergeant Brown saved me."

"They did?"

"They faked a shooting, and then Patrick thrashed him, stabbed him too. It was beast mode. I wish I'd seen it," he said.

"Faked. A shooting? Stabbed?" She closed her eyes. Why didn't that surprise her?

Luke's gaze landed on the bandages on her neck and chest that she'd applied from her first aid kit in her car. "Hey, what happened to you?"

"Nothing, just a scratch."

"I'm hungry," Luke said. "Can we eat? I haven't had anything in at least four hours."

She chuckled. Teenage boys and their bottomless pit stomachs. "Yeah. Just a minute."

She stepped aside and headed for Patrick, who was now standing and fidgeting with the buttons on his suit coat. He ran a hand through his hair.

She stopped a few feet in front of him and made eye contact.

He made no expression as he waited for her to talk, the only sign of his emotions coming from his fidgeting.

She took a deep breath.

He seemed to hold his. "You're hurt?" He sounded racked with guilt.

"I'm fine."

He nodded but didn't look convinced. "About last night, you were right. None of this would have happened if I'd listened, if I'd—"

She crossed the space between them and wrapped her arms around his waist. After a moment, he returned her embrace.

"Thank you," she said so only he could hear. "Thank you for saving my brother."

"You were right about me. I did let my quest for vengeance change me. And I didn't like who I was becoming." He rested his head atop hers. "Your way was the right way. I'll turn state's witness."

THE WORDS CAME POURING out of his mouth before he could stop them, think about them, about what they really meant. "I'll do whatever you ask of me."

He didn't care.

She smiled at him, and her gaze dropped to his ring finger. "You kept it?"

And here it was, the moment of truth. Ready for it or not. There was no holding back now. By going after Luke and abandoning his plans for revenge, he'd shown he wasn't the cold hearted monster he'd wanted her to think he was. He'd let the chips fall where they may. "Of course I kept it."

"All these years."

"It was important to me." Patrick wanted to make her understand. What it had meant. What she meant. "In moments when I was hopeless, when I thought everything was lost, when I thought I'd die a slave, this little band helped. It was a light in the darkness. It was you. Your friendship, your stubbornness, your golden gaze willing me to keep going. It was a reminder of why I needed to live. I love—"

Her eyes glistened, and before he could think, she went up on her toes and kissed him.

His eyes went wide in surprise, and then he smiled against her lips as he remembered the first time they'd kissed all those years ago. And now, just like then, he hadn't expected it. But now that it was here again, he knew how much he needed it. Needed her goodness, her stubbornness, her unfailing faith not just in God, but in him.

He needed her.

He pulled her tight to him, wrapping her fully in his embrace. All his frustration from the near-kisses, the irritation he hadn't realized was building, fled as her soft lips molded to his. Everything he'd seen, everything he'd been through, the years of his life lost had all been worth it because they'd led to this moment.

The kiss ended, but their embrace did not. They clung to each other, his hands rubbing circles over her back as she held tight around his neck and buried her head against his chest.

"I missed you," she said. "I missed you so much."

Patrick squeezed his eyes shut as the almost completely forgotten sensations of happiness and hope filled him.

"Patrick?" an older man's voice called from across the bullpen.

He glanced up in time to see an older man crossing to him. His hair was completely gray, cut short, and patchy, he had wrinkles around his baby-blue eyes, and he was thinner than Patrick remembered, but it was him. Rafferty.

He pulled back slightly from Elizabeth. She stepped out of his grasp as Rafferty reached him and pulled him into a hug. Patrick's arms went out.

"Patrick." Rafferty patted his back with one hand and squeezed him tighter with the other. "I'm so sorry. I should've done more."

After the shock lessened, Patrick hugged him back. "It wasn't your fault."

"I should've done more." Rafferty's voice cracked.

Patrick smiled. Yesterday he'd felt like no one cared, like no one had even noticed he'd gone missing. How wrong he'd been, and how lucky he really was. "You cared enough to keep looking for me. You cared more than my own father." He pulled back, taking the older man's shoulders in his hands as he made eye contact. "And I am eternally grateful."

CHAPTER THIRTY-NINE

Patrick stared out the passenger side window, watching his old trailer park as they got closer and closer. He stomach knotted.

"The one thing I don't get," Elizabeth said, "is how you remembered the account number."

He glanced over at her. "13, 14—"

"Yeah, I'm not going to remember it." She peered over her shoulder at Luke and grinned, then faced the road again. "How did you? Fifteen numbers you only repeated once?"

"Do you have a photographic memory?" Luke asked.

Patrick didn't think so. He remembered most things, but used tricks more often than not to help himself. He'd done the same thing with the account number. "I converted all the numbers to letters using the A1Z26 cipher. The letters made it easy to remember."

"A1Z26 cipher?" Elizabeth pulled to the curb and parked.

Patrick swallowed. Maybe he wasn't ready for this after all. He'd spent the last week working with the police, giving them all the info on the traffickers and different rings that he'd decoded for Vadim. He remembered everything, and so far thirteen victims had been rescued.

Patrick had also spent a lot of time thinking about the bishop and what he'd said to him before he died. That he wanted him to be good and do good, to learn to trust, and not give up on God. Mostly he thought of what the bishop had meant when he'd told him that men have free will to do good or ill.

Patrick knew what he was going to do with the money in account 1314 now. He was going to use it to bring down as many human trafficking rings as possible. He would start a nonprofit and call it Westkeys in memory of the bishop. Even Zakhar wanted to get involved, anonymously, of course. He'd quite liked throwing those human traffickers off the ship.

Patrick had found a lot of peace in the last week and a new purpose in life, which was a big reason why he didn't want to come back here, to his home from before. Not again. It was too painful looking back. He wanted to look forward.

Luke pulled out his cell and looked up the A1Z26 cipher and was reading how it worked to Elizabeth.

Patrick felt queasy. He'd already done this.

But Elizabeth and Luke had spent the last week talking him into it. He'd said no until two days ago when they'd invited him to their apartment, and Patrick had spotted the drawing of Maggie Luke had given him ten years ago.

He'd trailed his fingers over the scotch tape—the bumpy edges that Luke's six-year-old self couldn't quite flatten out.

Elizabeth stopped next to him. "You know about Maggie, don't you?"

He nodded. Apparently, he was the only one who'd had no clue what'd happened to her.

"Is that why you don't want to go back?" She leaned against the counter.

He faced her. "Why do you want to go?"

She looked down for a moment, then glanced up. "We had a deeper connection with your world than most do. We loved the people. We loved Maggie. It was a magical, *safe* place. And yes, we would love to see Tilde and Jay again." She moved to stand in front of him. "Mostly, I want to see you happy."

He waved her off. "I can't have my old life back. No matter how I wish it. I'm different."

"I get it. But Tilde and Jay are important to you and having them in your life will make you happy. So, yeah, I want to go." She took his hand. "What do you say? We could take a bushel of apples to share in tribute to Maggie."

He'd said yes. Not so much because he'd wanted to, but because she'd wanted it, and how could he deny her something that would make her happy, especially after all this time?

From their parking spot, Patrick's gaze fixed on the sparkling white mobile home across the park.

Luke hopped out of the car first, stretching his long skinny arms above his long skinny frame, then removed the bushel of red delicious from the back seat. As Patrick opened his door, he remembered chubby, little two-year-old Luke. If that wasn't a sign of changing times, then he didn't know what was. It'd been too long.

Luke offered him an apple and stepped back when Patrick reached for it.

"Just kidding." Luke laughed and tossed Patrick the apple.

Patrick grinned and turned the apple in his hand.

"Tilde! Jay!" Luke ran off as the couple exited their home waving.

Tilde laughed. Luke crossed the space in seconds and rushed into Tilde's arms.

Elizabeth reached across the center console and touched Patrick's arm. "You ready?"

"As ready as I'll ever be." He got out, waiting by the front end of the car for Elizabeth.

She came around and took his arm.

Tilde saw him, and even from across the park he could hear, "Jay, look. There he is."

Jay waved his massive arm over his head. "Smiley!"

Elizabeth smiled, a look of pure contentment on her face.

Warmth suffused him, spreading from his heart outward.

"Come on." Elizabeth grabbed his hand and tugged him toward the rest of his family. Jay was smiling from ear to ear. Tilde wiped a tear from her cheek.

Patrick glanced up then, staring at the clear blue sky, and remembered the last thing the bishop had taught him.

To trust people, and above all, God.

ALSO BY ELLIE THORNTON

Thank you for reading *Account 13,14* by Ellie Thornton. If you enjoyed this book, you will love the other books in the series available on Amazon.

Regencyland: The Bristle Park Murders
Dead to Rights

ABOUT THE AUTHOR

Ellie Thornton is an award-winning author who has been writing since she could lift a pencil and making up stories even longer than that. For years she worked part-time jobs so she would always have time to write, read, and travel. Some of her favorite filler jobs include working as an editor, at a nursery (flowers not children,) as a driving instructor (not as harrowing as one might think,) writing a blog called Confessions of a Property Manager, and being a ghost tour guide. If she's not at her computer, you can typically find her reading, listening to podcasts, at the local library, in her garden, in her kitchen, or with her sister and her sister's kids.

Made in the USA
San Bernardino, CA
17 January 2019